The Legend: Revealed

Cheryl Rush Cowperthwait

Book Two
The Legend of the Dragon Child

© Cheryl Rush Cowperthwait 2018

Graphic Designer: Lily Dormishev

Print ISBN 978-1-73148-9-456

Forward

My dear readers, in the note below is the experience I wish for each of you as your read this series.

After my friend received my first book and a companion Dragon Tear necklace I created, she sent me this note ... I would like to share it here since it touched me so deeply.

A note from a friend~

"It's beautiful and full of ... I'm not sure if it's the memory of the feel of scales, a breath of warmth on the skin, or the heart speeding up from the free fall of flight.... But then, you know that, don't you?"

Becky Scott Nickolson

Dedication

Since I was in such a mad dash of excitement to get the first book published, I realized too late that I had forgotten the dedication, so, this will be longer than usual.

First, I would like to dedicate Book One of *The Legend of the Dragon Child* to my mother. She taught me you could be and achieve anything you desire, if you applied your whole heart and effort into it.

To my 'publisher,' not the one who actually printed the book, but for the one who wanted more than anything else, to see my book come to life. Eternally grateful to you, my dear husband!

And now, two other very special people. Susanne Nelson and Tom Cleary. When I started writing, there wasn't a Book One. What I had was only a blurb and the picture which I created for fun to share on Facebook. They both enjoyed it very much and encouraged me to write more of the story. Because of their interest and continual comments, *The Legend of the Dragon Child* had begun and now is published!

And I also need to thank Mia Botha who opened her heart and group to the writers of the 12 Short Stories in 12 Months challenge. It was the constant writing challenge that ingrained into me to write daily. This was the first 'audience' I had to submit my writing to other writers. They have all helped me, challenged me and became friends. If it had not been for this group, I doubt I would have had the courage to pursue my lifelong dream of writing and publishing.

For Book Two, *The Legend: Revealed* of *The Legend of the Dragon Child* series, I dedicate it to my loving family. They have all pitched in with their love and support throughout this journey.

A special thank you to my editor of *The Legend: Revealed*, Johnathan Rush, who not only cleared away my typos and continuity issues, but offered outstanding advice.

Thank you Norman, Johnathan, Jenni, Sandy, Tony, Justice, Ezekiel and Kelly for your constant support and great ideas.

And to you, my brothers and sister, for reading and enjoying what your annoying little sister wrote.

For cousins and nephews and nieces, who must have always known there was a good reason for my craziness!

Oh, and for all you wonderful people in West Virginia, a HUGE thank you! You have, by far, bought more of my printed books than any other state.

Come on the rest of you states, catch up!

With love and deep appreciation,

Cheryl Rush Cowperthwait ~

Prologue

Wyrtregon, in a burst of frustration, bellowed roars of thunder. Flames licked at the secreted rock door to his hidden chamber. Three moss-green heads whipped around, looking for something to hurl.

"Why do these Dragons get into so much turmoil?" he ranted to the empty room as he stomped towards the table. "Writing their Histories used to be so simple, but now after the Dragon Hails fled Verlaunde and came to Urthe? Impossible." Six red eyes blazed at the massive book open on the table before him.

The Historian paced the room in thought. *Too many events to recount, too many Dragons to trace their steps.* His hand raised to rub the ridges of his central head. He lumbered over to the slab of rock which had been his table for too many thousands of years to count. It had been worn smooth and had indentions where his arms frequently rested. A loud groan circled the room as he sat, glaring down at the pages filled with the archaic symbols of Dragon language.

His thick black talon thumbed the pages backwards seeing scattered details of the Histories of the Dragons zoomed past three sets of weary eyes. He stopped on a page.

"Here is where the great changes started. Before this time, I only needed to record Dragon History." Plumes of smoke rose from his snouts. "The birth of the Dragon Child...."

He read on to what he had recorded.

Kiayla, the blonde-haired human woman, known as 'a peoples' had stumbled into the caves of the Mursei Dragons during the great quakes of Urthe. She was heavy with child and in troubled labor. Rynik, a magnificent blue and gold Mursei Dragon and a favorite of the Queen of Mursei, spotted the woman as a swarm of his Hail flew out of the cave towards the battles in the sky.

He landed as the woman passed out. The Queen came upon them and saw that the woman could not finish the birthing of her child. "Rynik quick, bring her to me! She is fading away; we need to save the child."

After laying her against the Queen's leathery tail, it had become clear the woman could not finish her task at hand. The Queen had instructed Rynik to pull the child free. The squirming infant screamed to life when Rynik's talons ripped her left shoulder during his extraction, marking her with four deep gashes. The Queen held the child close, her long forked tongue sealed the child's wounds and her fate. The Legend of the Dragon Child had been born. Rynik removed an item the mother had clutched in her hand: a strange white orb. He gave it to the Queen for safekeeping.

Wyrtregon tapped gently on the next entry and mumbled, "Here, the Queen touched the sacred place between Rynik's eyes. She had chosen him for her king only a Dragon's breath before taking the vast majority of her Mursei Hail to Verlaunde. Her mission was to block the portal from Verlaunde, to stop the onslaught of warring Dragons. Her Chosen, Rynik, stayed behind to protect their new home."

More pages flipped as he stared at the horrendous battles recorded on Urthe from the Dragons that slipped through the portals. Next, he read of the Queen's return to Verlaunde to seal all the portals she could find and return home to Urthe with more allies.

The Historian's face registered a smile when he read over the naming of the child. She had been named, Kaida, meaning 'little Dragon.' *The hatchling years*, he reflected. Kaida had been placed in the nursery with the other Mursei Dragon hatchlings and was raised with them. Kaida's favorite was Zlemtec, with his enticing eyes of blue, purple and flashing white. He never failed to hold Kaida's attention, and much later on, her heart.

A slow shake of his head filled his mind with remembrances. *She never ceased to amaze her Dragon family. She learned their language as easily as any other hatchling, having never known the 'peoples' language. It was soon to become known she had an ability few others possessed, she could hear and call Urthe's creatures, even Calling up fish from the waters for their food—so much I had to record of her early years! She possessed inherent Magic and added to it the Magic the Dragons taught her to pave her way to her special destiny. All too soon, she was lost from Zlemtec in a battle against warring Dragons and was left hidden in a forest close to where the peoples lived ... then her years of living and learning the peoples ways and language, began!* His chest released a tender sigh as he turned the pages.

His full palm suddenly slammed against an opened page, throwing a light dusting into the air. His eyes squinted, sparking red daggers as he read the entries. *So many entries for the warrior Galdean ... and now even more than should have been. This lifelong friend to Rynik had already logged in numerous battles before that fateful day when the scale was tipped against the Dragons.*

Wyrtregon's roar filled his chamber, shaking loose embedded rocks from the cave's ceiling. Smoke blew out from his mighty snouts. He reviewed the details that had thrust even him into chaos created by Dargenoin the Immortal; the ever present Great Deceiver. He mused angrily, *Where there is one force, where is always the other. It was the Nature of all things. All things were bound by the Laws of Balance ... but Dargenoin? He brought on the ultimate deception.*

It had all begun during the great battle on Urthe when the warring Dragons from Verlaunde used the portals and filled the Urthe's violet skies with terror. The Queen of the Mursei and her allies rallied against them, driving them back towards a portal. They cut a path through their enemies in a fiery bloodbath, and positioned Rynik and Galdean close to the portal. During the battle, Galdean dodged close enough to the portal to toss the special box Zelspar had created to blow the portal up, forever sealing it shut from intruders.

Unfortunately, the backlash of the explosion caught Galdean and crushed his chest, where he fell to his death on top of the many slayed Dragons below.

Zelspar, the Elder White Dragon from the Qyrdrom Hail, known as the Healer and Teacher, was far away. He had heard a warrior's Call from his spirit and made haste to answer the Call, not knowing it would lead him to his friend, Galdean. The Call grew fainter. Zelspar knew time was of the essence to save his life. He arrived and saw the crushed body and thought he was too late, but still the spirit called.

He worked furiously to save Galdean, calling upon his Ancestors to bring him the strength and power to reunite the spirit to the body. Finally, the Life Spark took hold. It would be much later when Zelspar discovered the trickery used against him and indeed, against all Dragons, had started at that moment.

Wyrtregon's talon made wide sweeping circles around Zelspar's name and pulled up his history. He traced the symbols with reverence for there are many, many Dragons but none to compare to Zelspar. *The turmoil Dargenoin created hit us all*, he remembered in utter disgust. *No one would have ever thought Dargenoin could have used Zelspar in creating a Chaos so devastating it could kill every last Dragon on Urthe ... however*, Wyrtregon chuckled with a smirk carved into his face, *Dargenoin gravely underestimated Zelspar's cunning and deep knowledge of Magic and potions.... All he needed was a little outside help*. Smoke flared from his many snouts, *That is what brought the Immortals into play ... myself, Pravietis and even one of the Weavers of the Strings. Had it not been for Pravietis, the Future Walker's help, all would have been lost*, he thought as he tapped lightly against the page.

Pravietis, the Immortal Sea Dragon, was known as the Future Walker When any event touched a Dragon's life, it could start a ripple in the waters that would alter the future of that Dragon, but never before had an event touched a Dragon where it stood to change the future of *ALL* Dragons, and *that* future was of total annihilation. *It took the combined help of Zelspar, Pravietis, myself and a Weaver of the Strings to sort out all of that Chaos*, Wyrtregon rubbed his long muzzle in thought. *Oh! how frightened that Weaver, Spedgjek was when he*

4

found out he too, played a part in the great Deception, then to learn only he had the ability to help remedy the error through Pravietis' plan and one thin strand of my hair.... Laughter boiled up from his belly and exploded across the room as the thought came to mind, *Never underestimate the collective minds of the Immortals and the powers of the White Dragon known as Zelspar.*

Wyrtregon rose from his seat and paced in a slow circle. Urthe was changing. He felt it in his bones long before the assault of the fireballs started spraying down from the sky, long before the Urthe started its furious shaking upheaval. He pinched the small soft scales next to the flare of his nostrils. *After all that the Dragons have gone through, their testing has only begun. And Kaida ... the Dragon Child, would have to survive it all to bring the prophecy to fruition.*

He returned to his long table and sat. History was being made every second. He flipped to an empty page, his hand poised to strike down the current moments into the book.

Chapter 1

Low grumbling rose from the belly of Urthe. Molakei, the old warrior and Elder of the peoples ventured out from the inner hidden chamber filled with dangling crystals. He looked at his daughter, Flower Bird and then to Kaida, the young child who was found alone in the forest, curled around a Dragon scale of Blue and Gold. His warrior's heart pounded heavily against his bones. He had to ensure their safety.

"Stay here. I will make sure it is safe to return to the upper chamber. It sounds like the fireballs from the sky has stopped. Wait for my return."

The smell of smoke and ash burned his nostrils as he cautiously made his way up through the winding tunnel. Peering into their cave, he saw it had been hit with a firm shaking. Scattered across the floor were the contents of their broken storage pottery and baskets thrown down from their niches. He gingerly picked a path through the strewn shards and stepped outside.

He held his tunic up over his nose to filter out the smell of the smoke. The sight in front of him caused his hand to drop and his jaw followed suit. Giant splinters fanned out in odd directions. The downed trees that once towered close to their mountain now lay prostrate against the broken back of the ones in front of them. Out-dwellings were still smoldering, their blackened corpses dotting the edge of the stream. Tears trickled silently down his face. *So much destruction!* Ash continued to drift down, making it hard to breathe. His ears filled with the death cries from the beasts of the ground that echoed across their valley.

Being an old warrior, Molakei had experienced Urthe's groanings before but never with the assault from the sky too. He felt like a stranger in an unknown land. All the beauty he had known and loved was now enveloped in a shroud of dust. Two wolves appeared from behind the broken sentinels of the mountains, their mouths carrying rabbits.

These were no ordinary wolves. They had come to Kaida as pups and Kaida had a gift of being able to talk and understand them as well as many other creatures. The wolves had become her Protectors.

Molakei spoke to them and pointed to the cave. "Go find Kaida. She will take your gifts. We thank you," he said as the wolves trotted towards the cave. It was in that moment the truth sunk in. Their food and medicine supply would be gone, or at the very least, greatly diminished. He must go get Flower Bird and Kaida. They needed to check on the others and start gathering food before it was too late.

Kaida ran to meet the wolves at the inner cave's threshold. "Look Flower Bird, they have brought us food." She took the rabbits they had dropped at her feet. "When we eat them, we will give you each a share."

Sigrunn, the white wolf, answered her, "We have fed. We will find more food to bring. The screams of the dying are numerous." She nodded to Tyrianua, her male counterpart and said, "Let us bring back all we can carry."

Kaida's jaw dropped in a shocked silence. Her mind grasped their words, *numerous are dying?*

Molakei reached the inner chamber as the wolves trotted away. "It grieves my spirit to tell you both, the outside of our dwelling is a strange land. Come, we must act quickly to ensure the safety of our peoples. The air is full of ash and dust, take a cloth to cover your nose and mouth," he motioned towards the tunnel.

They plotted a path through the upheaval in their cave and stepped outside. All the glorious colors had dulled into a shadowland of grays and black. Kaida's lips trembled. Molakei placed his hand gently on her shoulder. The three of them stood alone, absorbing the shock of their newly exposed world.

Soon, others ventured out, crying and pointing in great distress. Heads darted over to look at the three and pointed towards Kaida. It wasn't long before they heard the peoples blame the Dragons for this disaster. Molakei grabbed tight to Kaida's shoulder before she could run towards them.

"They are blaming the Dragons for all of this Molakei, it isn't right. I know Zlemtec and I know those he lives with would never bring us harm," Kaida said fighting back angry tears.

"I know Kaida. Fear does terrible things to the head. The peoples are afraid. They look around and see all they have lost. They try to make sense of it by putting blame on someone. How could they release their anger to the flaming rocks? How could they expect revenge against the very ground that shook?" Molakei shook his head sadly. "I will go talk to them and see if I can help them understand. I believe it would be better for you and Flower Bird to go inside and start cleaning up. If any more big shakes come or flaming rocks, go to the inner chamber at once."

"I want to go with you, Molakei. If they hear it from me about the Dragons, maybe they will believe. I will tell them about Zlemtec and…." Kaida's argument was interrupted.

"No, Kaida. Not now. They are looking for someone to punish for the things that have happened. I don't want you to speak of Zlemtec. Their fear has closed their eyes and their understanding. I worry now that they also wish to blame you," he answered, his face lined in deep concern.

He stooped and looked into her watery eyes. "I understand such thinking does not make sense to us. I need to find a way to explain it to them and turn their thinking. Now go inside and wait for my return. I go to visit all that have survived."

Flower Bird took Kaida's hand and looked deep into her father's eyes. She felt his pain and knew it would be hard beliefs he had to move. Her heart was too heavy for words. Instead she took her free hand and placed it on her heart then extended her open palm towards him. Molakei returned the gesture and walked towards his peoples.

Once inside, Kaida gathered broken pottery and placed them into baskets as Flower Bird straightened shelves and took inventory on what was not ruined by falling. *Much was still usable*, she thought. *This is good*. The wolves, Sigrunn and Tyrianua, returned dragging a deer and stopped at the cave entrance. Flower Bird and Kaida ran over and graciously accepted their gift.

Tyrianua explained as they dropped the deer, "This one was hit by a falling rock. It killed him. We brought it so his life was not wasted."

"Thank you both," Kaida said as she scratched their necks. "I will help Flower Bird save the meat. Come in and rest, you have worked hard."

"Yes, a rest would do us well. We will bring you more soon," Tyrianua said as he circled looking for a spot to sleep. Sigrunn sprawled out, head on her paws and quickly closed her eyes. Kaida moved her hands over their fur, thankful for their friendship. With that thought, her mind wandered to Zlemtec, her Dragon friend, and wondered what was happening with him. She missed her Dragon friend dearly.

Chapter 2

The King of the Mursei Hail of Dragons took Galdean with him to check on the other Hails after the ground became more stable. As they took to the ledge, they surveyed the area for damage. They had been spared massive destruction. True, the fireballs had left their marks all across their vista but the mountain held strong.

They flew to their neighbors and found all the Hails had survived without much incident. At the far end of their mountain, there had been rock slides but the Hails were not using those areas. A fine film of dust had settled on the lush green foliage making that area less desirable for collection of greens but they still had a sufficient supply closer to their home.

They returned to give a full report of the good findings to the Hails. Queen of Mursei, relieved, guided the Dragons back up through the mountain and into the common area where they all felt their worries diminish.

Zelspar, the old White Dragon and Elder of the Qyrdrom Hail, pulled the King of Mursei away from the others.

"Rynik, I have need to go the place where Kaida lives. I am worried that she may have been in danger from the recent events. You have told us of the dust covered plants just south of us and Kaida lives further. I fear they have experienced ash fall out from the destruction of our second moon and homeland of Verlaunde. I wish to make sure she is doing well," he stated.

"I understand your concern, as I had also thought about it after seeing the blanket of dust. First, hear me out my friend. It would be far easier for me to go check on her. I can hide my colors as to not alert her or the peoples she dwells with. Let me make this journey. We would all like to be reassured," Rynik said, pleading his case.

The old White Dragon rubbed his whiskers and thought it over. "You make good points, Rynik. I would not want to raise alarm and I also didn't want Zlemtec to go in case there is ... devastation."

"You are correct, my friend. Zlemtec would plow through them all to get to Kaida. I know he will want to go and that is why I will leave it to you to let Starleira know where I've gone. Talk to her privately, so Zlemtec won't hear. I can't take the risk of him charging in and causing any unnecessary problems."

"When would you leave?" Zelspar inquired.

"Straightaway. If others approach you, only tell them I've gone to check caves for falling debris," he answered

"Agreed. I'll join the others while you take your leave. I will take Starleira to the side and let her know the details of your departure."

Sigrunn and Tyrianua jolted upright and growled, hair stiff and standing on end. Sigrunn quickly expressed to Kaida for them all to get back down through the tunnel, immediately.

"Molakei, Flower Bird, come! There is great danger. The wolves said we must hurry back down the tunnel and stay in the inner chamber. Hurry!"

A rolling motion pitched them forward. Deep rumblings echoed as they hurried downward into the chamber of crystal fingers and the River of Life which flowed through it. Before they could get situated, the sound of explosions filled the cave. The mountain was lurching in a sickening way, tumbling the inhabitants from side to side.

Large crystal fingers snapped, crashing down and exploding pieces across the cave floor. Screams and howls joined the chaos of the mountain's movement.

The man, woman and child clung desperately to one another with the wolves tight in the circle. The ground made an ear-splitting screech as it suddenly dropped from underneath them and tilted on its side.

The chamber became engulfed with dust. All covered their faces with their sleeves to filter the thick air. They gasped for breath. It was darker than a moonless night and they had been swallowed whole in the belly of Urthe.

Rynik flew in the direction of the Urthe peoples and Kaida. The closer he got to the land the peoples inhabited, the more destruction he saw. His eyes flashed green, worried for the safety of Kaida and those with whom she was entrusted. His large wings tore at the air, pushing his body faster to search for Kaida.

His eyes scanned the ground and mountainside as he approached the land where Kaida lived. A sudden *whoosh*! hit his wings. The air pushed him up just as the range of mountains popped with dust and smoke. Before his eyes he saw part of the mountain rise, and another part slide downward. His heart hammered wildly against his chest. A few tiny dots scrambled across the ground before a large jagged crack opened up, swallowing everything in its path. From Rynik's perspective, it looked like a lightning bolt lying flat against the ground. He gasped at the sight.

He hovered above in great shock. His eyes blurred. In minutes the landscape transformed into the unrecognizable. Part of the mountain had heaved upwards while another part had disappeared completely.

The Urthe had become still and silent again. Painfully silent. Dust and smoke gathered forming thick clouds. Rynik bellowed a mighty roar which echoed across the wasteland.

Rumbles of thunder began to form inside the clouds. He dove underneath them searching the mountain for any life. His Dragon screams made even the thunder sound muted. Rynik circled what had been the place of the Urthe peoples, searching for any movement. He searched for life. He searched for the tiniest of hope. The only movement he saw were the boulders breaking loose to fall down to the decimated ground below.

A hot wind blew, pushing against him. He flapped his wings in fury and roared until his throat could utter no more sound. He turned and headed back towards the Hails. His mind had not come to grips with what had happened. How could he begin to explain this to anyone? His mind locked onto one word. Kaida. The only word that flew with him towards the Hails.

Chapter 3

Zelspar took Queen Mursei away from the others and walked with her towards the Queen's lair.

"Starleira. Rynik has left to check the place where Kaida lives. We both felt a strong concern for her and the peoples where she lives. He will hide his colors as to not draw attention and return to us shortly," Zelspar quietly said to inform the Queen.

"That will put my heart and I am sure, that of many others at peace. Perhaps the quaking did not reach them?"

Zelspar lunged and grabbed onto Starleira's arm before he pitched forward and down upon his knees. His jaw dropped open and his eyes glazed over and twitched.

Starleira knew he was taken into a Vision and held tight to her friend.

Zelspar saw the Urthe being torn asunder. Mountains rose and fell. Screams of all life blended with the upturned mountains and valleys. The sky thundered and turned dark, lit only by the lightning flashes: long fingers stretched out to grab any life below. Tears streamed down his deeply etched face as his eyes raced from side to side. He quickly took a breath and held it. He squeezed Starleira's arm with a great force, then exhaled a long and slow breath.

"What is it Zelspar?" Starleira asked in alarm.

"It is...." Zelspar began but could not find the right words to describe the Vision. His heart weighed him down like a mighty boulder was on his chest.

He braced himself against Starleira's arm and his walking stick and made his way to a bench. His head hung down low, looking for the words as if the dirt might give them up.

"Starleira. It is the great season of Change. It has come. Urthe has stirred and is in the process of the Change. Mountains will rise and fall. Great cuts are slicing through Urthe's skin. Life is changing."

"The season of Change began with our home planet's destruction. A giant hurtling rock of enormous proportion slammed into it, turning it into nothing more than huge chunks of flaming rocks, a few of which rained down upon us. Urthe has but one moon now. The Urthe is going through ... well, birthing pains I would liken it to."

"Will we survive?" Starleira asked with trepidation.

"Yes, oh yes dear friend. But we too, as with all things, will and must change. Even as we had already begun to do so when we came to Urthe. It will not happen overnight, but changes will occur and we will change along with it." Zelspar patted her arm and cleared his throat before he continued.

"I must tell you..." and then he shook his head. "Starleira. This is most difficult to say, so I ask of you to hold your thoughts until I finish with the Vision," he gently said.

Starleira kept her words but impatient eyes already asked several questions as she stared at Zelspar.

Zlemtec rounded the corner to the Queen's lair to speak to Zelspar and Queen Mursei just as Zelspar began to talk again.

"The great season of Change has taken Kaida. She is alive but ... she is in a place removed from us. I see it as a world within this world. She must take this journey without us," Zelspar was saying before Zlemtec's voice broke in.

"No!" A scream broke through the Queen's lair. Starleira and Zelspar both spun their heads towards the sound.

Zlemtec stood in the entrance, his talons digging deep into the rocky edge, aiding him in standing. His eyes were filled with pools of water and a low moaning crept up from somewhere deep inside. One solitary word escaped.

"Kaida!" he roared, his head thrown back in agony.

Somewhere distant, a place where Zlemtec had never been, came an answering call.

"Zlemtec!" Kaida's voice bounced against the back wall of the crystal cave and flew out the side which was recently exposed. Her word traveled deep within this new place and kissed the unseen ceiling of this hidden world.

Zlemtec's eyes grew large. He had heard Kaida.

Chapter 4

Kaida wiped her eyes, smearing the dust into finger trails down her face. Her heart knew she was severed from him but she heard his call. *He is alive.* She would find a way to him, somehow.

The dust had begun to settle. The wolves stood at the newly exposed side of the cave and sniffed the air as Molakei, Flower Bird and Kaida joined them. None of them spoke for a long time.

Kaida, the Dragon Child, flanked by her wolves took the first step out into this new land, her eyes wide in wonder.

What is this inner world? Her mind raced as she absorbed her new surroundings. *Has this been here all along?* She longed for the answers and knew she would find them.

Molakei and Flower Bird joined Kaida and the wolf pups and looked out with disbelief.

They had been dropped deep within the belly of Urthe as the cave in which they had hidden within was plunged into the depths of the unknown. The cave itself had been ripped from the guts of the mountain and plummeted far below. Like a nest caught up in a tremendous storm, it tilted on its side. The occupants were left staring wide-eyed at the new surroundings.

"What is this place?" Kaida whispered half to herself and half to Molakei.

"I have heard stories, in the songs of old about such a place," said Molakei as he looked out over the lush foliage. The ground they walked upon was thick blue-green moss, which cushioned each step and sprung back as their foot moved to another spot.

Flower Bird reached out to a plant that snaked across the ground bearing heart shaped red berries as large as her hand. "Father, look!" She exclaimed. "These look like the heart berries I use to make sweet treats. One of these berries would easily replace ten of the ones in our land up above."

"We do not know if these are safe to eat, Flower Bird. They may look the same but how are we to know if it is bad or good?" Molakei warned.

Tyrianua sniffed the huge berry in her hand and spoke to Kaida. "You may eat. My nose will detect any harmful food." He grabbed a large berry from the rambling vine and took a large, juicy bite. He sat and waited for the others to pick the berries.

"Mmmmm." Kaida responded. "These are so good."

Flower Bird placed a few berries in her gathering bag to have later. First, they needed to explore. If there was a way in, there must also be a way out. Her thoughts turned to their peoples, hoping they had survived.

Light illuminated everything as if by the sun but they could not see it. Trees grew taller than any they had ever seen, easily fifty times taller than Molakei. The ferns that usually nestled beneath the trees on Urthe, towered over their heads, nodding the deeply notched leaves which sprinkled dewdrops down as they passed. The air was a spicy scent of berries and exotic flowers, filling their lungs.

"Look!" Kaida said as she pointed at a large skybird. Its magnificent wings of white and gold made it difficult to watch, flashing the feathers brilliance in competition with the light emitting from above. The bird's caw sounded like music drifting through the air. As his face turned towards Kaida she saw he wore a mask of golden feathers around his eyes. The skybird steered towards them. As Kaida watched mesmerized, it dropped down closer, grazing the top of Molakei's head before climbing skyward again.

"That was close." Molakei muttered, exhaling his breath.

"Did he harm you?" Kaida asked.

"No, but he could have. Did you see how long those golden talons were? They were a match to the size of my hand," he said turning his hands over. "We must not seem like a threat. He could have lifted me up without a problem. I am thankful he did not."

Flower Bird looked back at the way they had entered this place. She could not see to the top of the mountain but their cave of crystal fingers looked like a tipped-over bowl exposed near the bottom of the mountain. Something about the way it looked struck her as odd. She had never looked at the cave in such a manner but now it made the skin on her arms prickle. The crystal fingers looked like they were glowing. She was enticed to go back to take a closer look but just then she heard her father call her name. She hurried to catch up with them as they had already started down the mossy trail.

Chapter 5

"Shhhh…"

Her eyes glowed with an impossible color of a phosphorescent green. "They pass across the Meadows of the Moss. I can feel their slippery sideways saunter."

She held a bronzed finger to her lips as she moved slowly around, trying to hone in on their exact course.

"Aha!" She exclaimed as she quickly pinpointed their location. Her verdigris wings veined in gold, captured the light, as they gently folded and unfolded. She rose from her Throne, the beautiful Faery Warrior Queen, standing at the full height of three and a half feet.

Her hair was flowing down in cascades, the colors of molten bronze, swaying as she moved her head. Flashes of reds, orange and golden yellow bounced down the length of her back, threatening to blind the casual looker. She is Jengar, Faery Warrior Queen of the Solteriem folk, protector of the Greens.

Heavy steps followed by … *what is that*? Her head tilted sideways, straining to conjure up the images of the footfalls.

"They must be the Uplanders. The ones who live in the land above us. I do not like their kind," she said wrinkling her nose as if their odor had permeated her very being. "Uplanders disfigure the Urthe. That is part of the reason we left them to that realm and chose to come here, long ago. We will watch them, yes?" Her question was met by throngs of buzzing wings.

Jengar once again took her seat on her Opal Throne which rose up from the Inner Urthe. The throne, a platform from a boulder carved and polished to show off the veins glimmering within its hold. She rubbed a particularly large slab of the transparent opal on the armrest and looked within the Watching Stone.

The points on her ears wiggled as she followed the Uplanders progress along the Meadows of the Moss. They would have a long journey to ever get close to the Solteriem. *Still ... one never knows*, she mused. Just to be cautious, she thought, perhaps she should alert the Squadron, those immense Dragonflies who do her bidding. *Time will tell*, she thought, eyes riveted to the Watching Stone.

The Solteriem folk established their presence on Inner Urthe at a time almost forgotten, back when the Ice slowly crept. As the Ice moved, it devoured their Greens. They were forced to retreat inside the mountains. The bitter cold threatened to wipe out their race. Food was in short supply. They had to find a way for survival, and that was when they stumbled across their answer.

As they explored their enormous cavern, they found tunnels branching off in every direction. One such tunnel wound deep into Urthe. One of the Solteriem scouts followed this tunnel until he hit a wall at its end. At the bottom of the wall, he detected a small fissure where light broke through. He chiseled through enough to peer inside. The scout, Aghar, stretched his arm through the opening and pulled out a large vine. *Paradise,* he thought. He practically careened through the tunnel to bring back the good news.

The Solteriem folk celebrated Aghar for his discovery. A team of scouts returned with Aghar to enlarge the opening. Once done, the Solteriem folk flew down into the newly discovered land. In honor of Aghar, this inner paradise was named after the him. They called the place, Aghar Found-land.

Chapter 6

Kaida pushed through the foliage and caught her breath. Before her stretched out a vast meadow where rivers cut through its blue-green landscape. Large trees clustered around the rivers casting off shadows, inviting the weary travelers to rest beneath the umbrella of their low sweeping branches.

"Molakei, look ahead!" Kaida could hardly contain her excitement as she took in the vision.

Molakei answered, "I see, Kaida. A beautiful retreat. Let's make our way to the river and trees. There we can eat and rest for a spell. Keep watchful. We do not know this land or where danger may arise."

Kaida and Flower Bird answered with nods of understanding.

For Kaida, it was difficult to think of danger in such a beautiful place. It seemed as perfect of a place as one could ever imagine. She was eager to get to the river's edge. With sweeping strides, her legs propelled her across the springy moss meadow well ahead of Molakei and Flower Bird. Unaware, each bouncing footstep transmitted their exact location to Jengar and the Solteriem folk.

Once at the river's edge, Kaida dropped to her knees and skimmed her fingers through the clear water. Sigrunn and Tyrianua approached and sniffed the water before drinking.

Tyrianua licked his muzzle and announced, "Drink your fill. The water is sweet and pure."

By this time, Molakei and Flower Bird had arrived. They all scooped up handfuls and quenched their thirst while Sigrunn and Tyrianua kept watch.

Jengar kept watch also. Her wings quivered and her eyes glowed green. Her mind buzzed with questions. *Who are these uninvited guests? Why have the Uplanders come to Aghar Found-land?* Her eyes narrowed as she unconsciously adjusted her arm shields. She was torn between the urge to tear them apart and the notion of learning their mission.

She reached behind her and plucked an arrow from her quiver. Her bow reclined against her Throne with a small cage woven from willow branches next to it. She took one arrow and thrust it through an opening and pierced the frogs back. Not deeply, just enough to coat her arrowhead with its poison.

The golden frog carries a poison on its skin which will kill. To keep the frogs highly prized poison flowing, the Solteriem trap a special beetle to feed their pets. In exchange, the frogs suffer the superficial wounds to their skin which quickly seals over and heals.

Jengar loaded ten arrows with poison and replaced them into her quiver. She glanced around her fortress with its stone walls which had been erected and fortified throughout the years. The battlements stood ready for her warriors should the Uplanders choose to invade. She pondered, *Those which she watched may be a scouting party, more may find their way inside.*

They had been able to protect their kingdom from most any attack, and there had been many. She did not mind a fierce battle, to the contrary, she fought valiantly along side of her brother, Togar, on their raids against the Nomliacs.

The Nomliacs are the Forest people that live far to the east in the dense forests. They are a decent people, for being clumsy giants. The battles between the Solteriem and the Nomliacs began long ago, after the killing of a young Solteriem. The Nomliacs said it was an 'accident.' Accident or not, the Solteriem folk never forget a harm. And as such, delighted in causing mischief against the giants. They had not killed a giant in hundreds of years but ... a harm is never forgotten nor wiped clean by time.

Chapter 7

I t was a time of great despair for the Dragons of Urthe. They had lost their Legend, Kaida, to a world within the one they flew. Queen and King Mursei tried to console Zlemtec to no avail. He flew solo now and across great swaths of ravaged land, searching for Kaida in every crumpled mountain range. He had become a rebellious hatchling, not listening to his Elders. They brought him no answers, they brought him no comfort. Even the Great Zelspar, the Elder of the Qyrdrom Hail, could not quiet the inconsolable roars of Zlemtec.

When Zlemtec was not charging off in one direction or another, scouring the landscape for Kaida, he took a perch on their mountain and thundered his loss to the sky. He flung boulders down to crack against the Urthe, punishing the ground itself for taking Kaida away.

This is the reason why Zelspar called a meeting with the Queen and King of Mursei as well as with Galdean, the mightiest warrior in Dragon history.

"By all that is Dragon, I can no longer tolerate Zlemtec's pain. He is tearing himself in two. Do you realize he hardly eats enough to sustain a beetle? He cannot go on this way," Zelspar told his friends.

"I do agree with you Zelspar," replied the Queen. "But what can be done for him? We are all in despair but Kaida is unreachable."

"She is right Zelspar. I saw the mountain fall away in front of my eyes. She is gone from us," said King of Mursei.

Galdean looked on but held his tongue. Something gnawed at him. It buzzed through his mind and would not be silenced.

Zelspar noticed Galdean's unusual quietness and raised his shaggy brow. "Galdean? Have you no words to exchange?"

He muttered something the three did not hear.

Zelspar asked again, "What is it, Galdean? I know you must be thinking of something. That is the only time you aren't constantly wearing our ears out!"

Galdean rolled his head to the side and looked straight into Zelspar's eyes. He said softly, "That is the nature of things."

Zelspar's eyes narrowed. A flush of anger rose to his cheeks ready to explode when in that instant, he understood. "By all that is Dragon, you are right! Indeed. That *is* the nature of things. For every good there is a bad, for every tear there is a laugh and by Dragon, for every exit there is an entrance!" declared the wise old White Dragon.

A small smile crept up to Galdean's mouth as his eyes flashed green. "I suggest we search for an entrance, my friends."

Starleira added, "But Galdean, there isn't one. The mountain fell in on itself in the Urthe's quaking. It took away the place where Kaida was, it swallowed her, and those with whom she lived. Rynik saw with his own eyes."

"Yes. He did. But Zelspar has seen Kaida in his Visions. She lives in a world inside our world. Which means, the 'nature' of all things still exists. There must be a way out for Kaida if she found a way in. We only need to find the way."

The group of four Dragons sat and discussed plans and when the sun faded against their cave, a plan was hatched. In the morn they will tell Zlemtec. They knew it wouldn't come easy, nothing of great value ever does. But they now had a plan. They will find a way to rescue the Dragon Child.

The sun gently washed the opening of the cave in the soft tones of morning light. Zelspar was already waiting at the entrance. A quick thudding against the ground announced an arrival, before his appearance. Just as he had thought, Zlemtec was making his way to ledge again.

"Good morn, Zlemtec," the old White Dragon called out.

"What? Oh, Zelspar. You are up early." Zlemtec muttered, being caught off guard.

"Indeed I am. I calculated your early arrival. One must catch the first rays of daylight to run into you these days, Zlemtec." The old Dragon stood his ground watching Zlemtec shifting his weight from foot to foot.

"Look, I just need to get out, stretch my wings a bit. I'll see you tonight."

"No." Zelspar plainly answered.

"But...." he began before the chorus of voices behind him pinned him down.

"Zlemtec. Follow us. We are sure you will want to hear what we have to say," King of Mursei said as he came up on one side of Zlemtec.

Zlemtec looked at the ground and kicked up the dust before responding. "I understand each one of you think you can help me. I listened when you said, 'give it time,' like that is supposed to do something. I can't do the things you want me to do anymore. I can't just sit here while Kaida is ... out *there* somewhere. I can't!"

"No you can't." Zelspar answered, making Zlemtec's head pop up in surprise.

Zlemtec glanced from Zelspar to the King and Queen and then to Galdean. They didn't look angry, they looked ... *sympathetic*? His mind felt muddled. He had been prepared to push his way through Zelspar if he had to, but now? He was confused by their reactions.

"What is it that you all came here to tell me?" Zlemtec managed to sputter.

The Queen, in her innate motherly fashion calmly slipped her arm through his and said, "Not here, Zlemtec. Come to my lair. We have a plan to discuss with you but ... well here is not the best place to discuss it." The Queen's eyes were soft and reassuring as she slowly turned Zlemtec's direction towards the lair.

"What do you mean, 'a plan?' To do what?"

Zelspar, instead of erupting in frustration, gave a soft chuckle. "Give us the time to speak and you will be informed. We were awake longer than the sun last evening, to formulate this plan."

By the time he finished speaking they had made their way to the entrance of the Queen and King's lair. They each entered and ushered Zlemtec to a seat by the table. Galdean bent over and retrieved a hastily made map and unfurled it across the table facing Zlemtec.

Zlemtec's eyes flew wide with surprise. As he gazed at the map he immediately recognized the landmarks. The landmarks of where Kaida lived with the Urthe peoples, the place as it was before the terrible downpouring of flaming rocks and the quake that swallowed her into Urthe. He reached out and touched it with a golden talon. His eyes were misty when he raised his head.

"What does this all mean?" He asked with a nudge of hope in his voice.

"It means," remarked Zelspar as he placed his hand on Zlemtec's shoulder, "we are going to look for Kaida."

Zlemtec jumped up from his seat in such a hurry, leaving Zelspar to catch the table before it tumbled sideways.

"We, all of us, will go hunt for her?" Zlemtec could hardly believe what he heard.

"Well, no. All of us cannot go and leave the Hails unguarded." The Queen of Mursei smiled as she responded.

"But, you will have us three." The King of Mursei added as he gave a sideways nod to Zelspar and Galdean.

"Alright! Let's go." Zlemtec was trying to leave the table so they could dash off.

"Wait," the old White Dragon said as he clamped down on the hatchling's shoulder, "we haven't laid out our plan yet. Fold your wings for a moment, hold still and listen." Zelspar gave him a wink and a reassuring smile.

This time, Zlemtec smiled back. His mind took flight and quickly soared to the moment they could rescue Kaida. His heart found its beat again, and his eyes? They carried that sparkle of purple, blue and white that once held the vision of Kaida in its grasp. He felt like flying solely for the sake of joyous flight.

Around the table, they spoke and laid plans and made notations on the map. Where first to search, what caves to explore and how to mark off where they had made attempts to enter into the world below. Their heads were bent in planning mode long after the sun had passed overhead.

The Queen had slipped out and went to the gathering room to fill platters of food to bring back to her lair. As she entered with her arms laden in food, it awoke hunger pains in Zlemtec he had not felt in many days. His stomach roared its intent to the laughter of the others in the room. They had what felt as a feast and agreed to start out in the morning so they could take full advantage of the light.

A new motto was shared across the table of the four Dragons. *Leave no stone unturned*. They will move, dash or pulverize boulders to find access to Kaida. Zlemtec had fought to keep hope alive but now, shared with these three legendary Dragons, it was alive and burning brightly in each of their hearts.

At first light the four Dragons gathered at the entrance to their cave. Beside them were travel worn bags which carried a few supplies to aid them on their journey.

Zelspar had the most bags and parcels to strap around his hide. He carried both daily supplies and medicinal supplies. He strained to fasten his side bag he always carried, but this time it was laden with a variety of Magic enhancers. Casting spells was a learned technique but when one used the Magic enhancers, the spells worked at their optimal ability. He had no idea what they may stumble across, and considered being prepared well worth the added bulk.

The Queen of Mursei joined them to send them wishes for a safe and productive journey. They had all reached an agreement that the four would return home after one complete cycle of the moon. She could see the anxiousness for them to depart, so she made quick her goodbye. Her king, Rynik, embraced her in his arms tightly before stirring the dust on the ledge.

Zelspar cupped the Queen's hand in his. "Starleira, do not worry for us. We shall look after one another. I have brought what I need to speak to the Ancestors, to seek guidance to find Kaida. Much time has passed, perhaps the newer quakes have opened accesses that were not there before." He patted her hand before turning to go to the ledge.

She caught her breath as they took to the sky. They did not utter the normal 'Fly fast, Fly direct' call. They looked from one to the other and then shouted to the sky and mountains, 'To Kaida, we go!' It made her hide tingle and her scales ripple. Dampness seeped down from her eyes, proud of each one of those Dragons. She leaned back into the cave's wall and watched the mighty Dragons until they were only specks in the distant sky.

Chapter 8

Molakei watched as Kaida raced ahead.

"Flower Bird, do you see anything different with Kaida?"

"Yes father, she is growing quickly. I also notice the change in you." She softly smiled as she placed his long braid over her father's shoulder. "See? You have been given silver strands to adorn your braid."

Molakei picked up the braid and held it in front of his eyes. "I have never seen these before. Now I surely look like an Elder," he laughed. "I wonder if it is this place? Does it make us grow old faster? I think I see the change in Kaida because she is ... or was so young. Easier to see those changes."

"Perhaps father. There is something else about this inner world. I feel more agile and, I do not have the words for it, I would say younger but that is not the right word." Flower Bird's words stopped as she searched for a better description.

"Yes daughter, I know of what you speak. No, not younger but more vital. Full of energy."

"Yes, that is it. Vital. I think it is good even if it gives silver threads in the hair." She shared a smile with her father then watched Kaida suddenly stop.

Alarmed, Molakei called out. "Kaida, is all okay?" He and his daughter made quick tracks to catch up to her.

By the time they arrived the wolves were pacing, hackles up and spiked. Low growls came out between their bared teeth. They had bumped Kaida backwards and were staring down into a hole. A long slithering monster showed its head and quickly lunged towards Sigrunn. Kaida let loose a squeal and Tyrianua leapt forward and caught the enormous viper under his jaw, snapping his neck. He shook the snake vigorously until he knew the threat was neutralized.

The wolves pulled and tugged until they pulled the full length of the viper from his hole. The snake's body was at least five times the length of Molakei with its head almost as large as Kaida's. Long sharp fangs protruded from the mouth, dropping venom to the ground.

Tyrianua chewed the head free from the body and told Kaida, "You may eat the body but not the head. The poison is deadly. If we were bitten ... we would not survive."

"Oh thank you! You and Sigrunn saved me. I'll be more careful when I look at holes from now on. I thought I might find rabbits," she answered. Kaida told Molakei the wolves said the snake meat was safe to eat, but leave the head alone.

They got busy butchering up the meat. Flower Bird loaded up a pack and drug it over to the nearby trees. She found enough deadwood to start a fire and forked the meat with narrow branches to roast them over the fire. As their meal cooked, she cleaned the snake hide and rolled it up for storage. She would find a use for the shiny hide.

Molakei had wrapped the head in the thick moss and tethered it with creeping vines and brought it back to their makeshift camp. The wolves growled and snarled.

"Kaida, tell your wolves it is all right. Molakei knows how to work with the snake and not be harmed. I will collect the poison and keep it in a container. It may help us in the future. The teeth I can use in some way, maybe a weapon? We must be prepared for anything."

Kaida explained but the wolves still were not happy. Their low growls continued as Molakei did his work. It was only after he completed his tasks that they finally quieted down and went to lie by Kaida.

They ate a hearty meal of crispy snake meat and stretched out under the trees. Another nightfall was approaching. At least, Molakei thought, they had made it to the tree line. Being out in the open meadows for such a long time grated his nerves. He felt exposed and easily watched. Here, by the trees, at least he felt more protected.

And watched, they were. Jengar and Togar watched them closely and felt their movements across the Meadows of the Moss.

Togar wiped the Watching Stone clear. "They have moved close to the Giants. They should not be a problem for us."

Jengar shifted in her Throne, "But, we can't be sure. What if they make friends with the Giants? What then? They could come to us and make war. I think we should seize those sidewinders now before they find allies."

Togar studied his sister queen. Her advice is usually more sound and grounded in the protection of the Solteriem folk but this time he wasn't as sure as she was about the Uplanders. "We will continue to watch. We have seen no others following. I think it was an accident they are here, like others in the past. They will wander around haphazardly and eventually die away. I see no threat."

Jengar's eyes flashed and narrowed as she clamped her jaw firmly shut. She did not expect his response, and she watched as her plans disintegrated before her sparkling eyes. She would just have to go about this another way, she thought as she replied, "If that is your wish Togar, yes. We will watch."

She abruptly rose from her Throne and flitted away.

Chapter 9

The sun was high overhead by the time the Dragons reached the land where the Urthe peoples and Kaida had lived. Although much time had passed, there showed no indication of the peoples reinhabiting the same area. Huge zigzag scars opened large crevices along the ground, cutting a path through where the river once flowed. Now the waters which had flowed freely from the mountain plunged into the deep crevice and disappeared.

The four landed close to the edge, peering downward.

"Do you think we can gain entrance here, Zelspar?" Galdean questioned as he looked down the narrow gap.

"It may be wide enough for us to fit but not enough room to alter our directions. Unfortunately, the sheer cut left no ledges or landings that I can see. As we look down, the light fades away. It does not give indication of an opening to reach Kaida."

"I think we should try," spouted Zlemtec. "I could test it out since I'm the smallest."

"I understand your eagerness but don't let it lead you into danger," Zelspar replied. "It is better for us to look for another way which would have the markers of a possible opening. I do not relish the thought of losing you before finding Kaida." His yellowed eyes rested upon the hatchling's and he knew he had hit his mark.

"You are right. I only thought it is a large opening...." he said shrugging, still staring down into the deep cut.

"Quite understandable. But we must look for as many markers as we can find, otherwise we would do no more good than hatchlings chasing their own tails," he let out a tumbling laugh and Zlemtec joined in with him.

Rynik said, "I think it would be safe enough to land on the broken mountain. There is no sign of the peoples here so we shouldn't be a cause for alarm. Since this is the last area Kaida was, perhaps there are noticeable markers."

"I agree with you. What do you think Zelspar?" Galdean asked.

"I think it is the best starting point. Perhaps we will find some indication of where she left. We know it has to be somewhere close to the mountain, it is the place the Urthe peoples made their homes, either in caves or the out dwellings."

"Kaida told me of the cave she lived in with her teacher, Molakei and his daughter! She was fascinated by the pictures on the walls. She said a lot of the pictures told stories of great hunts, but some of them had no stories she could understand. There were even pictures of Dragons flying in the sky." Zlemtec looked at the older three Dragons and his eyes threatened to pool over in his thoughts of Kaida.

"By all that is Dragon, Zlemtec! You have given us the type of markers we need. There are caves all through the mountains, much like our at home. I have been pondering how we will be able to differentiate one cave from another. This is good news, indeed," said Zelspar as he gave a hearty slap on Zlemtec's shoulder. "We will fly up one at a time, land carefully for we do not know how stable the mountainside is."

The King of Mursei looked over the broken mountain and pointed, "I'll fly up top from where the mountain split and look for markers. Galdean why don't you look for any loose rocks that could be covering an opening closer to the ground level. Zelspar and Zlemtec, fly around the backside of the mountain where half disappeared into the ground, there may be some sort of markers around that side but be careful, it could be more unstable than the rest."

They agreed and watched as the King of Mursei flew up to the shorn mountain and purchased a firm landing before they took off to their appointed search areas. Galdean found a landing spot midway to the side of King Rynik's search. They both lost sight of Zelspar and Zlemtec as they flew to the backside of the mountain.

Zlemtec was explaining to Zelspar, "I saw the Urthe peoples celebrating by a large fire pit one time. Maybe if we can find that area, we will know if we are close to the place Kaida had lived."

The old White Dragon gave a nod and a wink and allowed Zlemtec to take the lead. *It is good*, he thought, *that Zlemtec did come to see Kaida. If he had not, we would just as well be blowing Dragon smoke.*

The ground area was in total shambles. As the two made their way across the uneven terrain, it was hard to tell if there had ever been any dwellings in the area. Nothing but crumbled rock and dust in thick layers met their eyes where the ground leveled off.

Zelspar noted the look of defeat already rising in the hatchlings eyes. "I know this looks as if no one ever lived here because of all the rock slides. I think if we were to carefully move some of the rocks close to the mountain, we may have a better view."

Zlemtec made a grunt of agreement, his eyes not daring to look away from the ground. They started heaving small boulders to the side and looked underneath for any indication of a dwelling for the peoples. Rock after rock they tossed aside. They both had to be quick, sometimes when displacing a boulder, others tumbled to take its place. They were finally making some headway when Zelspar rolled a boulder out of the way and found remains of the peoples. He let out a deep groan at the sight, bringing Zlemtec close.

"We have the remains of some of the peoples here. They may have been running into a cave or out, we do not know, but they were caught by the boulders crashing down upon them. They have gone to be with their Ancestors now. They are at peace and we do not bother them by looking where they once were, Zlemtec. After we have cleared enough to see if there is a cave, we will once again cover their remains."

Zelspar was an old Dragon and had seen much death from the battles constantly fought on Verlaunde and the battles here on Urthe. But Zlemtec on the other hand had been raised on Urthe, and has not been to battle. Death still was an unexpected sting from an unseen arrow.

Zlemtec's eyes were open wide in the unanticipated find. He started backing away quickly sending small boulders running down the hill. He began to lose his footing, threatening to send him falling backwards when his arms flailed behind him.

His left arm disappeared halfway into the rubble.

Zelspar leapt over to see if he was alright and when he looked down at Zlemtec he saw a strange look.

"Zelspar, go get the King and Galdean. My arm...."

"Did you break it? Here, let me tend to you first." Zelspar immediately switched into his Healer mode.

"Nooo." Zlemtec said with the sound of awe in his voice. "I don't want to move. Go get them, my arm—it's in an open space! I don't want to move it only to have the rocks pour down to close it up before we know what the space is."

"Good thinking, good thinking. Don't move, well ... we just discussed that didn't we? I'll bring the others." Zelspar said with his tongue still in a dither. It was rare to see the old White Dragon flustered. Zlemtec held the smile hidden until Zelspar crested the top of the shattered mountain.

Zlemtec's eyes actually were beaming by the time the three Dragons flew over the ridge and made their way close to him. He didn't know what was below him but he knew he was a lot closer to Kaida than he had been in a long time and for him, that was enough to fan the small spark of hope.

King Rynik, Galdean and Zelspar flew over the top of the mountain and swooped down near Zlemtec.

King Rynik called out to him, "Zlemtec, does your arm move freely under the ground?"

"Yes, I can move it back and forth and not hit anything. I was afraid to pull my arm away for fear it would fill in with rocks before we could see inside."

"You were right to wait. We will start moving the rocks away from you slowly. Let us know if anything changes."

"I'll be fine. If it feels like it will cave in, I'll pitch myself forward. Go ahead and move the rocks."

Galdean grabbed up a boulder above Zlemtec and paused. It did not start a landslide so he pitched it free of the area. Rock by rock they proceeded to clear the area immediately surrounding the hatchling.

Zlemtec asked, "Can you see anything yet?"

Zelspar rubbed his chin hairs and remarked, "Still too many rocks. We will have to move more before we can get a better look.

King Mursei hefted a large boulder and was casting it aside when a loud crack was heard and the King of Mursei disappeared.

At the sound, Galdean and Zelspar were airborne and fluttered around the flying dust. Zlemtec had pitched his body forward, kissing the dirt with his snout.

Galdean roared, "Rynik!"

Coughing and sputtering, the King replied. "It is all right, I'm fine. A few scrapes across my hide but no injuries. Stay back until this dust settles, then I will be able to see where I am."

Zlemtec was still in the process of blinking away his startled look and getting to his feet. He had come to rest a Dragon length below the pocket which had snared his arm.

Galdean's wings beat in a fury, moving the dust away from the hole where his friend had fallen. Zelspar and Galdean began to fly tight circles overhead, pushing the dust away. At last, they were able to see down into the hole. It was still sending up dust, but they could see the King of Mursei.

After a moment, the King called out, "Zelspar, I need you to get Zlemtec. I want you to use your magic to levitate him over the hole and lower him in. I don't want to risk him walking over to the edge."

"It will be done. Give us a few minutes."

Zelspar dove down to Zlemtec and told him what to expect, but most importantly to stay still and silent as he wove the spell of Levitation.

Zlemtec nodded and watched the old White Dragon in awe. He had witnessed when Kaida levitated and it always fascinated him. Dragons fly. They hover but they do not do anything similar to the slow controlled movement of Levitation. Unless, of course, through the magic Zelspar wove.

Zlemtec kept his wings folded and tucked in towards his sides with his arms down. Soon he was floating inches and then a Dragon's foot above the clutter of rocks. He moved steadily up until he was over the collapsed part of the rock slide. Slowly, he saw the edge of the rocks disappear as he was lowered into the hole.

"He's on the ground, Zelspar. Thank you. Give us a bit to look around."

The King of Mursei turned to Zlemtec, "This is what I wanted you to see. I know you haven't been in the caves, but look at this wall where I wiped the dust away. Tell me what you think you see."

Zlemtec went over where the King was standing and squinted his eyes through the filtering dust. And then he saw it. His scales prickled as his fingers traced the lines of several running deer and hunters on the wall. Up above them he saw flying Dragons and stars of different sizes and shapes. His jaw dropped in wonder and his eyes grew large and damp. He turned to the King.

"This wall is exactly how Kaida described their cave. This is where she lived!" He pressed his palm flat against the wall trying to absorb her presence. Without a thought his lungs inhaled a mighty gulp of air and the cave rumbled with his call. "Kaida!"

Behind them, the wall rattled and dust began filling their chamber as the King of Mursei took one arm and pushed Zlemtec flat back against the wall, shielding him from the dust, dirt and rocks pouring down around them.

Zelspar and Galdean circled above, flying fast to sweep the dirt aside to see what happened below. Painful minutes passed until they were able to once again see down through the hole.

Zelspar called out, "Are you both okay?"

"Yes. A bit of a cave in. We have to let it clear again but...." King Mursei answered as Zlemtec interrupted.

"Look! Back there. I see some light piercing through the dust."

Rynik rubbed the dust from his eyes and squinted. Where there should be nothing but darkness at the back of the cave, there was a dim light penetrating through the dust and rocks. He turned with a smile to Zlemtec and squeezed his shoulder. "Light."

Then he called up to the others and said, "We see light! It is dim but we shouldn't be able to see any light at the back of the cave. Be cautious but start clearing away enough rock to be able to fly down here. Make sure there is enough of an opening for us to fly out in case the cave is not stable. We will stay by the wall until you have finished."

Galdean being the warrior he is, quickly grabbed boulders and cast them away like they were pebbles. Zelspar moved the boulders from where Zlemtec had been, opening a wider hole on that end. Soon, their work opened up a large slightly jagged hole, resembling a freshly hatched Dragon's egg. Instead of the Dragon's exiting the egg, they flew down inside and were reunited with the King of Mursei and Zlemtec. The four Dragons looked towards the dim light and at a slug's pace, moved cautiously forward.

Rynik was in the lead. His foot slid slowly forward until it hit a ledge. Or edge. But beyond his foot was open space. The faint light they had seen was being emitted from far, far below reflecting against some crystal formations. He spit a large flame of Fire and saw what before him was a vast void, where part of the mountain had disappeared. A huge hollow but still, that faint light emitted from far below....

Chapter 10

"**M**olakei! Listen, did you hear him?" Kaida sprung up from the grass and ran looking far up into the sky.

"Kaida, who? Who did you hear?" Molakei looked around and did not see anyone except Flower Bird tending to the fire.

"It is Zlemtec, he called me! He sounded so close, Molakei." Kaida's eyes shown the kind of sparkle the river makes with the sun overhead, flashing and bright.

"Kaida, come to me." Molakei knew she thought or wished to hear from her Dragon friend but also knew it was very unlikely, unless the Dragons fell through the Urthe. His lips puckered in thought. *There was no knowing what has occurred above ground. Maybe the Ancestors wiped the top of the ground clean and opened the Urthe until the outer Urthe was fresh and new?*

Kaida came bounding forward to pull at Molakei's hands. "We have to go look, Molakei. I know I heard him. He was very loud."

"Did you hear with your ears? Or did you hear with your head, the way the wolves talk to you?" He asked.

"I ... I am not sure. He called my name so loud I thought he must be right above me but I could not see him."

"I did not hear anything, so maybe he is able to reach you like the wolves do, but this I do know, if your friend Zlemtec is down here he will have a far easier way of finding us than for us to run all over the place looking for him."

Molakei gave Kaida a soft hug to help ease her thoughts and asked, "Is he still calling to you?"

Kaida looked down and shook her head no. She looked up and said, "I don't think I imagined it. I think he is looking for me. For all of us." She began to smile and added, "if a Dragon goes looking for something or someone, it will be found!"

Molakei could do nothing but scruff up the top of her head and wink. He could have said the same thing about her. She is one of the most determined little warriors he has known. An odd sound caught their attention as the wolves came running and jumped into the air.

Huge winged insects came shooting out from the trees. Their wingspan were longer than a full sized man and were a kaleidoscope of dazzling colors. They darted and bobbed all around them, circling and sizing them up. Kaida started waving her arms above her head, trying to shoo them away. One of them scraped her arm with his sharp feet as he buzzed past.

Tyrianua leapt and partially clipped the edge of a wing causing the giant Dragonflies to fly away. "Kaida, these are not just insects. They were sent to watch us. I do not know the name Jengar, but that is who sent them. Tell the others to use care. We are not alone. Whoever or whatever Jengar is, we are not wanted here."

"I don't care who this Jengar is, I don't want to be here either." Kaida glared and stomped her feet solidly. "If they want to show themselves then maybe they could show us how to get out of here. I mean, it is nice enough with plenty of food but it is not where our kind are, the peoples of Urthe and Dragons."

Tyrianua pawed at her elbow and issued a low whine. "Stay alert. I feel danger. They do not care that we wish to be back above. They only ... I sense they plan to attack us."

Suddenly alarmed, Kaida quickly explained to Molakei what she learned from Tyrianua. He nodded in thought and brought Kaida back close to the fire. "I had also wondered if there were others down in this place. It makes sense that there would be. I had hoped we would find some of our peoples. If we got here then I had hoped...."

Flower Bird saw the cloud pass over her father's eyes. It is hard having so many losses in our own family but now there is a great probability they have lost many of their own peoples. She hoped some fell down here too and survived. She stirred the coals in the fire until they burned brightly and let her heart fill with that hope.

The wolves, Sigrunn and Tyrianua, darted past Kaida and moved to the first outcropping of trees at the edge of the towering forest. Their teeth bared and muzzles curled back in deep snarls, they paced the line of trees.

Flower Bird grabbed up her bow and fumbled for an arrow as the trees swayed like a storm caught in its center. The air was pierced by the warning howls from the wolves as the trees began to part. Towering pines bent sideways as the creature stepped into the Meadow's light. Shocked gasps blended with the wolves howls. The wolves backed slowly to stand guard by Kaida.

The beast was enormous with large twisted branches as horns protruding from his head and a long scraggly beard falling down from his ruddy face. His arms resembled chiseled boulders. His huge round nose sniffed the air and turned full-faced towards the forest intruders.

His bellows sent a heavy vibration across the ground. "Who be ye? What brings ye nigh?" He thudded his club down to the ground and leaned against it squinting his forest-green eyes at the intruders.

Kaida stood up to her full length and puffed her chest out. "I am Kaida, the Dragon Child and...."

At this, the giant let out a humongous roar of laughter. "Ye be the Dragon Child of lore? This cannot be truth, ye are but a tender sapling! Aye, even the

Giants have heard this lore." He leaned his head closer and a pudgy finger pointed directly at Kaida's nose, "Who ye be and who sent ye?"

Kaida latched onto his finger and roared, "I am Kaida! No one sent us, we fell through the mountain and we are now here. Stop being so grouchy, we didn't do anything to you."

Kaida's brave speech caught the Giant off guard. He brought his hand with a dangling Kaida close to his face and a laughed heartily. Kaida quickly shielded her nose as his breath was hideous. She noticed his teeth looked like big slabs of wood set in a crooked line. Her stomach churned with the thought of being swallowed whole.

Tyrianua attacked the boot of the Giant and made hardly a scratch. Sigrunn took running leaps and bites but could not make it above his calves.

"Put me down!" ordered the defiant young warrior, Kaida. "You better listen up before I call my Dragons to roast your old hide."

The Giant paused and looked skyward, twisting his mammoth head from side to side. He gently lowered the girl back to the ground. Tugging on his wiry beard, he asked, "Where be thou Dragons?"

Kaida stared straight into his large round eyes and said, "Close by. They remain invisible until I tell them to show their colors. They will allow no harm to me or the Urthe peoples." Her eyes bore holes through his. "Who are you?"

"Ughedar of the Giants. Ye doth no harm, thou shalt stay as a freond."

Kaida tipped her head upward and repeated, "Freond?"

"Aye, freond. Friend. I shalt speaketh plainly as thou doth. Friend to Giant."

Molakei and Flower Bird lay down their bows and stood closer to Kaida. She motioned to the peoples and gave their introductions. The Giant Ughedar rolled their names around in his mouth until something similar came out. They nodded greetings to one another.

"Be wary," Ughedar said as he bent his head low, "the Solteriem travel hither and are pudh ... um, horrible. They durst come and steal. They knowest we wilt bring no harm. Aye, er long ago a horrible mishap and we pay e'er more."

"Who are the Solteriem and what happened?" Kaida asked.

"The Solteriem were once peaceful Faery folk living above the crust. They wandered and found their way hither in times long bygone. They began peaceful and stayed far to the east ... mostly. But soon enough a um ... problem arose. It has nary been the same since that time." Ughedar's head hung low and his lips pursed in memory.

"So, what happened that was so terrible?" Kaida prodded for better understanding.

"It was long before even I was boren. A lovely Faery, Aribriatem, fell in love with Guston, a Giant. They wed in secret for the Faery folk did not approve. Aribriatem boren twins but the last one died at birth, as did the mother. Guston was of a broken heart and held her in his hand. The Faeries rode in on giant Dragonflies and saw Aribriatem dead in Guston's palm. They stole the living child from us and promised we would pay for her death e're more. They did not listen or understand the death was from child birthing. The second child was far and away larger than the other and Aribriatem could not boren it. They both died because of it."

Sadness marked his eyes and words as he continued the story. "After the Faeries took away Guston's son, he ran up the mountain you see behind me. His heart became like hardwood and splintered. He flung himself from the top of the mountain into the Forest around us and died. Our Elders say before that happened, no Giant was boren with twisted horns of wood in their heads. Now, all boren Giants here have these," he said as he pointed to his head. "Some say it is a curse by the Faeries, some say it was because Guston was found with a tree splintered through his head. But know this thing, no harm to a Faery will e're be forgotten."

Kaida walked over to Ughedar and patted his foot, for that is as high as her reach would go. "That is so sad Ughedar. What became of Guston's son? Have you ever seen him?"

"Aye," he said with a mouth of bitter sadness, "he lived and boren twins with his Faery wife, Hirayella. Her twins, Jengar and Togar are the Quekings of Solteriem. They share queen and king titles, as twins. They have been taught to hate the Giant that lives within them so they prove this by raiding us when e're they chose."He shook his colossal head and tugged at a wooden horn. "We only want to be freond...." A massive sized tear rolled down his ruddy face and caught in the scruff of his beard. He rubbed his horns and said, "E'vn boren with these, we are a peaceful lot."

Kaida was moved by his story, it circled her heart and landed deep. She said, "lift higher" and floated up to be next to his face where she leaned in to him and gently brushed his coarse cheeks. He trembled at her tenderness and went to his knees, weak with the gentle kindness shown.

Kaida floated down and sat upon his thigh, looking upwards to his face. She said one word. "Freond." A friend she found and had become.

Chapter 11

T he Squadron of Dragonflies barreled across the Meadows of the Moss and made a streamline approach to the Castle of the Solteriem, called Rutenthrall. As on they flew, their wings set off bursts of brilliant shimmerings on the moss below.

They made their way through the large sentinels of trees towards the inner meadow. Over the moat and past the outer walls, they flew. They vaulted up over Rutenthrall's drawbridge, flew towards the castle's keep. A hum of wings buzzed the air, beckoning Jengar to emerge.

Jengar swung wide the massive rough hewn doors and stepped out into the dazzling light. The sway of Jengar tresses caught the light and flashed a blinding dazzle of molten hot reds, yellows and oranges.

The Dragonflies could not look upon the Queen. Their superior eyesight with thousands of facets in each eye stood to be blinded by a mere glance at the Queen in full light of day. Eyes properly downcast, they came with their message.

"Queen Jengar, the Uplanders camp outside the Giants Forest. There are only three small peoples and two fiendish wolves. They look as mere travelers lost in our world."

Jengar head swung to the side, glaring down at the scout. "What would you know of the unruly Uplanders? You know nothing by simply flying over them! How do you know they are not laying plans for an attack? Did you ask them?"

"No Queen Jengar, we only...."

"I could have said as much simply by the vibrations they gave across the Meadows of the Moss. Yes? With them camped outside the Giants Forest we must assume they are plotting against us with the aid of those nauseating Nomliacs. Those wretched Giants continue to be a thorn wedged deeply under my nails. I have tried, with no avail, to express their danger to Togar, this time he will listen." She set her jaw with clenched teeth. "Go to gather your cluster, I will tell Togar of their devious plans."

The air filled with the buzzing of the Squadron as they flew off into the trees to gather the full of their cluster and return to Rutenthrall's ward. They knew better than to clash against Queen Jengar. She had no problem with plucking the wings from a traitor, and those who disputed her opinions were at the very least, traitors in her eyes.

She flew across the Great Hall and lit upon her Throne. Togar had just entered and adjusted himself into his Throne.

"Togar, troubling news has just now come from the Squadron of scouts. 'Tis as I had thought. The Uplanders are camped with the Giants! They were seen making battle plans against us."

"The scouts saw this? When did this happen? I watched them long through the Watching Stone and only saw them traveling and eating as wanderers would naturally do. Where are the scouts, I wish to question them."

"It is too late, Togar. They have seen the immediate danger and have gone to gather their cluster. We must leave soon and attack before the Giants fall upon our land to destroy us. We know they have no scruples and will kill our Solteriem folk as they did long ago. We must once and forevermore rid Aghar Found-land from the threats of those long legged lumbering Giants."

"You show your aim, Jengar. The whole of your conversation was directed towards the Giants. You aren't in the least concerned that the Uplanders have come here with the intent of making war. It is your quest to obliterate the gentle

Giants. How can you be so narrow minded with Giant blood flowing inside us both? To hate the Giants is to hate yourself and me, your brother."

"Forgive me brother, yes? I am distressed you see it that way." Jengar hung her head low and her shoulders shuddered. Her bronzed hands clasped the arms of her Throne.

Togar saw the distress he caused his sister and frowned. He reached over to embrace her with a hug. "Ow! Jengar...."

Jengar slipped the poisoned arrowhead back into the hidden compartment under her armrest.

"Guards!" She called out from the Great Hall. "Quick, come get Togar. I'm Faery fairly sure he took a mild dose of poison to escape battle. Take him into the Keep and lock him there. I will bring the antidote. He must stay locked away, for I Faery fear he may sabotage our call to battle!"

The guards drug the King away and placed him deep within the Keep. The groan of the metal gates clicked shut as the guards locked the padlock and stood outside. When Jengar came, they unlocked the heavy gates to give her entry.

Jengar placed a dollop of honey on Togar's tongue, the sweetness infused with the antidote for the poison. It would take awhile for the full effect to flow through his veins, so for now, he remained paralyzed. A glint in her eyes sparked as she looked down at her helpless brother. She mumbled a word close to his ear. "Fool." She turned and flitted out of the cell.

Chapter 12

The four Dragons gathered along the edge of the abyss. The darkness so complete is was hard to tell if it was a bottomless chasm, except that one sliver of light which radiated outwards into the void. A slight breeze filtered up, followed by a tendrils of smoke which danced and formed the head of Dragon. The Ancestor!

They caught their combined breaths and waited, perfectly still. The image swirled and the mouth opened and sung a haunting song.

"His roars covered land and ground
She went down, deep down ~
He caught his breath
Hearing a sweet sound!
His lady fair
Calling from down, deep down ~
Mountains tumbled as Urthe rumbled,
She must be found, deep underground.
He must find Kaida!
She went down, deep down ~
She is hidden down,
Deep down ~
He would spend his lifetime, scouring the deep
To rescue the maiden beyond the Keep.
He'll go down, deep down ~
Roars will fly up ...
From down, deep down.
Four will fly deep, down deep

Underground.
They will battle against the Faery Crowned.
Avert your ears to the tinkling sound!
They are spells they cast, down deep,
Deep down ~
Trouble a plenty there abound,
Before the Legend will be found.
You must travel down deep,
Deep down!"

The smoke tendrils collapsed and disappeared leaving the four Dragons gazing deep into the chasm. King Mursei turned his head to Zelspar saying, "Any thoughts?"

Zelspar's yellow eyes glinted back at King Mursei. "We Fly Fast, Fly Direct!"

Their battle cry echoed within the chasm, four Dragons thundered as they swooped from the ledge, "Fly Fast, Fly Direct!" They spiraled down towards that thin sliver of light which separated their Future and Past, the Outer and Inner, the Dragons and their Legend.

Down and down deeper still, they flew, keeping their eyes focused on the crack of light. As they got closer they saw a hint of a curved surface where the light issued from and escaped outwards. It seemed to be a rough ball of rock which caught down deep inside the chasm. They landed on top where the crack shone light. It was not even a Dragon's talon wide of a crack.

Zlemtec leaned down and called through the crack, "Kaida!"

A sound returned swiftly, "Zlemtec!"

The four Dragons looked at one another and the beam of light caught their glimmering smiles as they perched on the huge rock ball. Rynik turned to Galdean. "Ice and then Fire?" A smile formed on Galdean's lips.

They flew above and cast Ice flames down against the rough surface followed quickly by thunderous Fire flames. They listened as the rock cracked. They assaulted it repeatedly until the small fracture of light exploded, leaving a large hole for entrance!

The bellows of the Dragons echoed through the chasm and into the Inner world. They made their way through the cave of crystal fingers and out into a new world.

The Dragonfly cluster filled the Ward. The saddles were on and bound tight, ready for their riders. The Squadron and cluster stood silently, wings stilled.

From the Keep, the sound of the creaking door echoed as it flung open. Jengar and the Solteriem folk spilled out of Rutenthrall castle. They were dressed for battle, woven leather arm bands ran the full length of their arms, leg bands fastened under their knees with leather pull tight through the buckles. All had their quivers slung across their backs filled with poison-tipped arrows. A few brought their frogs in cages.

Jengar stood in front of the Squadron of Dragonflies. Her war mask gleamed in the sunlight. It fit snugly over her eyes and half the length of her face. She gave a warbling yell, a call to battle. The air was filled with the buzzing of Faery wings as they all found their mounts.

Her bronzed arm lifted into the air. The noise stilled.

"We go to the forest of the Nomliacs. The Giants will not form an alliance with the unsightly Uplanders to come and take from our Solteriem folk. They have been seen making plans of war against us. We will *not* let that happen, upon that I am Faery fairly certain!"

She glanced at her army, making sure none disagreed.

But not all Solteriem folk were like Jengar. It would be fair to state *most* Solteriem folk were not like Jengar.

The Solteriem folk would do her bidding or risk being harmed themselves. And that is how she gathered her army to go wage war against the Nomliacs, even though they knew the Giants as gentle folk. Togar was not to be found. The Solteriem folk had no other choice.

Jengar addressed her army. "Shoot as many of the grotesque Giants as you see but those stinking sneaking Uplanders are mine." Her eyes raged beneath the shield of her mask. "They will be my prisoners." Her laughter made wings buzz with an uneasy air.

Three scouts from the Squadron of Dragonflies soared over Rutenthrall's towering walls and lit upon the ground near Jengar.

"Queen Jengar, the Uplanders are on the move. They have left the forest canopy and trudge towards the Vale of Valdross."

"Are the Giants traveling with them?" Jengar's face contorted with rage.

"They travel alone," replied one of the scouts.

"Arrrg! Those no good, no count Nomliacs must have told them to head towards the Vale of Valdross."

The front scout flickered his wings. "Queen Jengar, there is more. The smallest of the Uplanders was overheard saying her Dragons are coming."

Jengar shot up in the air, spinning so fast her hair looked like a dancing flame suspended overhead. She quickly darted over the Squadron and the cluster of awaiting mounts. Her fury was palpable. She returned to the ground, her toes skimming a line in the dust.

"They are up to something," Jengar replied. "Why else would they seek the Magicians in the Vale of Valdross? Fluttering Faery wings, why bring the death delivering Dragons upon us? You see, all of you who suspected they came here innocently, stumbling into our world by accident ... what do you say now? Arrrg!" Jengar spit her words out in a contemptuous shrill.

Not a single Solteriem folk nor Dragonfly made a noise. It was in such a perilous moment, Jengar could easily be enticed to bring harm. She possessed more than one hundred different charms to give to her Faery dust and some of them are too horrendous to think upon!

She paced in front of the Squadron, her bronzed and verdigris wings fitfully twitching.

When she spoke, her words were painfully quiet. This was the type of seething rage which boiled only a thin hair below the surface. All strained to hear her words for none wished to ask her to speak up.

"We will have to alter our course, yes? We need to intercept the incipient Uplanders before they reach the Vale of Valdross. Solteriem, do not shoot your arrows at them. Use only your charms with the Faery dust. The charm of Confusion should be enough to bring them peacefully back to Rutenthrall Castle. But ... if you should see a Dragon, fire upon it immediately! We cannot have those sky warriors in our realm! They, like the ground shaking Giants are nothing more than destroyers. We will not stand by and have our realm destroyed by their likes, yes?" Jengar's flaming phosphorescent eyes stared down the line of her army. Not even a breath was exhaled. She flitted onto her mount and grabbed onto the vine wrapping the saddle in place and yelled, "To the Vale of Valdross!"

A sudden blinding brilliance of wings catching the light, moved across the ward of Rutenthrall Castle. They gathered the air as they crossed the inner walls and buzzed past the towers and continued beyond the outer walls.

Chapter 13

Ughedar moved the trees apart with one arm and took a mighty step forward, letting the trees shake back into place.

Kaida, startled, yelled out, "Ughedar, you scared me!"

"Not meant to." His enormous head hung low with a deep frown carved into his whiskered face.

"Don't be sad, it's all right. I didn't know you were nearby." Kaida gave him a radiant smile to show she wasn't upset.

"I saw ye a traveling. Thought I could'st make yourn journey quicker."

Kaida looked at her companions and then back to Ughedar. "How?"

"I carry thee. In me hands and me pockets. Not had many freonds. Ye still freond?"

"Of course we are Ughedar." Kaida looked at Molakei and shrugged her shoulders. He replied with the same motion.

"We accept your offer," she replied.

Ughedar's face lit up with a big woody grin as he gently scooped up his friends and made them comfortably settled. He slipped Sigrunn and Tyrianua into his shirt pocket and held the others in one hand, close to his chest.

"I only go to edge of trees, but it will save ye from walking for a long journey," he said.

"You are a good freond, Ughedar. We thank you for your kindness," Kaida said loudly, hoping he could hear her tiny voice.

A loud rumbling started below them and in a huge rippling wave, rose from his belly and out his mouth with a giant sized laugh. "Likes when you call me freond. Feels like hot soup in my belly. Warm and ... and ... filling!" He gave another enormous laugh and his companions joined.

Kaida, Molakei and Flower Bird took the advantage of being lifted up high to look around the new world they were in. Their range of vision was much greater sitting up in the Giant's palm. They spotted a beautiful valley ahead, strewn with marvelous colorful plants, some vaguely familiar, even though their sizes were not.

Flower Bird nudged her father and pointed, "Look, those are like the mushy umbrella plants that grow on the wood bark and in the wet places, but look how tall they grow. They have bright blue edges that glow!"

Molakei nodded. "A land of mysteries. All things grow much bigger here in the world within our world."

Kaida pointed. "Take us to that valley, Ughedar. It looks so beautiful."

"I only can walk to the edge of trees. Not goes out of our forest. Too scared out in big open land of no trees. Nomliacs are forest Giants, not people of no trees."

"That is fine, Ughedar. You have saved us many hours of walk time. We will explore the valley ahead," Kaida replied.

The gentle Giant went to one knee and set his new friends down softly. He held his hand near his pocket and Sigrunn and Tyrianua leapt out. He lowered them down, looking sad to see them leaving the forest.

Kaida said, "Thank you, freond. We may pass your way again." She smiled warmly and hugged his finger.

"Be watchful. Therin be magic folk about ... ye be entering the Vale of Valdross, knowen to be filled with Magicians."

"Is it a bad place?" Kaida asked, her face splashed white with alarm.

"No place is e're good or bad." Ughedar said, thinking. "The stories been told since I was boren says most the Magicians and their folk be kind. Never goes into the Vale of Valdross so I not knowen more to tell."

Kaida unknowingly had clutched her neck chains. A soft warmth filled her hand as she held the stones, and a soft peace covered her. She looked at Ughedar and gave him a wink.

"We will keep our eyes open and be aware. We know magic too so we aren't worried. We may make more freonds!"

"Be well, freonds. Ughedar e'er ye freond. I be lone sick with ye gone." A massive tear formed in the corner of his eye, threatening to splash down.

Kaida's lip quivered. She felt sad to leave her new friend but they had to continue their journey. She waved goodbye. Sigrunn and Tyrianua rubbed their sides against Ughedar, marking him as a friend.

Chapter 14

Flower Bird pointed, "Look up ahead! Do you see those, father?"

Molakei shaded his eyes and looked. It looked to be a gateway. Stones seemed to sprout from the ground in odd shapes but neatly fitted on top of one another and tightly against the next one until it formed an arch.

As they approached, they saw strange markings on the large keystone. Molakei placed his hand against the arch and felt a tingle that made his forearm hairs stand up. He uttered a chant under his breath as he passed through the arch.

In front of them the ground made a gradual slope up on both sides and trees and shrubs crowded against jutting rocks. Molakei reached to grab Kaida's arm. Flower Bird had already stopped and was staring at the thin tendrils of smoke up ahead. The breeze was blowing against their backs. The smell of wood smoke hadn't warned them. The smoke could only mean one thing, someone was nearby.

A branch cracking had Flower Bird armed and ready to sail an arrow as a boy darted forward from the shrubs. He looked stunned to see the newcomers. Suddenly, a blue-white bolt shot from somewhere behind him and latched onto his waist, reeling him backwards. A voice sprung out loudly, "Kiel! You haven't finished."

A man, pale of skin, breached the bushes. His focus was on grabbing the mischievous young man and lead him back when he became aware of the group watching.

"Er hum," he cleared his throat. He took large strides to stand face to face with the newcomers, his piercing eyes sizing up Molakei. "What is your business here? You have entered the Vale of Valdross without invitation."

"We only pass through. We search for our way home," Molakei replied.

"Home? Where is your home?" the pale man asked as he pulled on his long mustache.

"It is in the land above. There were terrible shakings...."

"Yes, certainly. We felt those. It rained dust on us for days! We, the Magicians of Valdross, that's where you are, you know ... Valdross, we had to dome our area with a protective spell, otherwise our place would have been made foul." He shook his long dark brown hair tinged with broad streaks of gray.

Forgotten in the grasp of the pale man's hands, the young man spoke. "I'm known as Kiel." He managed a smile towards the visitors. "The man still digging his bony fingers into my shoulders is called Perthorn. He is my guardian and Teacher."

Perthorn quickly let go his grip and righted his lopsided cap. "Er ... Yes. I am Perthorn." His left brow wiggled as he asked, "Heard of me?"

Molakei had to bite the corner of his lips to not smile. "No, but then we are from.."

"Well, perhaps you are less informed living way up there!" His staff reached overhead and jabbed above his head. "What my overzealous student was trying to inform you of is that I am the Master Magician of Valdross. Perhaps he felt the need to warn you." He narrowed his eyes to intimidate the newcomers.

Kaida took a step forward and spouted, "I can do magic too!" She grinned and asked, "Why do you lip hairs grow so long?"

Kiel stepped back, laughing, making sure he was out of range of a sudden Magician's magic bolt. In a sudden flash, a crisp white bolt stretched out to zap Kaida's foot but only hit the dirt in front of her.

Perthorn's brows knitted together in surprised dismay. "Girl, your feet should be hopping up and down. How did I miss?" His puzzled look had even Kiel doing a double take. He said, "What manner of spell was that?"

Kaida looked down and released her hand from her stones around her neck. She looked at Kiel and said matter-of-factly, "It is the great magic of the stones I wear. One of them is a Dragon Tear and the great White Dragon of Urthe put a great Magic in every stone tear. The Dragon Tear protects me."

"Dragons? Girl, I would not have harmed you, it was only a little burst of energy to chide your quick tongue," remarked Perthorn.

"My name is Kaida." She held Perthorn's stare until he answered.

"Kaida. Odd name, it is." Perthorn mumbled.

"You haven't heard of me?" Her eyes flashed the challenge at Perthorn.

"Heard of you?" Perthorn gave out a burst of laughter. "Heard of a wisp of a girl from up above who stumbles into the camp of Valdross's Master Magician? Why should I, Perthorn, hear of a girl such as you?" Amusement flashed in his violet eyes.

"Then, you have not heard of the Legend of the Dragon Child? It might be you are uninformed down...."

Molakei quickly buffered any further words with his hand clamped gently over Kaida's mouth. "She means no disrespect, Master Magician. And we mean no harm. We are simply travelers in your world, trying to find the way home."

"What did she mean by mentioning the Legend? Is she to say she is claiming to be the girl of the Legend?" Perthorn asked.

"Perthorn, it is my honor to present Kaida, the child of the Legend." Molakei replied.

"Thunder and Lightning! How can you be sure?" Perthorn asked, his violet eyes snapped enormously wide.

Molakei replied, "Everything about her is in the Legend. How she would be found, what she would be like and the things she would know. She even flies with a Dragon."

"Thunder you say! Is this true?" He replied absently twisting one side of his long drooping mustache between his narrow fingers.

Molakei nodded as he released his hand from Kaida's mouth.

Kiel stepped forward with a smile. He said with unrestrained excitement, "Is it true you can ride a Dragon?"

Kaida chuckled, "Yes, I guess that is true. I have always thought of it as flying. Zlemtec, he's my friend, we fly as One. I never thought of it as *riding* a Dragon, but now I see that is what it would look like. We just fly. He ... it is hard to put in words. It isn't like he becomes my wings or I become his rider." Her face scrunched up trying to find the right words to say but none translated to their ways. She could only repeat, we *fly as One.*

"There hasn't been Dragons in our world for thousands of years! They lived here, you know? Long ago and before the Outer World was hospitable. So long ago, they are but a small entry in our history. It is recorded, they all left at once and were no longer in our sky."

Kaida latched on to the meaning. "Then, they had to find the way out! That is what we need to do, find how and where they got out!"

"You could leave the way they did, but it will be tricky," said Kiel.

Kaida's jaw dropped. "You mean you *know* how they left?"

"We know what was written. They left through a passageway, but it is on the other side of Rutenthrall Castle. That's where the Solteriem folk live. They are Faery folk, not much of a bother to us but...."

"Then they won't be a bother to us, either," Kaida said confidently.

Perthorn said, "Come into our village. Rest up a bit. After we eat, I'll pull out our Book of Days and we will go over it with you," Perthorn eagerly said, hoping to learn more about the travelers.

Molakei leaned heavily against his walking stick. "We will be honored to come to your village. I am tired and food always sounds good," he answered, giving a wide smile.

Little did they know a Squadron of Dragonflies and the Solteriem folk were quickly making their way to their location.

Jengar made the Squadron and their cluster stop along the way so she could dig her toes into the ground to hone in on the direction of the Uplanders. The last stop made her let out a shrill that threatened to burst all eardrums.

"I knew it! They have joined the Magicians in the Vale of Valdross!"

All held still as they watched the Warrior Queen pace and kick at the ground. It made the Solteriem folk shudder. They could feel the heat of her anger as her face resembled molten bronze, ready to incinerate anyone close. In a flash, she darted through the sky leaving a streaming trail behind her. After a short time, she discharged her anger and landed heavily with a 'thump'. In the corner of her eye, she saw movement.

Jengar called out, "Quick, to the bushes and trees! Dragons!"

Hidden in the brush, the Faeries looked on anxiously as three Blue and Gold Dragons and one White Dragon sped to the West, towards Rutenthrall Castle.

Perthorn led the newcomers into the small village where some of the villagers were forging swords, some were practicing spells and others were mixing concoctions into a large black kettle simmering above a fire.

The newcomers looked on with great interest, surprised to see so much magic in one place. Kiel sported a proud gleam in his eyes. It is rare any outsider had such a privilege.

They came upon a rocky hill covered in a vine that hung down with cascades of flowers caught up in clusters, much like a cluster of grapes and of the same color. Way down at foot level stood a small, bright purple door.

Perthorn stopped and said, "This is our home. Please, come inside."

Kaida looked at the wee door and then back at Perthorn. "How do you get inside?" Her eyes were filled with confusion. The door was too small for anything but perhaps a rabbit.

"We use the door," Kiel said. He tried diligently to suppress a chuckle. He had been raised here most of his days, so to have a newcomer see things with fresh eyes gave him a new perspective and he was delighted. He knew the next thing would downright shock them.

He pushed up his sleeves and said, "Abracadabra! Open." The whole of the front in the hillside swung wide, large enough to accommodate a man of great height. He was right. The newcomers staggered backwards, sending Kaida tumbling over Tyrianua.

Perthorn burst out in a jolly laugh. The villagers grew quiet as all work suddenly stopped. It was a momentous occasion to hear the Master Magician laugh, for he rarely was inclined to do so.

Kaida dusted off her tunic and asked, "How did you do that? What means this 'abracadabra'?"

Kiel, barely able to contain his laughter, answered. "It is a magical word. It is one of the first Magic words ever to be written in our spell books. Its meaning is as old as Magic itself. It means: *it came to pass as it was spoken.*"

"Yes, it is true, Kaida. But it only works for those carrying strong Magic in their bloodlines," Perthorn replied. "For instance, the Solteriem are Faery folk. They have their Faery dust and charms. Their Magic is not of Sorcery or Wizardry. It is a weaker link in the Magical realm. Therefore, it will not work for them."

"Is that why you make your door look so small, to keep the Solteriem folk out?" Kaida asked.

"Hmmm, well partially. We have no great fear of the Faery. As I stated, they are weak. It is mainly ... the *Others* that we hide. But it is of no matter, now please enter and sit." Perthorn said.

With a grand gesture, his arm swept before them to create stools upholstered in a fine and colorful purple brocaded silk. A low table was set with bowls of fruit and stone goblets encrusted with gleaming jewels were filled with refreshing drinks.

Sigrunn and Tyrianua gave a low growl. Kaida opened her hand and cast it down low, her signal for them to halt their menacing sound.

Tyrianua replied, "We will stay outside and watch for any trouble. You will be safe on the inside, but ... if you have any worry, remember your stones."

Kaida softly smiled. "Thank you, Tyrianua. I have my Protection worn around my neck."

Perthorn sat and motioned for his guests to do the same. "Let us share a meal. The journey ahead will be long. We eat, we rest, we shall share stories before we venture forth."

Molakei repeated, "We?"

Perthorn stopped tying his long mustache under his chin. "Certainly, *we*. I could not in all good conscious allow you to make this journey alone."

"We will be honored to have you come on this journey," said Molakei. "It only surprised me that you would want to travel with us."

"Ah, we may be of help to you, and you to us!" Perthorn said with a sudden smile.

"What help could we be to you?" Molakei questioned, looking puzzled.

"All of that in good time. It will be told as we go through the Book of Days. Now, eat. Let us enjoy the food and friendship forged around this table!" Perthorn finished tying back his long lip hairs, in an effort to keep them out of his food.

Kiel stole a look at the Master Magician. It was odd to see him in such good humor. The energy he was putting off in their hut was palpable. Even his own hair on his forearms tingled and rose. Since he had been brought to the Master Magician, he had never seen him so happy. He wondered, *was it the newcomers or the talk of the Legend and Dragons*? Whatever it is, he liked seeing this side of him.

Chapter 15

Zelspar called out, "Look ahead!"

The four stared at the large out building rising straight out of the ground and fashioned of peculiar stones fitted one upon another. As they flew closer, they saw a small river that circled the building. The river had no beginning, nor end. They flew over it and saw the inside of the stone building. It had a great open space with no sign of activity. They circled twice, then landed to explore.

Zlemtec called out, "Kaida!"

The four Dragons had barely had time to scratch the ground with their talons when a mighty wooden door swung open. They stared intently at what came through the door.

Two Solteriem guards stood at the entry, visibly shaken to their core. One was able to mutter "Dragons!" The other passed clean away and fell back into the entry. While the Dragons looked upon the fallen guard, the other guard blew a fine dust into the air.

The Faery dust rose on a breeze and fell lightly upon the Dragons' snouts causing them to sneeze. They blinked, looking bewildered. Their eyes grew heavy and they sat down. They blinked slow and with heavy lids, then fell into an apparent slumber.

The guard then ran into the keep, calling for King Togar. He passed the guards standing sentry before the King and said, "King Togar, Dragons!"

The guards shook in their bronzed slippers and quickly unlocked the padlock, saying, "King Togar, protect us! Send them away."

King Togar quickly fled his dungeon and asked the guard, "What did they do? Are you harmed?"

"N-noo," the guard stuttered. "They landed *in* our ward! I ... I was surprised and ... Regclive fainted. I blew dust at them. I was so frightened, I didn't even say a charm but they fell into a heavy sleep. Quick, before they wake! We must ... must...."

King Togar stepped through the massive opened doors. There in his vast ward, lay four sleeping Dragons.

As soon as the guard had ran through the massive doorway, Zelspar had said, "Feign sleep until we see a threat. They are small people, Faery folk, only grown to this stature by their environment. Their dustings brush off, our own Dragon Tears reflected any magic they could muster. We must learn more. Do not startle them. Keep your eyes closed and ears, attentive. Zlemtec, no matter what we hear, stay silent."

"But what if...." Zlemtec began.

"Shhh, they return." Zelspar warned.

Togar looked upon the massive beasts sleeping in his ward. *Amazing*, he thought. *Dragons have not been in this realm for longer than his memory. Only the tales of Dragons lived on.*

He took a cautious step forward. No movement was seen from the Dragons. He took another step. His curiosity of the marvelous creatures before him drove him closer still. He stood just feet away from a blue and gold colored Dragon, his head resting upon his chest, breathing deeply in his sleep.

"King Togar, I'll get your bow and poison arrows. Get rid of them," called out the guard.

Zlemtec flinched.

King Togar held up one hand, "Shhh ... Do not wake the sleeping Dragons! His eyes squinted at his guards. "Even you must recall what is said of waking sleeping Dragons? I want to learn more about them and why they came here."

The guards shuddered in remembrance. One guard found his voice and sputtered, "Queen Jengar said it is because of those Uplanders! A scout said a Dragon will come for the girl. They will burn us up!" The guard's eyes were wild in fear.

Zelspar knew he could not contain Zlemtec's silence and sat up.

King Togar's mouth dropped open. Fear and shock robbed his tongue of words.

"Zlemtec, sit slowly. Tell them we mean no harm, we are searching for Kaida," said Zelspar.

At Zelspar's voice, all Dragons opened their eyes and sat up. They knew the Faery folk could not speak charms to bind Dragons but they kept watchful eyes. Arrows can find their way through their armor.

Zlemtec said, "We didn't come to do any harm to you. We are looking for Kaida, a yellow haired girl. She may be here with a few others. They fell through the Urthe and disappeared."

Zlemtec stopped speaking. He recognized the look of shock in the man's eyes. It was similar to the way Molakei looked at him the first time. He waited for King Togar to digest his words.

King Togar looked at the Dragons, then spoke. "My sister queen has said the one you look for, an Uplander, is on the way here. She said they are coming to make war against us."

Zlemtec jumped up to full height, excited to hear word of Kaida.

King Togar scuttled backwards, fearing he had upset the Dragons.

Zlemtec continued, at Zelspar's urging. "I'm sorry I startled you. We only want to find those you call 'Uplanders' and bring them home. Trust us, Kaida and the others do not wish to war. They are looking for the way home. We are here only to lead them back. We will not bring harm or war to you, that is, if they are not harmed."

King Togar dropped his head for a moment in thought. "It may not be safe for you ... or for them."

Zlemtec's eyes flashed out in warning. "What do you mean?"

King Togar replied, "I have no quarrel with you or the Uplanders. It is the Queen, she has war in her blood. She looks for reasons to battle when there are none. She ... she is angry at her birthright." He ran his fingers through his auburn locks. "We have mingled blood. Not just Faery but also of Nomliacs, blood of the Giants mix with ours. She would cut it away, if she could. I do not understand her anger or shame but it has made her ... quarrelsome. Now, she sees the Uplanders as threats. She went to find them."

Before Zlemtec could inhale a lung full of air, the King of the Faeries said, "Shhh ... I feel Queen Jengar!" He slid his feet across the ground and said, "They have turned back. She flies with her full Squadron back to Rutenthrall, our castle. The Uplanders are still far away in the Vale of Valdross, the land of the Magicians. Something has turned them back. Did they see you?"

"I don't know," said Zlemtec. "Where is this Vale of Valdross? We must go there!"

"I ask you to wait. She is unpredictable. She has made poison arrows and I know what great harm they would do, even to Dragons. You could take shelter behind the castle. They will come in from the front and never see you. Let me diffuse this and tell her why you are here. It could save us all from a fight none of us want."

Zlemtec told his companions what King Togar said and they agreed to wait in hiding. They slipped over the walls and fell back behind the towering

Rutenthrall Castle. The Mursei Dragons used their Invisibility Magic and hid their colors. Zelspar conjured a spell and blended in with the rocks. They would wait.

Hastily King Togar ran back into the castle barking out orders. "No one say a word about the Dragons! Put me back into the Keep, Queen Jengar will come to me. We will bring no harm to the Dragons or the Uplanders, understood? Give me time to convince her, if I cannot ... I order you to overpower her and lock her in the keep!"

The guards nodded and were relieved to hear the King stepping in. Queen Jengar must be stopped before her fury brought an end to them all.

Chapter 16

Kaida jumped up from the table. "There! Did you hear him?"

Molakei said, "No Kaida. Did you hear your friend?"

"Yes! He is here somewhere, I heard him call out to me."

Perthorn stood and looked cautiously around. "Who is here? Where?"

Molakei said, "Kaida hears her friend, a Dragon, call her name. She thinks he has found the way inside, to lead us home."

He tilted his head and spoke to Kaida. "Remember Kaida, what I told you before. If Zlemtec is down here, he will find us easier than us rushing out to find him. We must take a rest, eat and learn the path out. Agreed?"

"Yes, Molakei." She sighed heavily. "It's just that I hear him. It seems he is close to me but ... I ... maybe it's because I want him to be close."

Molakei smiled to her. "It is all right, Kaida. If he is close, he will find us. If he isn't, we will find him."

Kaida found her seat again, her heart still fluttering. She would know Zlemtec's voice anywhere.

Perthorn cleared his throat. "If you have ate your fill, I'll remove the clutter and get out our Book of Days."

With a '*whoosh*' of his arm, the table was cleared. Kaida grinned watching the Magician.

Perthorn made his way around the table, back towards the wall. He mumbled some incoherent words and pushed the wall. A portion of the wall slid back and he reached deep within the cavity and brought out a large book. A hush filled the room as he placed it on the table.

It was a fascinating piece of work with its deep green color emblazoned with golden scrollwork running a border around the edges. Perthorn took his sleeve and brushed away the dust to let the wording show their dynamics.

All at the table crowded forward to look upon this relic. Light gasps filled the pause in conversation. Silence has a sound and *reverence* is its name.

The cover of the book was moving. Symbols danced slightly above their imprint. The Magic radiating from the book sent sparks flying up to the rafters. Perthorn placed his hand over the cover. Symbols and words of sizzling gold crawled up his hand to his arm and around his neck. They slithered across his face and touched his lips.

All eyes were open wide, mesmerized by what was unfolding before them. All but Perthorn. He spoke to the book. "It is I, Perthorn. Grant me entry as the keeper of the Book of Days."

The letters and symbols gathered across his mouth. "You may enter, Perthorn." After they spoke, they slid back down his neck, his arm and hand. They fell onto the book's cover and disappeared inside. The sound of three locks being sprung open rang loudly in the sudden silence.

Perthorn reached down and pulled the cover back, exposing the first page.

A loud clap hissed in the room, of lightning contained and squeezed down into a smallness unaccustomed, went suddenly free. Stools slid back, scraping the wooden floor. Flames from the candles leapt into the air and danced in frenzy before settling back to a normal glow.

Perthorn's face took on an eerie glow, illuminating the room. Kaida latched tightly onto Molakei's arm. Perthorn whispered, "This page chronicles the beginning of Magic. It is known only to the Magicians."

Eyes reverently turned away, but Kaida saw it. It will forever blaze in her eyes. The outstretched hand ... the spark, the touch. She was in awe. She shivered next to Molakei, even though the room felt hot.

Perthorn slowly turned the pages, looking for the particular entry. Words danced up from the book, rising to meet him, feeling his familiarity and embracing him. It was as if they hungered for him to read their words, to say them out loud, to release their Energy. As he would lift to turn the page, they collapsed and fell back into the page, once again held prisoners by the book.

Perthorn looked up from the pages and to his guests. "I must always start at the beginning. This is the full account of all Magicians. The Book of Days is our history, and our Future. As anyone will tell you, the Future is never written in stone. It weaves and rearranges itself, like the words you just saw dance from the pages. When there is a change, or a new element given Life, the Future rearranges itself to accommodate. Now, let me find where the entry of the Dragons leaving is written."

The crackling of the ancient pages turned one by one. Words leapt from the page, longing for utterances. Perthorn scanned the entries, his eyes ablaze with archaic symbols twined with letters, words, and paragraphs.

His long bony finger suddenly stopped at the bottom of page seventy-five. The words gathered and encircled his finger.

"Here it is!" Perthorn announced.

Upon his acceptance, the words flowed like a river uphill, finding a course to his mouth and rested across his lips.

The heads of all five leaned closer to the page, its smell pungent with the aroma of Time. The entries were illegible to the guests, the constant swirling of letters making it impossible to read.

Kaida whispered a question, "What does it say?" Her blue eyes were held open wide by awe, wonder and a dash of fear.

"This is the part marking the Dragons departure. It reads, '*The sky became filled with a moving cloud of fanning wings. Not clusters, nor squadrons but legions of Dragons, called the Sky Warriors, moved rapidly to the east. Middle Ground was in its shadow, for the mass of Dragons blocked the light from above.*' It continues on the next page," said Perthorn, licking the tip of one bony finger before turning the page.

"*They flew and the air was split by wings and roars, casting away the days of being the overseers of Middle Ground, to become the co-creators in the land above. A new opening was birthed beyond the Rutenthrall Castle and above Mount Leonju. All on Middle Ground stood witness as the Dragons skimmed the side of the mountain and appeared to be inhaled into the thick, cloud-capped top.*" Perthorn looked at those gathered around the table, and smiled.

As his eyes returned to the page, golden letters fell down from above their heads and showered the page. They formed and reformed and then shot like an arrow to Perthorn's eyes. He sucked in his breath. The Book of Days shook on the table and bounced up and down. A whirl of wind cycloned above it, then calmed.

Perthorn stammered, "A new entry has been made!"

Kiel asked, "How, who made a new entry? We were all here and watching."

Perthorn said, "Then you bear witness. The Future has written the entry. Did you not see the letters falling from above your head?"

Kiel was at a loss of words, as were the guests around the table. Slack-jawed faces stared at Perthorn, even their eyes had forgotten how to blink.

A slow smile crept up the corners of Perthorn's lip. "Here is the new entry. *Watch for the return of Dragons. They carry Change upon their wings. Middle Ground will be your home but up above, you now shall roam. A young one meets the old, a remarkable Future is now foretold.* So, your Dragons coming here is in our future as well, Kaida."

Perthorn stared down at the newest entry, then closed the book. He reserved the rest of the entry for another Time and place. The Time is at hand. He gave a silent thanks to his lucky stars to have been born for this Time.

Chapter 17

A loud buzzing drifted through the air, the Dragons kept hidden, but ready. As the noise grew closer, Zlemtec could barely contain himself. He did not like this Jengar who wanted to harm Kaida and her companions.

As soon as the Squadron and clusters landed, Jengar slid off her mount and threw open the doors of Rutenthrall yelling, "Bring me Togar!"

Behind her, the Solteriem folk slowly lit upon the ground. Nerves were on edge, visible by the shimmerings of wings, anxiously waiting for the Warrior Queen's next move.

King Togar marched through the door with the remaining guards who stood watch over Rutenthrall's castle. Before he could address Jengar, she quickly discharged her venomous accusations.

"Togar! You did not believe me when I told you those unruly Uplanders were teaming up with the Magicians—and yet—they are on their way here. Here! To our Rutenthrall. If that isn't enough for you to grasp our dire situation, perhaps knowing that they called upon their Dragons. I've seen them with my own eyes! The whole thing has been a plot from the beginning, they are coming to take our castle. They seek to take the whole of Aghar Found-land. They must be stopped!"

"Jengar. Calm yourself. Your rant regarding the Uplanders does not make sense. For that matter, nor does your fear of the Nomliacs or the Magicians." Togar paced in front of his sister-Queen, his jaw clenched.

"How *dare* you speak to me in this manner! I have always had to look after our Kingdom because you refuse to rule jointly with me. You never see the threats that surround us. You believe our Kingdom is simply the land of butterflies and Faeries, but it is not so."

"It once was, Jengar. Before you decided we should rule our Kingdom with your bronze fists. Remember? Think back. Think about our heritage, remember the fun our Solteriem folk used to enjoy?"

"Stop. You make my blood boil with your talk, brother. Guards, escort Togar back to the Keep. Lock him away!" She spit her words out as a poisonous venom, her eyes boring holes at her brother king.

No guard nor Solteriem moved. A silence settled over Rutenthrall Castle, such as was never heard before in memory.

Jengar turned. Quickly she spouted, "Dissolve the Wings of Flight, I remove your power and Might!" Her hand quickly cast the dust into the air to attack all those present.

Thunderous roars came from behind sending a shock wave through the ward. The massive Dragons flew up over Rutenthrall's walls and froze the airborne dust to fall harmlessly and shatter on impact.

The Solteriem folk and Dragonflies buzzed in anxiety as the Dragons circled the ward.

Jengar pointed a finger at Togar, staring back at the Solteriem folk. "See what he has done? He has brought the Dragons down upon us! How can you not see the threat he brings against us? Don't be persuaded by his pathetic ploys. Seize him!"

Then slowly, first one and then a few more moved forward until the Solteriem folk all joined in the advance forward. Jengar could not hide her delight. Her eyes flashed their brilliant green at her brother until the moment they surrounded her.

"What? No!" She lashed out, "Dry up to a bag of bones!"

Before she could toss the dust in the air, Zelspar was ready. With one swift movement, he turned the Draga Stone towards her. It burst in a flash of Lightning and shrunk the whole Solteriem folk down to half a talon length. All but King Togar and his guards were shrunk.

The Dragons landed.

Zlemtec spoke to Togar. "We had to, er ... minimize the threat. Zelspar can undo the Magic of the Draga Stone."

After the sudden shock of the sight, Togar's face split wide in a smile. "I will take your offer under consideration," he answered. Then he burst out in laughter.

The Dragons couldn't help but join in too.

Togar eased his way forward towards the cluster of buzzing wings. As he approached, the Solteriem folk moved away from Jengar, leaving her helplessly exposed. He reached down carefully and snatched up the kicking Queen and deposited her into an empty Faery dust bottle.

Jengar kicked and fluttered inside the bottle mouthing muffled insults and threats to her brother. He responded by slipping the bottle back into a small bag fastened to his side.

He looked softly upon Zlemtec and said, "Give my deepest thanks to the great White Dragon. He has quickly stopped the constant threat our Kingdom has been ruled under for hundreds of years. There has always been a split in the Kingdom due to the threats Jengar held against our Solteriem folk."

Zlemtec told his friends how grateful King Togar was for their help.

King Togar said, "If you fly due East from here, you will reach the Vale of Valdross. I am certain you will find the one for whom you search. The journey should not take but a day with the great distance your wings can carry you.

There is a way to the upper world, behind me. I realize you entered another way but I ask of you to come back this way. It will give me time to set things right again in our Kingdom. I will know by your return if I wish you to change Queen Jengar and our folk back to size. This requires some thought."

Zlemtec winked a sparkling purple eye at King Togar and asked his companions their thoughts.

The King of Mursei made his thoughts known. "He does not ask more than our ability to give. It is good to have bonds with the peoples who live in this world inside of our world. Zelspar? Your thoughts?"

The old White Dragon needed no time to ponder. "Yes, agreed. He is an honorable king. I believe in this season of Change many new things will be discovered. Some good, some bad, for this is the nature of things. Having allies who are honorable is good for us."

Galdean said, "I have no quarrel with returning here after we find Kaida. Here's my thoughts. We already know where the place is that will return us back to our beginning. It could be a risk to us to use this new place to return home. After all, we have no idea where it will take us."

Rynik, the King of Mursei, smiled at his friend, then spoke. "Can it be? The mighty warrior is worried for a new adventure?" His eyes radiated warmth in his challenge.

"The Dragon, you say! It is you whom should be worried. How many times have I had to rescue your reckless hide? Why, if it wasn't for me...."

Zelspar cautioned, "I know you two love a quarrel but you are worrying our host!"

They all turned their attention to King Togar who was steadily creeping backwards at the Dragons sudden thunderous discourse.

The King of Mursei quickly told Zlemtec, "Please tell him we are thrilled to do as he requested. We were only teasing each other, it is the Dragon's way."

Then he did his best to offer and a non-threatening smile towards King Togar, granted it was hard to do with a mouth full of jagged teeth.

Zlemtec rapidly explained to King Togar there was no reason for alarm. His companions were happy to do as requested and were only teasing each other. Togar relaxed his composure and exhaled a deep breath.

"Thank you, my new friends," King Togar replied. "You do me a great honor. It is said of us that we never forget a harm done to one of us but it is also true, we never forget a kindness. For your kindness you will be greatly repaid."

Zelspar told Zlemtec, "Tell him we seek no payment. It is our way, to help our allies."

After Zlemtec set King Togar straight, his eyes sparkled at the King Togar's response. He turned and beamed brightly at his companions.

"He said he will show us great treasures upon our return, free for our taking," said Zlemtec who always kept a keen eye out for precious stones.

"Well," offered Zelspar, "if it is a gift ... we could not object." His quick reply brought on a sudden round of laughter from his friends. They all knew there wasn't a Dragon alive who could pass up such an offering! Their one weak point was in the collection of treasures, to the extent it often made them enlarge their caves to store them all.

Rynik replied, "Offer accepted!" He again offered his host a dazzling smile and this time it was returned.

The four regal Dragons slipped into the air with a brilliant display of color. They headed due East, towards the Vale of Valdross and more importantly, towards Kaida.

Chapter 18

Kaida looked from Perthorn to Molakei, then asked, "Molakei, does the Legend talk of this new world and the Dragons bringing about great changes?"

Molakei looked thoughtfully at the yellow haired girl. "No Kaida. It speaks of you being the change that comes. This is the way my thoughts flow. You are the critical element. Without your interactions with the peoples and the Dragons, things would continue in the old ways. But now, they cannot. You have already interacted with both and change has happened because of this. That is the truth of the Legend. It does not go on to describe all the particular changes, only that it must happen for the survival of all. Since we now see changes, we know our feet follow the right path. Change can be hard, but to not change can be worse."

His eyes scanned the girl and noticed her arms were now taut with muscles. Her skin glowed with the warmth of many seasons of the sun, her hair still wild, but fluttered around her waist when loosened. She could be the very meaning of change for she has changed so much in the short time they have been here. She has the look and confidence of a seasoned warrior. He now believed it was destined for them to fall into this inner world. His chest extended with pride to be the Teacher to Kaida. His eyes glistened, thanking the Great Ancestors for allowing him to walk this path.

Sigrunn and Tyrianua slipped out into the fresh air and waited. The others would soon join them.

Perthorn gave last minute tasks to Kiel to prepare for their journey as he slipped the Book of Days under his robe, into the cushioned bag which crossed over one shoulder and rested against the opposite hip.

Kaida, Flower Bird and Molakei went outside to wait. The two wolf pups had grown in size and flanked Kaida as they prepared for the journey to Rutenthrall Castle.

"Do you feel what's in the air?" Sigrunn, the female wolf, asked as she nudged Tyrianua, her male counterpart.

"Yes. It is time," replied Tyrianua. "We must be prepared for this new Season."

They shook their fur and stood in their regal transformation.

"We are ready," he said to Sigrunn.

Kaida stood transfixed. Flower Bird was captivated by the change of the wolves. Molakei looked on with great wonder, something unpredictable was occurring before their eyes.

Tyrianua shook out his fur, sending a ribbon of blue coursing through the recently exposed mystical markings. His river-blue eyes met Kaida's. He spoke to her.

"I have been sent for this Time. The outer and this inner world has entered a period of Chaos. All things will lose their path. I am the way to Harmony. I am the Teacher of those ways."

He looked around, then let his thoughts be heard to all. "Do not be frightened of the changes you see. I have come to you for this journey just as I had come to others before you and will come to those who will come after you. It is *this* Time which is the most precarious. Life has been rattled, there will be fighting for power and resources. I will help you find the path to Harmony."

A sudden buzz of shocked whispers filled the keen hearing of the wolves. Sigrunn walked in front of the group, her fur long and white. She answered the unspoken questions with a fluidity of gentle rain.

"Call us the names you have given to us. It *is* true that we have been given different names by different people at various Times. Our path on this journey is to bring all to a common path of Harmony." Sigrunn sighed heavily, charging her markings with a flash of ice-blue. "I am the Holder of Secrets. I know the hidden things and allow them to find their place amongst all in their proper Time."

Sigrunn spoke directly to Kaida. "Your journey is great. You have been given many Teachers to help you on this journey. Every Teacher you have been sent will help you with aspects of your destiny. In time, you will remember."

Kaida bit her lip lightly. "Sigrunn, Tyrianua, why does everyone think I can make a great difference?" She knelt to the ground and buried her face deeply into Sigrunn's fur.

"It is who you are. Who you were born to be," Sigrunn replied softly, leaning her whole body into Kaida. "Remember, you don't take the journey alone. We are all here for you. Kaida, do you remember the special ceremony Molakei gave you? The one where so many Ancestors came to bind the Magic to the stones?"

"Oh, yes! I will never forget," Kaida turned and gave a smile to Molakei. "The cave filled and moved with my Ancestors giving their power to the stones."

Sigrunn moved her muzzle and looked at Kaida, nose to nose. "I share this so you will never feel alone, no matter where you are or what you face. The powder used to mix into the Cleansing ceremony of those stones ... everyone tried to give you the best that they knew how to give. Your powder had the pieces held in your Heritage box of your mother and father but ... those who love you added in their own pieces."

Kaida rocked back in shock. "But how?"

"Shhh Kaida, let me finish." Sigrunn dipped her head and uttered a low growl." So, your powder was mixed with the pieces from your mother and father plus a pinch of those who first cared for you. The Dragons."

Kaida's eyes snapped fully open in surprise. This surprise was echoed to all those around her.

Sigrunn continued, "listen well as I fill in the information you do not know. As I tell you, you will begin to remember. First, the Queen of Mursei added a pinch from her Heritage box, then for good measure added a piece from the King's box, plus a pinch of scale from Zlemtec's box since you were the closest to him. They gave this to the great White Dragon...."

Kaida shouted out, "Zelspar! I remember, he was my Teacher!"

Sigrunn and Tyrianua shared a look and a gleeful howl.

"Yes, you are correct Kaida. But, I'm not finished. Zelspar mixed a dash from his very own Heritage box. He then gave the powder to your friend, Zlemtec. He brought the powder to Molakei to perform the ceremony."

Sigrunn casually looked over to Molakei, watching him shift nervously from one foot to the other. "Molakei added a piece of grounded nail to bring his Ancestors to the ceremony." Molakei slightly lifted his shoulders, then gave a crooked smile acknowledging his secret was revealed.

Tyrianua interrupted, "It didn't end with Molakei."

Sigrunn shot a fierce glance at Tyrianua, but he continued.

"While you, Zlemtec and Molakei were busy watching the gathering of the Ancestors, Sigrunn added a hair from the both of us into the brew. You will understand now, why you will never be alone, and why no one else could ever walk your path."

Kaida's face was radiant. "I never understood why I seemed so different than everyone else I met. Tell me more of my mother and father."

Tyrianua glanced to Sigrunn and said, "That is not my story to tell."

Kaida had followed his glance and hugged Sigrunn tight. "Oh, I know you must have the answer! Please? I don't remember them. Where are they? Do they look like me?"

Sigrunn prepared herself to give up the secrets. Her sparkling eyes looked long into Kaida's.

Chapter 19

Perthorn pointed up at the sky and yelled, "Dragons!"

Heads turned skyward to behold the sight. It was a new sight for most of them. Four Dragons were flying straight towards them in a sleek line of flashing colors.

Kaida broke from the pack and ran out to the field, tears flowing as free as her blonde hair. Her arms reached up as she called out, "Zlemtec! I knew you would find me!"

With all the might in his armored body, he pushed himself forward at breakneck speed. He dove down as he got closer to Kaida. She grabbed onto his neck and jumped onto his back, hugging the very breath out of him. After so long, they were once more, flying as One.

Zelspar flanked Zlemtec and dared a glance towards Kaida. She beamed sunshine to his eyes and reached out.

"Zelspar! I have missed you." She held his arm for a moment. The old Wise White Dragon snorted a puff of smoke. It seemed his words were extinguished by the river of tears as he took in her image. He finally was able to grunt out, "Our little Dragon." He pushed off to allow room for the King of Mursei and Galdean to fly up on the other side of Zlemtec.

"We came looking for you after the shower of flaming rocks and the quakes," the King began.

"I tried to find you after Zlemtec had lost you but the peoples had already found you...." Galdean offered gently.

Kaida said, "It is all right. You are here and I am back with you!" Her eyes gleamed. "I have to introduce you to the others I am with, we were heading towards a place known as the Rutenthrall Castle, the place where...."

Zlemtec interrupted, "We just left there to come find you!"

The King of Mursei suggested, "Let us land and meet your companions. Zlemtec has told us a bit about the peoples you lived with before the Urthe shaking. Let us met all who helped our littlest Dragon."

Zlemtec circled once and glided smoothly to a rest a few steps in front of Kaida's companions, smiling at Molakei.

Flower Bird, Kiel and Perthorn were still slack-jawed at this new sight. They involuntarily stepped backwards as Zlemtec and Kaida approached.

Tyrianua stepped forward. "Zlemtec. We welcome you and the others. I will make your words more easily understood with the peoples. I can only unscramble the languages for brief exchanges but soon you will be able to speak fluently to one another."

There they all gathered and met. The Dragons, the peoples of Urthe, the Master Magician and his apprentice, all bound together on this journey with the Dragon Child. It would be thousands of years before any other assembly would be so powerful or legend.

Tyrianua and Sigrunn wagged the tails of wolf gods. For gods they were, in every language and every faction of people. They were and would be, forever.

Zlemtec nodded and helped introduce the King of the Mursei Hail of Dragons, Zelspar and Galdean to the group in front of him. Slowly, those unaccustomed to Dragons relaxed, albeit they retained a healthy distance between them. The peoples in return, introduced themselves to the Dragons.

Zelspar asked, "What does it mean, this Master Magician title?"

Perthorn, his chest suddenly puffed up, answered. "I have been tested by the best and have been found unchallenged. I have learned all that my predecessors could teach. All come to me for my Magic, spells and enchantments. When the time is right, as the Master Magician, I chose an apprentice to teach and ensure Magic will never be lost."

Zelspar tugged on one bushy brow, absorbing the information. His eyes shone brightly with keen interest. "So then I may conclude, you do not have a direct line of Magicians, an Ancestor that passes the power on?"

"Oh, some have laid claim to an ancestor of renowned abilities but that is mostly unproven. And even if so, they must still go through the rigors of testing. A Master Magician isn't simply born, he is made." Perthorn's eyes narrowed a hint, thinking this White Dragon wished to bring a challenge upon him.

"By all that is Dragon, Perthorn, your ways are similar to those of the Qyrdrom Hail, except we are given much of our power from our Ancestors. Yet, we still must practice, learn and be tested. I think there is much to learn. Perhaps, if you are willing, we might exchange our ideas and teachings?"

A wry smile started and spread across the face of Perthorn. "A wondrous idea! Our Book of Days recently added a new event and said we should watch and go with the Dragons. My apprentice, Kiel will have the greatest benefit of all. He will learn all the Magicians from the Vale of Valdross has to offer plus the Magic of Dragons!"

Zelspar chortled a puff of smoke. He thought, *Perthorn may be a Master Magician but he has a lot to learn about Dragons!* He cleared his throat and replied, "Indeed! We may all learn a thing or two."

The King asked, "If you are ready, let us head back towards the Rutenthrall Castle. We have made an ally with King Togar. He wishes to travel with us to the portal the Dragons used when they first went above."

"But you fly!" Kaida moaned. "We will have to walk the distance."

Zelspar scrunched up his face in a pretended thought. "Well, perhaps you should fly with Zlemtec and King Mursei. Galdean and myself will escort your companions if that agrees with all?"

Kaida and Zlemtec, at the same time, exclaimed "Yes!"

King Mursei winked at Zelspar and said, "How could I disagree with such a Wise Old Dragon? We will fly ahead and find a place to accommodate our group for a resting spot. It will give me time to catch up with our littlest Dragon!"

Kaida turned her beaming face towards him and ran up to give him a long-missed hug. The King's face rippled as his smile grew in depth.

Kiel looked first to Perthorn, then to Zelspar and finally back to Kaida. He shook his head. He would have never imagined meeting Dragons or talking to them but the amazement he felt at watching the Uplander girl run up to them and hug one, words would never be enough to express it.

Zelspar told the others, "Bring me your bags and traveling gear. I can easily carry it and ease your load."

With gratefulness, Molakei and Flower Bird made their way over to him and wrapped their bundles across his side. Perthorn and Kiel watched, still a bit in awe.

Zelspar grumbled, "Well?"

It was if a fire was lit under their feet as the two rushed forward with their burdens. It was all Zelspar could do, not to bust a laugh or spit out a flame, but he thought better of it. His eyes sparkled with mirth. *It will be exciting to learn more of these peoples,* he thought.

Kaida climbed up Zlemtec's back and leaned forward, her arms finding their home once again. It always was this way with her, the sudden deep breath like all the breaths before were lacking. Zlemtec's long tail gently swirled the ground around him. He, too, could finally breathe wholly.

King Mursei looked at the sight and his heart felt joy. The Hails will be happy upon their return. He turned and said, "We start our journey home," and they lifted to feel the wind.

Sigrunn and Tyrianua trotted ahead, leading a path for the others to follow.

Tyrianua turned and spoke to Sigrunn. "Isn't it always the same? The bringing together the ones that will make the necessary changes?"

She stopped and looked at him a moment in thought. "I was about to agree with you but this time, I feel a different ripple. A new spinning. We both know the outcome. But it's the journey to that future that resonates differently."

"Yes, I will agree. Knowing and walking the journey are two different things. But then, you are the Holder of Secrets. Perhaps you know things I have not seen?"

Sigrunn's eyes shimmered. She responded with a simple, "Perhaps." She felt a wild hair and suddenly lunged forward, long white fur flying, leaving Tyrianua behind staring after her.

He howled and rushed to join her.

The group headed out, exchanging thoughts and ideas along the way. The learning was taking seed. The eagerness to share, grew. They had ventured a short distance but it hadn't gone unnoticed.

Chapter 20

He watched them leave, his eyes black and narrowed. He could not have hoped for anything better unless it was the fruition of his dream, to permanently do away with his nemesis, Perthorn and his runt of an apprentice. Flegmorr pulled the rim of his drab olive hat down low and glared after those headed away. He thought, *had it not been for those Dragons....* As he turned and walked away, a rattle shook his hat and reached his ears. "Quiet!" he grumbled. "I have to think."

Flegmorr slunk around the bushes. Glancing over his shoulder, he called the Magic and slid through the door to Perthorn's house.

His companion, the Flaptail, whispered, *"there, check there!"*

"I told you to be quiet or I swear I'll turn your fuzzy wings into rocks!" Flegmorr, in one swift move, ripped off his hat and shook it vigorously, almost dislodging his cohort, a Flaptail which was a foul creature of a bat's body with a long snake's tail. Glik's tail rattled loudly as he re-positioned himself tightly around Flegmorr's hat.

He mumbled, "Where was I? Oh yes. The Book!"

He started rustling through the room, overturning chairs and opening cupboards. He ran his fingers over the walls, looking for a variance, some small hint of the deception. His pointing finger hit the crease. *Aha!* With a quick pound of the fist, the secret wall safe sprung open wide.

His black eyes peered inside. *"Nothing? Nothing!"* he exclaimed aloud.

Behind him, he heard snickering, his cloak swished as he turned. There, watching him from the back wall stood two candlesticks, flames flickering with their snickers.

His right arm shot out of his cloak as he yelled, "You shall regret! Be ye all wet!" Water gushed from his fingertip and extinguished both the flames and the laughter. His eyes narrowed and through the small slits he slowly took in the complete room before kicking the table leg and slamming the door upon his departure.

He climbed the hill above the house and stood staring out over the Vale of Valdross. His cloak rustled briefly caught by the breeze before it rested against the Magician. He pushed his way through the bushes and slipped into the dotted tree line which grew along the edge of the Vale and began his journey.

The corner of Flegmorr's lip twitched, adding depth to his scowl. He had to confront Perthorn and take back what was rightfully *his!* He had out-ranked Perthorn every year at their testings. It was only the final testing which Perthorn won that led to Perthorn receiving the Master Magician title. He knew there had to have been some trickery, some privileged access Perthorn was given, for him to have won the final testing. Somewhere in the Book of Days, it must be recorded! He would right his name or destroy Perthorn in the process.

His black eyes scanned the field. He would pursue Perthorn from world to world, if he must. Perthorn was an outsider, not born in the Vale of Valdross. A traveler who came to them in his youth, bragging of his Magic and lineage of Magicians. It had never impressed Flegmorr. It was his own family that had always held the title of Master Magician. He had vowed to learn how Perthorn stole the title and from where in Magicians' Lore did Perthorn sprout from? Seeing him and his apprentice following the Dragons made him seethe. *Dragons!* His twitch turned into a snarl as he spat a vile substance at the base of a tree. It melted into the grass and smoldered. A slight rattle from his Flaptail companion mimicked his feelings.

"Good Glik. Yes, we will get them. What belongs to us, will be ours!" Glik soothed his companion with the gentle rattles of his tail as they trailed behind Perthorn and his companions.

Chapter 21

I n flight, the King of Mursei wore a smile that gleamed off of his long sharp teeth. *It is good to have our Kaida back,* he thought. His heart felt the fullness of a bond that could not be broken.

Zlemtec soared and dove with Kaida firmly seated against him. Life returned to his spirit. His wings again found the hidden notes that streamed in the air, playing ancient tunes so softly, only the discerning ear could hear.

Kaida was once again in her element. She leaned forward, head inches above Zlemtec's, and wrapped her arms around his neck. Her body awoke as if from a deep slumber. She closed her eyes. She felt the surging of energy shooting through the internal rivers, moving rapidly over every part of her being. It felt like blue flashes of lightning, dancing within her.

She brought her knees up and shifted until she was standing on Zlemtec's back. Without thought, she threw her arms wide open, dropped her head back and gave a mighty roar! Instinctively, she was joined with the roar of two other Dragons. It was only after that moment, the King and Zlemtec swooped down to land.

Kaida slid from Zlemtec's back and leaned against him, adjusting her eyes as a thin membrane rolled up and out of sight.

"Kaida...," the King began as Zlemtec also spoke.

"Kaida!" Zlemtec's eyes sparkled the blends of purple, blue and silvery white.

"I don't know what just happened." Kaida struggled with finding the correct words. "I felt a deep urge, no ... not even that. I had a need to express my happiness. I..." She shook her head of sun colored hair, trying to capture the words again.

"Kaida," the King gently spoke, "you do not have to explain. Your Dragon voice is beautiful. It is understandable to speak and call as we do. You have be raised by us."

She met the King's eyes, unwavering. "I hear your words. This is different. I first felt this odd energy surge after the cleansing ceremony Molakei gave for me. I thought it was because so many Ancestors came to strengthen the magic of the stones. But..." Kaida paused to trace back the thread of memory, "I felt the energies sparking from my toes through my head. Powerful energies! Then, Zlemtec and I flew as One, again."

Zlemtec's added, "I remember that also, Kaida. You stood on my back then, too. You gave the Dragon Call. The one used for Victory or Celebration. Kaida? I wanted to ask you something ... something about that day and all the times after that we flew."

Her blue eyes flashed. "The answer is yes, Zlemtec."

The King tilted his head, looking from one to the other. "Would one of you do the honor and tell me what you are talking about?"

"I will try, Sipta King." Kaida looked back at Zlemtec and then to the King. "I don't think I'm one of the peoples. I think I'm one of the Dragons. I feel 'Dragon' when I'm flying as One with Zlemtec. It has always been so but ... after the ceremony, I feel this power flowing through the rivers inside of me."

"King, it is hard to describe." Zlemtec added. "I know many of the other Dragons think it strange for Kaida and myself to fly as One. But ... not only does it feel normal to me but it feels better than when I fly alone. Not simply that I miss Kaida flying with me, it's more! I feel more energy. I can breathe fully. It is like.."

Both Kaida and Zlemtec answered together. "We are complete."

The King's eyes were open wide. Several heartbeats passed. His talons scraped against his leathery jaw. Finally, he found his voice. "I don't have any answers for either of you but then, you need no answers. You have your own answers. I do think perhaps Zelspar might help us understand the reasons as to why you feel the way you do. Maybe the Queen will have more insight when we return...."

Kaida beamed. "Then, you believe me, believe us?"

The King's eyes crinkled as he smiled. "What a odd question. Of course I believe you. But how you feel doesn't require a belief from anyone, other than yourselves. It does, however, explain more clearly to why it is normal for you to fly as One. It is more than something that happened by accident. It was meant to be this way." The King could not help but think back to the day his Queen took the items from Kaida's heritage box, the strange orb that her mother had clutched tightly in childbirth. *Starleira knows more than she has said, I am sure of it,* he thought. *When we return, it will be time for her to share her knowledge of the secrets held within the peculiar orb.*

Zlemtec's chest produced a low rumble as Kaida leaned against him. A soothing sound to Kaida. Her eyes fluttered and closed gently.

It was only when she opened them again that the King saw her eyes. The inner membrane was slow to retreat and for a sliver of a second he saw her eyes, the eyes of a Dragon ... before they returned to normal.

Zelspar turned to look back at the stragglers. He shook his head in frustration.

Galdean lifted one brow as he looked at Zelspar. "What has set your bones on edge, old Dragon?"

"The peoples. They move so slow, how do they ever get from one place to another? This is an impossibility! By all that is Dragon, I would fade away if I had to travel that way all the time," he gruffly answered.

Galdean suggested, "We *could* speed it up a bit." He added a wink.

"Hmpfft. It would be far better than this crawl we are doing at present! We will see what their reactions are. Let us wait here for them to catch up," said Zelspar with the hint of amusement flashing in his gaze.

The wolves sensing something was in the air, headed towards the Dragons.

Tyrianua spoke to Sigrunn, "What do you think they are doing, waiting here?"

Sigrunn replied, "I believe they are about to teach the peoples about flight."

"Oh, this will be memorable," he said lightly nipping at Sigrunn's back.

Zelspar said, "We will need your help. We want for the peoples to move quicker. Each of us could easily carry two upon our back. Help them understand our words and desire to make the traveling easier on us all."

Tyrianua said, "I will let it be known to them. Even though the idea of such travel is new even to you, it is far from a new idea. There are worlds and times where this is quite normal and even worlds where it isn't only normal but a necessity. They will come to an understanding."

"I think it will be easier if you, Zelspar, take Molakei and his daughter. They would be the easiest to convince. Zlemtec had made great steps in learning and sharing with Molakei. He won't be frightened and will be able to reassure his daughter to do as he does. Once the other two see it is all right, they will be convinced," Sigrunn stated.

There was a pause as the four peoples ambled up to where the Dragons and wolves were waiting.

Molakei pulled his water bag up and offered it around. The peoples each took a drink. He then offered a drink to the Dragons which immediately won Zelspar's respect.

"Thank you Molakei, but we Dragons have a large reserve." He winked as he patted his belly causing Molakei to grin.

Tyrianua addressed Molakei. "Zelspar has seen your struggle to keep up with the Dragons pace. He suggested that you and your daughter travel on his back. Your journey will be made both quicker and easier."

Molakei smiled warmly and said, "It will be an honor to fly as Kaida flies through the air. I have watched her flying with Zlemtec and have wondered how it would be to watch the land below me."

He turned and told his daughter that they would fly with the Dragons, like being small birds carried by larger birds. Although Flower Bird's eyes grew very round, she only nodded yes to her father. Her excitement readily showed from her tunic fluttering above her chest, moving with her heartbeats.

Perthorn removed his hat and was slowly spinning it between his hands and mumbling under his breath. Kiel shot a look at the Dragons and then to Perthorn, not sure he had understood everything. The mumble that he *had* understood, was the chant Perthorn offered up for their protection.

Zelspar said, "Loosen the bindings up by my neck, then you will have a place to hold onto. Your daughter will be able to hold onto you." He turned his head and came face to face with Molakei and chuckled as he added, "I haven't lost a rider yet."

Molakei, the Elder warrior, burst out a belly laugh. He then climbed up onto the old White Dragon and leaned over to pull his daughter up. Waves of excitement rolled across his skin, causing a flurry of bumps to stand up. His heart pounded deep within his chest, not out of fear but out of a new adventure. *He would know flight!* Again he sent blessings to the Ancestors for allowing him to be born for this Time. *Not only the Time of the Dragon Child, but to fly with a Dragon!* His face had the glow of youth, dewy-eyed and flushed with adrenaline.

Galdean turned his attention to his would-be riders and that simple act had Kiel falling over his own feet, trying to back away. Galdean did all within his power to stifle his laugh as it crawled up his throat. The result was a quick snort and a puff of smoke which did nothing to soothe the nerves of the Master Magician and his apprentice!

Molakei asked Zelspar if they could take a short flight to show the others all was well.

Zelspar obliged. He took a few gigantic steps and climbed into the air doing a slow circle above those waiting below.

Molakei leaned into the gentle arc of the turn, his braids flapping gently as the air rushed against his face. Even the deeply etched lines of his face softened as a slow smile spread, becoming a huge grin. Those below were mesmerized by the watching of the riders on the Dragon.

As Zelspar coasted to a soft landing he noticed Perthorn had already climbed up onto Galdean's back and was in the process of helping Kiel get seated securely. Galdean gave a toothy grin and arched one brow. He bellowed as he caught air, "*Fly fast! Fly direct!*"

Zelspar returned the call, *Fly fast! Fly direct!*" His talons scratched at the dirt as he took to the wind, feeling the power of being a Dragon.

Galdean's sudden lunge to catch the air and his Dragon call, rattled his riders, causing Perthorn's hat to topple. Zelspar skillfully maneuvered under him and snatched up the hat and offered it back to the still shaken Perthorn. As Zelspar leveled his flight, he drew up beside Galdean, and shot him a warning glare but Galdean's jovial expression made even the Old Dragon bite back a chuckle.

Flegmorr watched from the tangle of trees, both mesmerized and defeated. He hastily ripped off his hat and threw it to the ground. Glik had but precious moments to scurry away and latch onto his shoulder before Flegmorr stomped his hat into the ground.

"Those cursed Dragons! I'll make them pay for helping my foe. I'll ... I'll...."

Glik, his tail buzzing in anticipation burst out, "T-t-t-turn them into t-t-toads? Bury them in the br-briars?" His fanged grin eagerly looked up at his master's face, waiting.

"I'll cast the spell of Confusion and have them circling the land until they drop," Flegmorr thundered out as he watched the Dragons quickly put distance between them.

Glik clicked his tongue rapidly, in devious delight.

Chapter 22

The King of Mursei looked at the Dragon child, full of pride, taking in for the first time the changes in their Little Dragon. Gone from her were the chubby cheeks of the hatchling that had been taken from them. In front of him stood a warrior who gently leaned against her no longer hatchling friend; but her warrior Dragon. *What strange land this is, this middle land,* he thought. *She has changed so quickly, as has Zlemtec!*

"Look," Kaida said," Zelspar and Galdean are coming!"

"That's not all," exclaimed Zlemtec, "they are bringing your friends, Kaida!"

"By all that is Dragon," uttered the King of the Mursei.

As the Dragons came closer, it was easy to see the faces of the peoples. Wonder was a language that was quickly understood by the shine of the eyes and the smile on the faces of the riders. Even the Dragons had a special gleam flashing in their eyes.

This will certainly make the journey quicker, thought the king as he watched his friends make a slow descent to the ground.

Molakei slid off the side of Zelspar and helped Flower Bird to the ground. Kaida ran forward to greet her friends, Dragons and peoples alike.

"Molakei, you fly! Now you know why flying makes Kaida so happy."

He replied, "I would watch you fly with Zlemtec and see the sun shine in your eyes. Now I know where the light of your eyes came from. It comes from inside and is so strong it bursts out from the eyes."

Molakei turned to Zelspar and said, "I do not have enough words or gifts to give you for what you have given to me, my friend. I shall remember always the gift of Flying. To see the sky so close and the land disappearing underneath me; it was like being carried in a Vision but I could feel, smell, see and hear everything. Thank you, my friend."

Zelspar eyes shimmered even though a flush crept across his face. "No need for all the fuss. We had to get to where we were going. Flying was the only practical way. Now, by all that is Dragon, are we going to spend all of our time talking or can we eat?"

This brought on a round of laughter, mainly from the Dragons and Kaida who knew Zelspar did not handle compliments well. Kaida hugged Zelspar and as she had his head bent low, Flower Bird pressed her face against his. His eyes flashed a radiance that all could see. He was well pleased.

Perthorn and Kiel had maneuvered down from Galdean and made a quick-step to not be in proximity of his feet, jaws or wings. Perthorn didn't need someone to tell him to make room for the Dragon to move, he had felt the powerful muscles of the Dragon under him and had no doubt he could be easily crushed if he got underfoot.

Rynik, the King of the Mursei, was amused and grinned at Galdean, which in hindsight was probably the wrong thing to do as his friend delighted in causing a bit of turbulence for fun.

Galdean quickly flapped his wings a few times and let out a hint of a roar. That was all it took to have Perthorn running and Kiel right behind him. Kaida fell down in a fit of laughter that soon led the group into rapid bursts of chuckles.

Perthorn's large round eyes looked at the spectacle around him. He did not find anything that was so funny. Kiel looked from the Dragons to Kaida rolling around on the grass and joined in. Perthorn scrunched up his lips, dusted off his cap and found a resting spot under a tree.

Galdean slowly approached. "Perthorn, my friend. I am sorry I startled you. It's the 'Dragon' in me that likes to play pranks."

Perthorn replied, "Ahh, so I've learned a new thing. Dragons like to scare the wits out of a person. I am sure if I had known you as long as the others here, I wouldn't have been so alarmed. But I see now that it was all in good fun and as my new friend, I have to share a laugh with *you*. *I* was about to turn you into a ground rodent! Now that I think of it, wouldn't that have been jolly?"

Galdean's eyes grew so large, they looked like they would pop. Rynik could not help but let a deep resounding belly laugh out as he watched his friend. It wasn't often Galdean was caught by surprise. Soon, all joined in with the laughter including Galdean and Perthorn!

They all settled down to an evening feast and found lodging beneath the trees. Four Dragons formed a circle, and inside the circle slept Kaida, Molakei, Flower Bird, Kiel and Perthorn. Protected and sound asleep.

Zelspar looked across to Kaida. She was slumped over Zlemtec's outstretched arm, under the cover of his wing. Both seemed to wear the identical soft smile on their faces. He noted, *Something is different between those two.* Before he could ponder more, two shadows approached and broke through the circle. They circled and came to rest next to Kaida. Sigrunn and Tyrianua had returned.

Chapter 23

Flegmorr shifted his weight on the hard ground and not finding it any more pleasant, gave a quick spell to add a mat of thick moss to sleep upon and a feathered pillow for his head.

Glik, who had hung upside down from a branch, slowly uncurled his tail and flew off into the night. His nose had picked up the scent. He would find it. His tongue clicked as he flew, dodging trees and low hanging branches.

His feet reached out and located his prize. A large maroon fruit had burst open and was dripping its sweet nectar. He landed and used his jaws to clamp down into the fruit, squeezing the juices down. When consumed, he tossed the deflated fruit aside and found a supply of bloated fruit spilt across the ground. One after another, he drank them dry, grinning a toothy lopsided grin. His tail twitched and rattled softly.

He had more than his fill, slobbering juice down his mouth and onto his engorged belly. He flapped his wings and was ready to head home. He tried to get airborne but his tail kept dragging him down. Angry, he bent down and bit into it sending sharp screeches into the air!

He tottered in a zig-zagging manner, causing his tail to rattle even louder, making his head pound at the noise. His wings flapped quickly as he turned around to grab his tail, to silence the intrusion but his tail turned too. Around and around he went until he flopped down, his head spinning faster than his body. Still at last, his tail curled around him and covered him as he whistled a light snore.

Flegmorr woke before the light could penetrate the foliage of the trees. "Glik! Where are you? You miserable Flaptail, I'll wear your hide if you don't get back here!"

Glik awoke feeling a stern vibration rippling in the air. He scratched at his tail, unwinding it from his wings and half-flopped across the ground, crashing into the bushes until he could climb above them. Finally he made his way and landed with a heavy thud onto Flegmorr's hat, sending it down over his eyes.

"Glik, I've told you to stay away from that fermented fruit! Ick, you smell of rotten fruit flesh. You better sober up or you'll be walking the rest of the way."

He didn't dare say a word. Instead, he just re-adjusted himself onto Flegmorr's shoulder and gave his companion an intoxicated grin.

"Hmpfft," was Flegmorr's only response as they followed behind his enemy and the Dragons.

Glik rode contentedly, giving an occasional crooked smile when his night feast squirted down the back of Flegmorr's once solid blue cloak. His tongue clicked happily on their journey. Flegmorr had made a habit of ripping off his hat and fanning in front of his face, trying desperately to rid the air of the foul smell around him.

Chapter 24

The morning broke with shards of light peering through the trees. Already, a fire glowed bright as Flower Bird worked on the morning meal. Its aroma wafted towards Kaida, stirring her gently from her slumber and rousing the wolves. One by one, the peoples awoke and set about repacking their bed rolls and packs.

Zelspar kept watch over the small group of the peoples as Rynik, Galdean and Zlemtec moved through the trees to collect enough for their morning meals. Among the standard greens growing on the forest floor, they had found trees which dangled large golden fruits. Upon further searching, along the front of the tree line, a cluster of trees which bore a bounty of purple fruits were found. They brought back huge limbs of the ripened fruits for all to enjoy.

Perthorn called out to Kiel, "Boy. Where is my roasted morning brew? You know I'm fuddle-brained until I've had my cup or two!"

Kiel muttered under his breath, *why don't you just conjure up one....*

"Be careful my young apprentice. If conjuring you want I could always conjure up something special for you!"

Kiel's head whipped back to look at the Master Magician. *Dash it all,* he thought, *his ears ring before my words pass my lips.*

"Quite true," Perthorn replied with a smidgen of a gloat lifting up the corners of his lips.

"I'll have my drink now, if you please."

Kiel stirred the drink and brought the large mug over to his Master. "Fresh from the fire and strong enough to wake a Giant."

"Giants I can do without, but not my morning brew!" Perthorn inhaled the steam rising from the cup and the first hint of a smile crossed his face. He tucked his long mustache under his chin and took a large swallow. He closed his eyes briefly, enjoying the passage from lips, to tongue, to throat. "Ahhh! Now that is worth waking up in the morning!"

Kiel visibly relaxed. He returned to the fire and warmed hunks of bread to smother with fruit preserves. He offered the same to the others and in return was given strips of cured meat. He took a leaf platter to Perthorn and set it down in time to get his offered mug for another pour. After returning with a fresh mug of steaming brew, Kiel finally sat to enjoy his meal.

The noise around the fire was the happy sounds of the food being enjoyed and sharing of how each made a particular food.

Zelspar looked on with amusement. He had never spent this much time around the peoples and they proved to be most interesting. His head tilted as he watched them interact. He had hardly thought of Kaida as a peoples, since she had been born and raised with the Dragons, but now as he watched them eating and conversing, he saw they were not much different than the Dragons.

Oh, to be sure, Zelspar thought, they were small wingless creatures but they acted much the same as Dragons. They ate, shared, talked and even poked fun at one another. In a moment of reflection, he thought of Starleira. *The Queen of the Mursei would be happy to watch the peoples*. This was her dream back on Verlaunde, to live in a place with peace. Now, with their Dragon Child, they have learned to communicate with the peoples and in time, will learn more from one another.

Flower Bird left the fire and approached the old White Dragon. "I bring you a sweet treat I make from the heart shape berries. I make good with nuts mixed in. Is sweet to eat and gives energy."

Zelspar's yellow eyes sparkled golden. He opened his hand and she filled it with the goodies she brought. He didn't know how to respond. This wingless female peoples had thought to bring him something she made. He felt a warmth spread from below his neck to his face which left him flushed.

"Thanks be to you," he managed to convey. Flower Bird smiled and stood still.

Zelspar took the food to his mouth and chewed slowly. His eyes sparkled as he tasted the unique mixture she had brought to him. The flavors he had not known together. Such a perfect blending! His smile grew large and pleased Flower Bird. She gave Zelspar another gift, her dazzling smile. She turned and went back to the fireside to clean up the area.

Molakei asked Kaida, "Where are the wolves?"

"They said they will run ahead of us. They know we will travel faster so they left to make better travel time. They also go to make sure nothing bad is waiting," she answered. She did not know the threat was somewhere behind them, trailing them with every passing moment.

The King of Mursei spoke. "We need to get ready to go to Rutenthrall Castle. Now since we are all together, we can spread out the loads. Kaida, you will fly with Zlemtec. Galdean, Zelspar and myself will carry the four of you."

Flower Bird quickly brought her packs and placed them by Zelspar. Molakei looked from his daughter, then to the King of the Mursei. Flower Bird smiled and waved him on towards the king. He answered her with a nod and brought his packs towards Rynik.

Galdean looked at Perthorn and smiled. "That leaves you and your apprentice to ride with me."

Kiel lugged their belongings up to Galdean and carefully stepped around the Dragon as he strapped them around his neck. Once everyone had their parcels in place, the Dragons lowered to allow their riders to climb onto their backs.

This time, Perthorn took firm hold of the strapping as Kiel clutched tightly around his waist. A new energy rippled within each Dragon.

The call went up in unison, "Fly fast! Fly direct!" Each Dragon took large strides and scooped the air with their wings bringing a quickened heart rate to the riders. The newness of flying with the Dragons had not worn off, as each rider again caught their breath and hung on tightly.

Time passed as quickly as the landscape underneath them. In the distance, the King of Mursei could see the first stony glimpse of Rutenthrall Castle. He dipped his head and pushed towards their target wondering if they would be met with a welcome or if something had gone wrong since they had left the castle's walls.

As they closed in, they saw the small river that had no beginning or end that circled around the castled. They flew up over the walls and swooped down to land within the large castle ward. Just moments later, the huge wooden doors that led to the interior of the castle, swung open.

King Togar walked out, flanked by his guards. The guards wings nervously shook as they looked anywhere except at the Dragons.

King Togar smiled broadly. "You have returned, my friends." He walked out to stand in front of the massive Dragons leaving the guards quivering behind him.

Rynik answered, "We have returned with our friends. Are we welcome here?"

"Yes, all are welcome. Have your friends climb down, I would like to meet them," replied King Togar.

Kaida was the first to jump down and walk towards the new creature. Her eyes were flashing a bright blue as she walked puzzled around him. She found her voice and asked,"What form of peoples are you? I have never seen peoples with wings!"

King Togar was not put off by her curiosity and smiled warmly to her. "We are known as a group, the Solteriem folk. We are Faeries."

Kaida stepped closer. "You can fly?" Kaida's face was both full of wonder and puzzlement. Her hand hovered mid-air. She longed to touch those beautiful wings that looked far different than a Dragon's wing.

To answer her, King Togar quickly fluttered his bronze wings and buzzed around Kaida, causing her and the others to catch their breaths before he descended.

Kaida, with eyes wide in wonder walked closer. She towered over King Togar. She asked, "Will you grow taller with age?"

This sent King Togar into a burst of laughter. "I am considered middle-aged being an adult of four hundred and seventy-three years old."

Kaida's eyes looked from the Faery to her companions and back again. "I am Kaida."

She turned and pointed to her companions and introduced them to King Togar.

"Welcome all." The King of the Faeries tipped his head to the peoples and the Dragons. "King of Mursei, I thank you for returning this way."

"King Togar, we are most grateful to you and your help in us finding our Kaida," he said.

Zelspar asked, "Have you decided on what to do regarding your sister and the peoples with whom I minimized with the Draga Stone?"

A ruffle of his wings and the sudden spark in his eyes answered before his words could.

"Yes, yes. The answer is clear! Even though Jengar is my sister and twin, she has caused our Faery folk more trouble than necessary." Saying this, King Togar laughed before continuing. "Now, the amount of trouble she can cause, is small! She and most of our people are now not much bigger than my littlest finger."

Rynik and Galdean roared a laugh that shook the very ground they all stood upon, causing an instant alarm in both Perthorn and Kiel.

The King of Mursei composed himself and asked, "Where are your Solteriem folk?"

"Ah yes. I was about to get to that. Jengar, even being so small, still has a large impact on those her same size. She convinced a group of the shrunken ones to release her from her prison in the bottle. I can only imagine the type of threats she used to get her way. My guards here," he waved his hands to his right and left, "overheard her plans. She has led them back through the tunnels in the mountain. The tunnels our folk originally took to find this land in times of extreme cold and dwindling food supplies. It will lead them to the Upper world."

"Thunder and Lightning!" Perthorn exclaimed. "So we will have to deal with the vile varmints there too?"

King Togar addressed Perthorn. "We, the Solteriem folk, even at my stature, have never been a viable threat to the Magicians, and certainly not to Dragons. No, there is no worry we will be in any danger from them, even if we cross paths. Besides, they have taken to the tunnels, our way is up over the mountain."

Zelspar asked, "How many of your folk remain here with you?"

"My loyal guards and myself, as well as a small group of followers. A total of eighty-two of us will make the trip."

Rynik responded, "We can take you up the mountain. It would take you far too long and too much energy to fly. Perhaps the smaller folk would not mind being carried in one of our packs? It would protect them from the winds weaving havoc against their wings."

"We gladly accept your generous offer. We have prepared items we need and have them just inside the doors. Would your friends help us carry them out?" King Togar's eyes shone brightly as he added, "There is also the treasure to consider...." Having the undivided attention of the Dragons he said, "First, you need to bring our belongings out and move them far away from the walls."

Kaida waved to Molakei and Flower Bird. Kiel and Perthorn joined them. They approached the large doorway and peered inside. Kaida caught her breath. The castle was filled with beautiful hanging rugs and polished slabs of stone on the walls that reflected the images in front of them.

It was not much to carry, for people of their size. Several trunks and bags and parcels but being items of the Faeries, they weren't very large. Once they all were removed and set towards the center of the ward, King Togar motioned for the King of Mursei to approach.

"From one king to another, I offer my treasury! You are far too large to fit through the castle doorway. You will need to tear off the top of the store house." Togar pointed to the tall tower above the Keep. "I am sure you will succeed. The power of all of you will open it up like splitting open a ripened fruit."

"King Togar, that would destroy your castle! What if you wish to return?"

"King of Mursei, our people have lived here a long time. We built our castle long ago. Whatever damaged is caused can be repaired if we ever return. The castle itself holds no fondness in my soul. It has been, for a very long time, a place of discontent. We go with you in the hopes of a better way of life. Tear down the storage house. Reap your reward!"

And so, with the mild persuasion from King Togar, the Dragons came to the storage house. Their razor sharp talons dug deep at the fitted stones and pulled them away. Dust and chunks of stone fell down into the ward. With a mighty pull, the top circular wall was torn away.

Those below gasped in surprise as a rain of sparkling gems and flattened circles of gold poured out from the storage tower. Chests of gold and silver fell into the heap of treasures, being jostled open, exposed flashing stones of every color!

The gleam in the Dragons' eyes nearly shone more than the treasure itself. They quickly went to work on packing the treasures into side bags. When those were full, they melted some of the gold to fashion a large box and poured the rest of the treasure inside. The large box could be strapped onto them for carrying back to their lairs.

"Your gifts are many," replied King Mursei. "Too generous for taking you up to our World. As your folk never forget a harm or a good, neither do Dragons. Whatever your need, you may always come to us. You have proven to be honorable and good to your word. You must journey with us to our land and meet our Hails of Dragons. They should come to know you and your desire to live in peace."

King Togar bowed deeply to the King of Mursei. "It will be our honor to meet the Dragons above. Our history tells us long ago, we were all allies. It is my wish to return to the old ways."

"Then, we should start our journey," said the King of Mursei.

Kaida spoke out, "But what about Sigrunn and Tyrianua? How will they find us? We can't leave them here!"

A low growl came from behind them. Tyrianua padded close to Kaida, shaking out his fur. "We will go through the tunnels. Do not worry for us, we will make our way. We will find you." He pushed his side against Kaida as a wolf embrace. "Besides, we need to see what awaits above. If there is any trouble...."

Kaida's eyes flashed with alarm.

Tyrianua pawed at her leg, "We will be safe. Remember, we are not mere wolves." He rippled his fur and once again the flash of bright blue traveled the hidden spirals and shapes across his body and transformed the wolf to the deity he was. "We will find you."

Kaida hugged him close and said her goodbye to him and Sigrunn before she climbed up on Zlemtec, ready for the journey.

There was a sudden bustle of activity and noise as the group of peoples, Faeries and Dragons prepared for the trip.

Sigrunn turned to Tyrianua and said, "Yes. We will find her. She is of the age to know. It will be her battle to fight...."

Tyrianua replied, "Yes. It is what she was born for. All Dragons know of the Legend but not all of them understand what particular part of the Legend Kaida plays. Not all will be happy with her path but it was cast in the stars, long ago."

They watched as all prepared to leave and then, made their way towards the tunnels.

Cargo, treasures and riders were loaded and ready for the adventure. The excitement and nervousness rippled in the air. For most, they had not ever seen the Upper World and could not imagine what it would be like, but even so, the prospect of adventure and a more peaceful way of life, led them on.

For the Dragons and Kaida, it meant going home. That idea alone was the driving force that beat fast in their hearts. All heads turned towards the King of the Mursei. As their leader, he took huge strides and broke away from the ground.

He roared, "Fly Fast! Fly Direct!"

His call was met by the thunderous roars of the other Dragons. "Fly Fast! Fly Direct!"

As the Dragons caught the air beneath their wings, an audible gasp traveled from rider to rider. They were airborne and climbing at an alarming rate, even for the Faeries who had wings and flight experience.

Galdean turned his head towards his life-long friend, Rynik. The glint in his eyes and the flash of shining teeth told all. *This never grows old,* he thought. The Dragons had always been accustomed to flight, the power of moving in the wind. Having riders experience their power brought both pride and an urge for the mischievous. Especially in Galdean. He flew and sharply dipped to his left giving Perthorn and Kiel a hard look at the rocky mountainside.

Perthorn shouted, "Thunder and Lightning!" He had to quickly snatch up his cap before it tumbled away. He felt an odd ripple beneath his seat and knew it to be the confounded Dragon snickering.

"Galdean, I'd change your wings into wisps of grass if it wouldn't mean I would fall to my death," yelled Perthorn.

Zelspar shot Galdean a piercing glare as a warning which seemed to make the desired impact, at least for now.

The higher they flew, the more dense the cloud cover until it was hard to see the Dragon next to them. Suddenly, they were rocked it flight, knocking them precariously sideways. Each Dragon fought to stay airborne as rain, no, *waves* of water poured all around them!

The King of the Mursei roared. Each Dragon answered and adjusted their flight to follow him. The beat of their wings slowed. Zelspar groaned under the pressure of trying to lift his wings and body upward. From the heavy cloak of clouds, sudden torrents of water crashed against man, woman, Faery and Dragon. The roars continued in the enveloping whiteness. Their hope was in following their leader, following the sound. The roars became muffled, swallowed up in clouds.

A Lightning flash shot directly in front of the Dragons. The King of Mursei had lit the way by shooting Lightning, and just in time. In front, the massive mountain loomed, water cascading down its sides. Abruptly, the Dragons reared back to avoid the collision and struggled to push their wings to pull them up higher and higher. Their breaths were labored and smoke rose from their snouts. A clear thunderous roar came from above.

The top. They had reached the top!

Chapter 25

E ach Dragon found purchase on the mountain top and looked around. No words were spoken, only gasps of wonder met their ears. Every head turned to look at the view. Never before had any looked at what met their eyes.

Kaida exclaimed, "I have never seen so much water! It surrounds us on all sides." Her blue eyes mirrored the reflection of the vast waters around her. One hand arched over her brow, shading her eyes from the brightness of the glistening waves.

The King of Mursei surveyed their area. They had plenty of windswept trees for protection. It provided a good place to rest and let everyone stretch a bit. After such a journey, all their travel parcels would need to be removed and re-tied before they could take their next trip. He made the announcement.

"We will rest here before any more traveling. All bindings will have to be redone. Please help remove all parcels from us. After that, stretch your legs but do not journey far. We have not returned to our familiar land. I am unsure if there is danger here. Eyes and ears open, be watchful of danger."

Zelspar uttered, "By all that is Dragon," as he took a hard look at their situation. "We must have hit some type of portal from the Inner Urthe. No wonder we were tossed sideways, rocked with so much water on our way up. His eyes had sprung completely open, in a sudden realization when he thought, *We could have drowned!*

"Thunder and Lightning! Is your world all water, Uplanders?" Perthorn walked in a slow circle, seeing a repeating image.

Kiel looked below. Several pools were trapped in bowl shaped carvings on the sides of the mountain. "Look down there, Master! The water is filled with fish!"

Kaida grinned a wide smile and said, "I will catch us some good food. Flower Bird, get us a fire ready and Zlemtec, get ready to catch all I throw to you!"

Zlemtec returned Kaida's smile. He knew this would be a surprise to the others and he found a spot a few feet from Kaida and watched as she used her special talent to fish. He glanced up to see all heads focusing on her and knew they would be in for a treat.

With waves of blond hair billowing out behind her, Kaida crouched over a large pool of water. She spied all shapes and sizes of fish swimming in the water. She held her hands over the surface and called out to them, "Come. We are hungry."

Fish leapt through the water and crashed around Zlemtec. The air sparkled with the spirits of the fish as they gave up their strength to feed the hungry. Zlemtec filled a large bag with the fish and the onlookers broke apart to let him pass.

Perthorn was tugging on his long mustache, puzzled with what he had just witnessed. "What form of magic did she just do?" He asked no one in particular, and it seemed he was asking himself the question.

The King of Mursei answered, flashing Dragon pride in the gleam of his eyes and his puffed-out chest. "It is her Dragon Magic that allows her to call the wild things. Only the very adept of our kind are able to do such Magic." He looked towards his special Dragon, Kaida and then back to Perthorn. "She could do this from the time when she was very young, much younger than any Dragon had done before her."

The Master Magician removed his hat, scratched at his scalp and shook his head slowly from side to side. "I would not have believed it. She's not much more than a scrap of a girl ... er, Dragon ... er, Dragon-girl. Well, Thunder and Lightning! What is this girl?" Perthorn looked confused and frustrated. Not many things baffled the Magician.

Zelspar chuckled softly. "She is Kaida. The Dragon Child. Never before has there been one like her. However, I must confess the term 'child' no longer seems to apply. She has grown and come into her youth while living inside your world, Perthorn."

Kaida, unaffected by their talk, climbed the rocky slope and trotted towards the campfire to squat next to Flower Bird as she prepared the feast with her special herbs and spices that made mouths water.

King Togar gathered the Solteriem folk and made their way close to the others, to share a meal and the conversation. The Dragons found the vegetation filling and found large round stones on the ground, that when cracked open was filled with sweet water and delicious white meat. After their shared meal, the process of packing and rebinding the parcels, bags and chests took place.

The King of Mursei looked at Zelspar and noted. "Judging by the place of the Sun in the sky, I think we will have to fly far to the West to find our home. I only hope we will find land before our wings give out."

"By all that it Dragon!" Zelspar shouted, suddenly. "I can call up Pravietis! He said I can always call him from the water. He might be the Future Walker but the water is his home. If anyone would know where we are and how to get back home, it will be him."

Before Rynik could reply, Zelspar had flown down the edge of the mountain and stirred the waves that lapped next to his feet. "Pravietis, we are in need of your help and direction."

The waves began to undulate and crashed into themselves, when out of the water, a great Sea Dragon broke through and crashed back down. The gleam of his multi-colored scales were dazzling and so bright in the sunlight, it caused a bow of colors to cross over the water.

"Zelspar, my friend, we meet again! You gave me quite a concern when I saw you and the rest floundering in the water before finding the mountain top. You altered your course. You did not leave the inner world the way you entered."

Zelspar asked cautiously, "Are you saying we have changed our Future?"

Pravietis' body swished through the water, like a towering tree, its body bobbing up and down in the waves. His eyes locked firmly onto Zelspar's. "No Zelspar. The Future has not been changed, only its approach."

Zelspar's voice was gravelly when he spoke. "What do you mean by that? For once, Pravietis, can you use a plain tongue? Are we lost out here? Will we be able to find our way home without plunging to our deaths in all this water?"

Pravietis' eyes closed softly. When he opened them he said, "When you are ready to travel, I will guide you to land."

"Well now, that is what I was asking! I will go and tell the others. We will follow you." He made his way back to the group and explained they would have a guide back to land.

Pravietis rippled through the water, flashing his brilliant colors as he moved. He thought, *There was so much more to tell, but then perhaps, telling of the Future this time would be too much for any of them to absorb ... and ... this Future cannot be altered. Yes, they are in fact, on the right course for their Future.*

The peoples and Dragons alike, strained to look into the water below, in hopes of spotting the One who was only whispered about, Pravietis. Hearing the buzz of excitement from above, Pravietis broke through the water. The regal Sea Dragon with his sleek glistening body, undulated in the air before diving back into the great waters.

Perthorn looked alarmed and had begun to stumbled backwards when Zelspar came to his aid.

"There is no need to be concerned. He brings no harm," Zelspar assured Perthorn. "Have you heard of the Future Walker in your world?"

Perthorn pulled at his mustache as he tried to find his words. "He was a myth! Yes, even in our World we have heard his name, remember, long ago our world had Dragons also. But ... but, we always thought of Pravietis as a myth!"

Zelspar's brows lifted. "He is no myth, as you can see. He has been very helpful to us in the past. Without his help, all Dragons would have perished. He and the Historian, Wyrtregon, came to our aid when the Great Deceiver, that instigator of Chaos, tried to kill us off simply for his sick entertainment."

Perthorn replied, "We know of the Deceiver, Dargenoin. We suspect he played his hand in our world, also. Creating hate between the Faeries, Giants and ourselves. I do not want to run up against that one."

Zelspar unconsciously rubbed his hand across the top of his staff, knowing the hidden compartment and its secret. He softly chuckled. "There is no need to worry about Dargenoin. I have heard from the highest authority, he is contained and can no longer meddle in the affairs of any in this world or even yours, below."

"I would like to know more. How did Dargenoin cause the Dragons so much harm?" Perthorn asked as he tugged on his lip hairs, thoughtfully.

"That is a long story. Perhaps a story better suited once we reach our home. Now, let's finish preparing for that journey. Do what you can to help reload and cinch up our travel gear. We don't want to lose our goods somewhere over the vast waters!"

That said, they made their way back to the flurry of activity as the others had already been busy preparing for the trip. Flower Bird, Molakei and Kaida hurried over to help load Zelspar up with his load. Once finished, all riders mounted the Dragons and cinched themselves tightly to their backs.

The King of Mursei strode to the edge of the mountain top. He glanced behind to take a long look at his Dragons, friends everyone. His hand reached up to hold his Dragon Tear which hung down from his neck. His protection. He hoped it would be enough to help him reach his home safely, with all his friends, the peoples and the Solteriem folk.

His call rang out, "Fly fast! Fly direct!"

All Dragons answered the call as they left the mountaintop, surrounded by the rippling waters.

"Fly fast! Fly direct!" Their sound thundered across the vast expanse of the ocean.

They followed the great Sea Dragon, Pravietis as he led them towards land. The sun was at their backs as it gained speed on them, eventually overtaking them on their journey.

They had flown for hours and the sun was moving ahead of them, to the west. The place where the sun would set in their homeland. Weary wings pushed on, following the crests of the Sea Dragon as he guided them to land.

As the sun threatened to disappear beyond the horizon, great birds had been sighted off in the distance. They were diving into the great waters and pulling out their meals.

The King of Mursei called out, "Look! The fishing birds. We must be close to land because their wings cannot carry them great distances."

It was as if a new wind found their wings. Each Dragon pushed onward with a renewed strength, their weariness forgotten with the hope of land, rest and home. It was not long before an outline of land was spotted.

"Just ahead," roared the King of Mursei, "a shoreline!"

The wings of the Dragons pumped the adrenaline through their bodies, using the last of their reserves to make landfall. The sun had dipped low and streamed the sky with amazing colors of reds and purples, all reflected across the water below. The King of Mursei dropped down his feet and made contact on the rock strewn beach. His Dragons followed and all gave a mighty roar, the sound of triumph over the waters. The sound of coming home.

Chapter 26

All were relieved to touch ground again. They made their way from the rolls of the waves kissing the shore, towards the trees and hillside where they made quick the unloading of their belongings. They all were in need of food and rest.

The Dragons had formed a loose circle around the peoples, a habit they had formed to protect their companions from any sudden threat. While the Dragons rested, the peoples and Faeries alike, prepared a quick meal from their packs.

Kaida, the first to wake and stretch whispered to Zlemtec. "I will be back. I want to climb the hill and look at what lies ahead."

"I'll come too. I can take you quicker than you climbing."

Kaida's face radiated the warmth of her heart. "You rest, Zlemtec. This won't take long. My legs need to stretch after so long in the air, just as you need the rest to prepare for the journey. I'll be back soon."

Zlemtec nodded and watched with groggy eyes, as Kaida climbed along the hillside. Weary down to his bones, he rested his head on his outstretched arm and closed his eyes. When his eyes opened again, he did not see Kaida. He was certain he had only closed his eyes for a moment because everyone else was still resting.

He sat up and stretched. His eyes traveled the area where Kaida had climbed but saw no sign of her. Something inside of him started to crawl. A worry so strong, his chest was pounding in loud thuds. He leapt into the air and landed solidly on the hillside. What he saw out in front of him, hit him with shock.

He yelled, "Kaida!"

His yell caused many heads to turn and reach for their arrows. Kaida spun on her heels, her arms spinning, knocking down the pulled arrows. Kaida made rapid hand signals and words, exerting all her efforts to communicate with these peoples. "Stop! We mean no harm."

After hearing the commotion, three more Dragons appeared on the hillside next to Zlemtec. They stared at the group of peoples around Kaida. There, surrounding Kaida were a cluster of people unlike the peoples near their home. These looked remarkably similar to Kaida with the same blonde hair and blue eyes. They were all of advanced age, and they had Kaida surrounded.

"By all that is Dragon, they have our Kaida!" Zelspar was on the verge of taking flight when Kaida implored her Dragon friends to stay where they were.

"Please wait. I'm trying to find out more from these peoples. I can only understand some of their words. I thought they were calling my name but it was only similar. They think I am 'Kiayla.' I have tried to tell them my name is Kaida but they don't understand."

The King of Mursei answered Kaida. "We want to come near. See if they will allow us to approach."

Kaida struggled to find the words and gestures to speak to these new peoples. When her attempts seemed in vain, her head shot backwards and a great thunder roared. The blonde haired peoples fell to the ground, Kaida's arms were thrust wide and vibrating. Her hair stood out on end as a bolt of blinding Lightning flashed. The accompanying thunder was deafening. Then silence.

The blonde haired peoples and the Dragons looked on in awe. Kaida was glowing and in her hands, a great staff with glowing gems. Kaida's head fell forward. She shook off her shock as her head rolled from side to side. That is when she first noticed what she held in her hands.

The blonde peoples uttered, "med sa tivar!" The loose translation given by the glowing staff was '*by the gods!*'

Kaida whirled to face the peoples and said, "I can understand you now. Speak to me."

A man rose from the ground and said, "Are you Kiayla? She disappeared from us many years ago when we left our homeland."

"I am not the one you look for," answered Kaida. "Do not be afraid of the Dragons, they are my friends, my family. They want to come closer."

The man said, "If they mean no harm, let them come."

Kaida had begun to tell the Dragons they could come but they were already moving.

The King of Mursei spoke. "Kaida, we heard and understood his words. It must be something with your new staff. What we could not understand before, we can now."

"Oh! I didn't think of that," Kaida said, turning the new staff around in her hands. She noticed the gems illuminated when someone spoke.

The King of Mursei asked the older man, "Where is your homeland?"

He replied, "It is not this world but another far from here. Our lands are known as The Seven Sisters. There was a strong uprising and battles broke out. Our queen was taken from us and our king sent us to take his daughter far away from harm. Her name is Kiayla."

The King of Mursei wore a face of sudden revelation, confirmed by what dangled from the man's neck. A white glistening orb, the same style as the woman wore who gave birth to Kaida. The same type of orb he gave to the

Queen for her to protect. The orb that held Kaida's secrets that he was now sure, the Queen of Mursei had already discovered.

The King of Mursei asked slowly, "Did you bring Kiayla here?"

"No," the man responded, running his pale hand through his yellow hair. "There were many of us. We all took different tunnels from the palace, each leading to a different gateway. Gateways are special places that lead to other worlds. Once we entered our Gateway, we disarmed it to stop the intruders from opening it. The group with Kiayla were supposed to send out a signal, so we could find her and all come together. Several years ago we thought we at last, found her signal. It grew weak and we lost it before we could go any further."

The King of Mursei nodded with full understanding. He was there when the soft glow of the orb had stopped. He stood conflicted with the knowledge he held. He thought, *What if their agenda meant them taking Kaida away from us? I cannot let them take her away, no matter the cost.*

"This girl is not the one you seek," the King of Mursei finally answered. "I can see how it would seem like it with her hair and eyes but she had been with us from day one. She is a Mursei."

The old man rubbed his heavy lidded eyes. He answered, "I suppose you make sense. Our Princess Kiayla would be much older than this girl. It is only ... perhaps it is nothing more than an old man's wishful thinking. We grow old and weary but cannot lay down our task. We have traveled many gateways here, searching for Kiayla. We have stayed in this location the longest because we had hope that the faint signal might repeat again." He ran his hand through his thinning long blond hair and let out a heavy sigh that took with it, his hope of the end of his search.

The King of Mursei nodded and asked, "You said your homeland was in battles. Did you battle Dragons?"

The man quickly responded, "No, they are or at least, were our friends when we left our homeland. We would journey to their world and they, to ours.

We shared ideas and commerce between our worlds. The battles came from within. An uprising took a foothold within our ranks. They sought to stop interplanetary travel and communication. They asserted that our heritage was being threatened by having close relations with others from different worlds."

"What if you were to go back?" The King of Mursei asked hopefully and followed up with another thought. "Perhaps you no longer hear a signal because the one you have searched for is no longer here. What if her and her guardians returned to your homeland? Do you receive signals from there?"

"No, we are too far from home to pick up any signals from there. That is why we were sure Kiayla was here. We heard a signal."

"I understand your thoughts. It is only...." the King of Mursei paused as if in a deep reflection. "I'm sure Dragon ways would vary greatly with your ways. Always when we have lost our bearings on what we seek, we return to the beginning. To find some missing piece. It has always made our way more precise."

The man conferred with those around him before he answered. "There is much truth in what you say. We have stayed here, waiting on an answer that did not come. As much as we hate to return to our homeland without Princess Kiayla, it could mean she has already returned with her guardians. If not, we may gain important knowledge by returning." He looked at Kaida and rubbed his hand across his chin. "We hope to meet you all again. We will make our way to our homeland. A gateway is nearby. Where does your journey take you?"

"We too, journey home. Good journey to all!" The King of Mursei said smoothly. "Come Kaida, we have to make ready to travel."

Kaida, a little startled by hearing her name, slowly turned to go. She had been staring so intently at the white orb the man was wearing, she seemed to be coming out of a trance. She answered, "Coming!" She took one last look at the strange looking peoples, looking somewhat like her but different somehow. She looked fondly at Zlemtec and said, "Let's go home."

Zelspar returned to the shoreline to speak to Pravietis. "Many thanks we give for directing us to land. Tell me, are we close to our home?"

"You have a long journey yet. Follow the shoreline and head north. You will once again see your home," he said.

"Pravietis, will we meet danger on our way?"

"There is danger. I see it much closer to your home."

"By all that is Dragon, is there an attack against our Hails?" Zelspar's sudden burst of anger made his face flush red.

"No, Zelspar. The danger is not brought to the Hails of Dragons, but to the Magician who travels with you. Be on guard. Flegmorr has followed the Master Magician and seeks to take his revenge."

"I will be on guard and warn Perthorn of this Flegmorr. We have not seen him yet."

"It is because he altered his course and took another route. He will reach the area close to your home soon after you arrive. Do not let him steal the Book of Days. He seeks to alter the Book which would alter the Future. Just as one stone cast in a lake produces large ripples, Flegmorr could greatly change the Future of the Magicians if he succeeds in stealing the Book." Pravietis replied.

"We will not allow that to happen. Whatever magic he tries to use, we will use stronger magic. I have a great interest in the Magician and his apprentice. There is much we can share and learn from one another."

"Yes, Zelspar. Your interest in them has been foretold. During this season of Change, ideas need to be shared. Urthe has lost many and with the loss a void is created. You know as well as I do, voids must be filled. It is the nature of things. Be sure to have the strongest seeds to fill those voids."

"It will be so, Pravietis. Once home, my teachings will begin again."

"Your Healer, Traylethon is doing remarkably well."

"Traylethon? Yes, well he has yet to shake all the yolk from his feet."

Pravietis splashed his tail through the water and said,"You would be surprised at how well your instructions have already set seed. His journey shall be long, just as your journey has been. With your instructions on Healing and Magic, he will be a great asset for the Hails and the peoples of Urthe."

Zelspar felt a cold tingle travel the length of his back. His brows lifted. "Are you trying to tell me something, Pravietis? Speak plainly!"

"All is well, Zelspar. You are at the right place at the right time. I only wished to remind you of the continuing legacy you are giving to the Dragon Hails. In times such as these, when you are away, you have left your Hails well-tended."

"Ah, very well then. Thank you for bringing us back to land, we will be continuing our journey home. I'll help Perthorn and his apprentice too. This Flegmorr that you have warned about, he will discover he came to the wrong place."

"Safe journey, Zelspar. Do not become overzealous in your plans of attack against him. He may not hold the title of the Master Magician but he is not one to take lightly."

Zelspar nodded and returned to his group who had made great strides in their departure preparations. He was fastidiously attended to by Kaida and Flower Bird. They made sure to bind the strapping on tight to hold the provisions securely during their travels.

The King of Mursei gathered the air beneath his wings and became airborne. The others followed suit. As they rose above the hilltop they saw the blonde haired people stop in front of an enormous tree with its trunk hollowed out.

Each had an arm outstretched in a farewell salute. The Dragons responded by dipping to their side to raise a wing in response. The people disappeared. One by one, it appeared that the enormous tree swallowed them whole.

The Dragons circled the tree once before setting their heading in a northwest direction. All made note of this location and of the tree that towered above all others. Another portal to distant lands.

Of all the Dragons, Rynik, the King of Mursei paid special attention. He knew the people which looked like Kaida would not give up their search. He had never imagined peoples would be looking for Kaida's mother. He wondered, *What would it mean to them to learn their Kiayla gave birth to a child? Kaida is a princess by her birth mother.* He liked Kaida's peoples but even if Kaida was not born a Dragon, she has been raised as one. He felt a deep ache knowing he must tell Starleira, his queen, of these people.

He wondered if Kaida was questioning how much she resembled them? *What if she asks the question? What do we tell her?* His thoughts were as many as the miles they traveled towards home. He needed time to discuss this with Starleira and Zelspar. They had to be prepared for what could come from this chance meeting.

Chapter 27

I t took two more sunrises for the Dragons to spot familiar territory. The land had been altered by the recent quakes leaving deep slices in the ground. Still, a smile and a surge of energy drove the Dragons homeward.

Rynik saw the towers of their mountain home, dazzling with the Sun's rays splashed against them. Natural instincts took hold. A Dragon's call ripped through air. One after another, his companions joined in.

Kaida filled with her longing for home, repositioned herself. She crouched on Zlemtec's back, slipped her feet under the bindings, and stood. Her lungs filled with air and she exploded a bellowing roar, which startled the peoples much more than the Dragons. Even so, Zlemtec craned his head backwards to look at his Kaida, as pride flashed in his eyes.

The call of the Dragons brought the Hails out of all their caves. They flew down to the open ground below and congregated in a large mass, each excitedly answering the call. Out in front of them all, stood Starleira, the Queen of Mursei.

She first saw her Bonded, her king, leading the others home. Then, *Kaida ... is that our young hatching standing upright on Zlemtec,* she questioned her own vision as she stared at the girl. *How could that be*? Her thoughts suddenly deterred as the next view came in sight. She caught her breath. All others saw too. An eerie silence replaced the deafening roars the Dragons had just made.

All flying Dragons were carrying riders! They brought strangers to their home. The silence was broken by astonished whispers which buzzed from Dragon to Dragon. The Queen of Mursei lifted an arm to quiet the noise.

The King of Mursei landed a few Dragon lengths away and allowed King Togar and his Faery folk to dismount. As the other Dragons landed, the King of Mursei greeted his queen.

"Starleira, it has been too long!"

She responded by embracing him and held tight to his arm. "My King!" She looked behind him and then back to his sparkling eyes. Before she could ask more, Kaida had jumped to the ground and ran to her.

"Sipta! I am home!" Kaida ran and threw her arms around the Queen, which brought tears and smiles to them both.

"My little Kaida," murmured the Queen, softly caressing her before lifting up her chin. "How is it you have grown so much in such a short time?"

Kaida, in a whirlwind of excitement and flooded memories, spewed out snippets of her story which included a quick introduction of the peoples assembled behind her. "I thought I would never again see you or the rest of my family after the mighty quake that swallowed us whole! It is so wonderful to be home again."

The Hails of Dragons had begun to shake off their shock and welcomed their Dragons and Kaida home again.

Perthorn and Kiel approached Zelspar.

Zelspar saw the look he first remembered seeing when they met. "Do not be worried. They will not harm you or any we bring to our home. You are a curiosity to them and I might add, they have only seen Zlemtec and Kaida fly as One. It isn't everyday you see Dragons in the sky with riders. Or for that matter, Dragons bringing peoples into our homeland. Give them time. I will address them all shortly. You may wish to stay close to me. They will accept you knowing I have." Zelspar had to swallow the temptation to burst into laughter as both Perthorn and Kiel quickly flanked him, leaving him scarcely any room to walk.

He called to Starleira, "Dear Queen, come meet our new friends."

Starleira and Rynik turned and made their way to Zelspar.

"Old dear friend," Starleira said as she leaned in for an embrace. "I see you have brought friends."

"Yes, indeed. Please meet the peoples from the down below, they lived in Inner Urthe, where we had to go to bring Kaida back. The tall older one is called Perthorn. He is the Master Magician of his peoples. The younger one is called Kiel. He is his apprentice, sort of like Traylethon is to me." He paused as the Queen of Mursei nodded to each one. "The two over there," he said as he pointed towards Galdean, "are the peoples who took care of Kaida. Molakei is the Elder of his peoples. Next to him is Flower Bird, his daughter. We could not have asked the Ancestors for better peoples to care for our Kaida."

The Queen of Mursei was filled with warmth as she looked at the people whom had taken care of their Kaida. She sent a silent blessing to the Ancestors for finding Kaida good peoples to learn and live amongst.

"Did the King make introductions of his travel companions?" Zelspar asked.

"My Queen," Rynik said, "This is King Togar. He is the King of the Solteriem folk, a few which you see darting around him. They are Faery folk which were living deep down under in a whole Inner world. King Togar helped us greatly in finding Kaida."

The Queen looked at King Togar and his easy smile and returned it to him. "King Togar, I hope you will understand my words as I have much to thank you for guiding our Dragons to find Kaida."

Kaida walked forward and said, "All can understand now, Sipta. I was given a staff and it makes the words of all clear in understanding." Kaida lifted her staff for the Queen to look at when Rynik spoke.

"My Queen, there is much more to tell but first let us make our guests welcome with a fitting banquet. I'm sure we can make an acceptable array of foods for Dragons and peoples alike."

"Yes, my King. I was too excited to have not sent our Hails off to prepare a celebration meal. Excuse me while I set them about in preparation."

The Queen of Mursei issued directions to the Hails as the weary travelers found a spot to sit and rest.

"Galdean," called Rynik to his friend, "check those low lying caves close by to see if they would make good sleeping quarters for our guests."

"Would any of you like to come with me, to see if it is fitting?" He looked towards Perthorn and Kiel but they appeared to be tied to Zelspar's side, every step he took, they took three to stay close to him.

"We will come with you," replied Molakei. Flower Bird nodded in agreement. "We like to make our dwelling face the rising Sun."

Galdean turned to Molakei and answered, "You are much like Dragons. We do the same to watch our Ancestors chase the Sun across the sky."

Molakei smiled. "Our dwellings face the rising of the Sun. It is the direction of Wisdom. It brings us the first light of the day in a warm embrace."

Galdean remarked, "The more we learn of each other, the more I see how much we are alike."

Molakei nodded thoughtfully. He pursed his lips and said, "Many things alike. Enough different to bring better understanding. But this thing I feel to be true...."

Galdean tilted his head. "What thing is that, Molakei?"

"That you can make campfire much quicker!" Molakei laughed heartily and sent a sudden burst of laughter through Galdean.

"That is a truth, Molakei! Let's find your dwelling and I will be honored to light your first fire in your new home." Their walk was shortened by a growing bond between the peoples and the Dragon.

Chapter 28

The King and Queen of the Mursei made their way towards their lair. Zelspar, Zlemtec and Kaida stayed with their travelers.

Zelspar addressed all those present. "We need to be alert. Perthorn, the Future Walker warned me of danger coming. Not a threat to the Dragons but to you, personally."

"What danger?" Kiel blurted out before Perthorn could gather his words.

"I was told a Magician named Flegmorr has made his way here. His purpose is to take your Book of Days. Pravietis said if he achieves his goal, it will alter the Future."

"Thunder and Lightning! He is a brash and jealous Magician. His family had earned the title of Master Magician for generations. He feels I cheated him out of his title and angrier yet that I was an outsider," Perthorn spat out, his eyes glaring around.

Zelspar answered, "You will have many a Dragon by your side. I would not be overly concerned but I had to give you the warning in case you spot him before we do. What do you mean you were an outsider? You were not born in Vale of Valdross?"

Perthorn paused and selected his words carefully. "Born there? No, no but then many Magicians were not and make their way there. Take Kiel here," Perthorn side-tracked the attention towards Kiel, "he was born elsewhere and brought to me to raise and train. His mother saw the spark in him as a small child." Perthorn gave Kiel a friendly roughing of his head.

"We appreciate the warning and will be prepared if his loathsome hide decides to show up for a challenge," Perthorn replied. "Don't worry. We won't let him bother you or the other Dragons. It is our fight."

Zelspar could not contain himself. "Bother? The day will never come that one of the peoples could be much of a bother to Dragons!" He let loose a thundering laugh.

Perthorn was lightly pulling down on his long lip hairs and shot Zelspar a sideways glance. "I make light of Flegmorr because I disdain him. He is a disgrace to Magicians far and wide. But this I also tell you is true. He is not one to take lightly. He ... he maneuvers in the Dark realms."

He continued by explaining, "When I deprived him of the title of Master Magician, he disappeared for several years. Not many in the Vale of Valdross were concerned at first because Magicians often make sojourns. But then, time wore on. People had begun to look at me as if I caused his disappearance. Before I was made out to be some sort of vile Magician, he showed up again. Him and that repulsive friend or fiend I should say, showed up. His friend ... is a Flaptail."

When the mere mention of a Flaptail didn't bring a response from those around him, so he explained further. "By your lack of astonishment, I gather you have not heard of these loathsome creatures? They are said to be birthed in the deepest pits of Fire. In this place they gather the Shadows of Lost Souls and glean from them all of their darkest thoughts. From that they create a magic. When they find a living Lost Soul, they befriend them and give off the Dark Magic. That is why, even after Flegmorr returned to the Vale of Valdross, he lived on the outskirts. Even his own family knew he had changed. Now, he seeks to take the title from me and return as if all of this is by my doing. If he succeeds, he will change the Future. All Magicians will be taught the Dark Magic instead."

Zelspar said, "I don't know much of what you speak, but what I do know is he will not stand a chance against me. I can assure you of this. I have not only Dragon Magic but the magic from the Great Ancestor from the beginning of our Time. Whatever he seeks to do, whoever he seeks to attack, he will not win. I will stand with you Perthorn. By all that is Dragon, we will make sure his Dark Magic will not gain a foothold here!"

Perthorn looked around him to discover he was surrounded by friends. He, in that instant knew his decision to go with this group of Uplanders was the right decision. He also knew a great Change was coming and he and Kiel would be at the right place at the right time. He would not allow Flegmorr to change what he saw in the Book of Days. It was imperative that Flegmorr was stopped and he felt more certain than ever before, he could stop him with the aid of his new friends.

Galdean had returned with Molakei and Flower Bird to let the others know where their new homes were found. Their conversations switched back to discoveries and new friendships being formed. They made their way to the caves which would be the homes of the travelers to help them get settled before the celebration meal ahead.

Chapter 29

The Queen of the Mursei made her way back through the gathering of Dragons. "Dragon all, we are prepared for our feast. Let us welcome our new visitors, our new friends!" The words had hardly escaped her throat when a thunderous roar of welcome sounded, shaking the very ground they stood upon.

So many Dragons roaring at once was a frightening sight to the newcomers, their eyes bulging and scanning from one Dragon to another. Kiel found himself tucked closer to Perthorn, who had plastered himself against the rock-face of his cave's exterior, inconveniently knocking his cap down over his eyes.

Zelspar stepped forward to quiet the Dragons to a dull roar. "We are grateful for your welcome, but as you see ... our guests are overwhelmed by such a hearty welcome. We will become more familiar with one another, in groups large and small as time allows. Remember my friends, the peoples above ground have at least been familiar with the sights and sounds of us in groups but the peoples of the deep, the Inner Urthe, have not seen Dragons in a very long time. We must give them time to adjust to our ways without causing unnecessary alarm. Let us welcome them by opening up a wide passageway in which they may enter our gathering room without the fear of being trampled."

As he spoke, Dragons moved creating a large path through the wall of Dragons. Kaida grabbed Molakei and Flower Bird's hands to lead them forward. "Come with me," she called over her shoulder to the other newcomers.

Zelspar led Perthorn and Kiel through the crowd of Dragons as Galdean motioned for King Togar and the Solteriem folk to follow him. King and Queen of Mursei fell in behind their guests with the other Dragons trailing behind in a dulled thunderous procession. The gathering room was filled to overflowing with all Dragon Hails eager to hear the stories of their returning Dragons, Kaida and the strangers that arrived with them.

Molakei and Flower Bird had reached their place at the banquet platform with a feast laid before them but their eyes were busy taking in their surroundings. It was similar yet different than their cave home. It was a huge cavernous place with light that shone down from large openings high above that were fitted with what looked to be translucent slabs of crystal ornately inlaid with workings in swirls of gold and silver. Huge gems were embedded all around the rim, catching the sunlight and streaming colors across the room.

Kaida noticed their wide-eyed stares and smiled. "Do you like my home? It's much bigger than you've seen. Many Mursei Dragons live in this complex of caves which wind all through this mountain. The other Hails have similar homes all across these mountains."

Molakei rubbed his rugged chin in thought. "Do you have a … a cave home here?"

Chuckling she answered, "I don't know anymore. I used to live with the other hatchlings before you found me. That time seems so long ago." Her eyes grew misty as she looked out across the gathering room. "I've changed so much in that time, I don't think I would fit back into the nursery with the hatchlings." She turned her gaze towards Zlemtec and said, "I don't think you will either!"

"I hadn't thought of it until now, but you're right. We will have to find new homes."

Molakei had been talking to Flower Bird and turned back to speak to them both. "We know you have only just returned home. We have a large cave and we are in a new land. We would be honored to share our dwelling with the both of you, if you would consider it." While the two thought over the idea he added, "We have already made friends with a few of your Hail but I sense we make most uncomfortable. To be honest, I too, am a bit uncomfortable being in a new place with so many I do not know."

Kaida placed her hand over his. "I think you have a great idea. I will talk to Sipta Queen after the celebration. I think she will agree, at least for now, it makes perfect sense." She saw Molakei fully relax with a smile that lit up their space.

"It is good. There is still so much to learn and share. Remember, we will not always have the advantage of your new staff to understand talking to Dragons. We must continue to learn."

The gathering room was filled with excitement which rumbled so loud, the walls shook. The Queen and King of Mursei stood up in front of all those assembled in their great room. The King's heart swelled in pride as he thought, *Whatever the call is, I will go. Whatever the danger is, I will fight. It is the return, the looking out over the sea of faces, that makes me know any sacrifice is worth it. It is good to be home.*

He raised his arms to quiet the crowd. "Guests and Dragons, all. I have but a few words before we all start the celebration proper. You have been introduced to our guests and I charge you with making them all feel welcome. They have proved themselves to be allies, no ... they have proved themselves to be friends of the highest order. As you know, we set out to find our Kaida who had vanished after the Urthe tore itself open. We had all but lost hope. We found the place of the peoples, the ones here today, Molakei and Flower Bird, who had become the guardians of our Kaida. It was knowing where she had lived that helped us find the way ... the way through and into the world within our world. We call it Inner Urthe."

Tears ran freely down Kaida's face as she watched and listened.

The King of Mursei continued, "The Inner Urthe is fascinating and very similar to our own except things and even people grow larger, faster and in an abundance. It will be worthy of future exploration, but only after we learn more from one another. Our Hails of Dragons are the largest beings of land and sky and with that comes the largest responsibility. Right now our greatest responsibility is to learn from one another. The Dragon's way is not to rule over, exploit or diminish resources but to share all things, including our knowledge. Our guests will live and move freely in our domain and be made as welcome as one of our own. Each one has proven their right to be here in thoughts and deeds. They are honorable peoples. So to you all, new and old friends alike, let the celebration begin!"

The roars became deafening but the guests, having been made welcome, lifted up their voices to join in the booming sounds. Voices united from different places and backgrounds but joined together through the bonds of friendship. Even Perthorn and Kiel seemed altogether comfortable in the new surroundings, celebrating with the thousands of Dragons sharing meals, drinks, jokes and conversation. New friendships were being forged. A foundation, a bridge between all was being laid, one stone at a time.

The celebration continued until the fading of the day with its long shadows brushed against the mountain homes. Dragons separated, making their way to their homes chiseled out of the mountainside.

Kaida, hair blonde flying behind her, surged through the thinning crowd to search for the Queen and King of Mursei. Spotting them by Zelspar, she hurried towards them, leaping over Dragon tails with Zlemtec close behind.

"Sipta Queen," she called.

The Queen hearing the voice of her heart, turned to see Kaida coming to her. She opened her arms for her heart to be filled again with her long separated hatchling. Starleira bent in order to scoop her hatchling to her, closed her eyes as her heart absorbed its missing piece. They embraced for a moment before Kaida let go and took a step back.

"Sipta Queen, Zlemtec and I have grown much too large to return to the hatchling nursery and will need to find homes of our own."

The Queen's eyes grew quite enlarged before they returned to normal, for the first time taking a long look at the two in front of her. "It is hard for me to believe how the two of you have grown in such a short time. We will find a temporary place for you both until the proper place for your homes are discovered."

"That is why we are here Queen Mursei," Zlemtec gushed, "Molakei and Flower Bird have asked us to join them in their cave!"

"What is this?" The King of Mursei having finished his conversation with Zelspar, had only heard a portion of Zlemtec's words.

Starleira took the King's hand and repeated what Zlemtec had said. Zelspar standing close by, curled his palm across his chin and waited for the Queen and King's answer.

The King thoughtfully replied, "I see Molakei's offer as a suitable one." He was stalled from continuing by the Queen's sharp intake of air.

"My Queen, my Bonded, do not look upon Molakei and Flower Bird as trying to keep Kaida from us. They live *with* us now. Besides, with Kaida and Zlemtec sharing their lair, err ... home, they will both continue to learn from one another. Another fact is, our Hails will see the interaction and soon come to accept the interactions of peoples and Dragons as commonplace, normal even."

Kaida shifted from foot to foot, waiting as her blue eyes met the Queen's green eyes, narrowed in thought. "I suppose it would do no harm, *temporarily....* " she said drawing out the last word for a few heartbeats.

Zelspar's eyebrows lifted as he spoke. "Do not think either of you can escape our continued lessons!"

"We won't Zelspar," said Kaida, "plus, maybe Molakei and Flower Bird could join us?"

A loud cough of surprise hit Zelspar. He blinked a few times and caught Rynik smiling at him. "Well now, we will take that into consideration. Highly irregular. Hmpfft!" The King could hold back his laughter no longer and released an explosive laugh from the vast fire pit of his belly.

The Queen chuckled with a low rumbling sound. "Go gather some of your things to take with you and do not be a nuisance to your guardians. Be helpful and do hunting for them and...."

Zlemtec and Kaida had already ran through the network of caves collecting their possessions before the Queen had a chance to continue her motherly list of to-dos.

Chapter 30

Rynik looked from Starleira to Zelspar. His heart both full and heavy, he said, "I would like to speak privately to you both. Let us go to our lair."

The Queen and Zelspar exchanged looks. Zelspar hunched his shoulders, answering the Queen's unspoken question. They turned to follow Rynik.

Once in the lair, Rynik paused. The words he had to say did not come easily to his tongue. He paced a moment before saying, "My Bonded, please bring out Kaida's heritage box."

Starleira was shocked. This was farthest thing on her mind as she followed Rynik to their lair. The coloring of her face drained as she replied, "You can't mean to hand her heritage box over to her now, it's much too soon! She only looks old enough, my Bonded. She still has many lessons to master...."

Rynik dropped his massive head and continued to pace. "I'm not suggesting that. Yet. There is something I wish Zelspar to see before I go any farther into explanations. Please bring it out."

The Queen's eyes found nowhere to rest as they darted between her Bonded and her dearest friend. She absent-mindedly picked at her talons and turned to go into the alcove where all the Mursei hatchling boxes were stored. Kaida's heritage box was easy to find, even in the dim light. It was different than all the others. She picked it up and clutched it tightly to her chest. This had been her secret, her discovery. True, Rynik had given it to her but he didn't know what it was, what it held....

Starleira slowly walked back to face Rynik and Zelspar, the box hidden between her palms.

"Hold it out, my Queen. I would like Zelspar to look at it," Rynik cautiously said.

The Queen opened her hands and allowed the box, the white orb, to dangle from its chain. Zelspar's eyes flew wide open as he gasped, looking at what the Queen had exposed. The Queen took a step back. She had no idea why he would act in this manner.

Rynik knew the answer before he asked the question, but asked it anyway. "Zelspar, does this orb, this heritage box, seem familiar?"

Zelspar could only nod an affirmative. His jaw had come loose of its hinge. *Could my old eyes be deceiving me? It ... It looks the same as the yellow-haired peoples we met.* He recovered his voice. "We have seen ... such boxes."

The Queen, confused, replied. "You couldn't have seen anything like this. It is the only one. Her birth mother wore it. We took it from her after her spirit left, to hold for Kaida. No other peoples have been seen with such an orb as a heritage box, it is unique and only Kaida has one."

It was as Rynik thought. "Come and sit, Starleira. I must tell you of our travels back to you."

Feeling uneasy, Starleira sat on the granite bench, her hand clutching softly, the white orb. She could make no sense out of her Bonded's words or those which Zelspar uttered. *Surely, they are confused,* she thought.

Rynik began the re-telling of their trip across the land as they made their way towards home. He sat next to his queen and told her of the peoples Kaida discovered. The very same peoples with blue eyes and yellow hair like hers. The Queen's face cracked with a newly registered alarm, as did Zelspar's.

"No!" The Queen's heart pounded with fear.

"There is more to tell, my Queen. The peoples are not from here. Just as we used portals from Verlaunde to come here, they used what they called *gateways* to come here. They have been in search of one of their own. They followed a sound from a beacon to this planet in hopes of finding this woman. Her name is Kiayla. She is or was the princess of their world."

Starleira's shoulders heaved as a volume of tears flowed forth.

Rynik continued as he leaned Starleira's head against his shoulder. "I recognized the orbs they wore as being the same as I removed from Kaida's mother and gave to you. We had only just found Kaida again. I could not tell them that the woman they sought died in childbirth. I could not tell them Kaida is the woman's daughter. They did call Kaida by her mother's name when they first saw her but I told them Kaida is a Mursei and has been with us from her very first breath. I was able to get them to return to their home, to see if the missing woman they were searching for had returned to their world. I am not happy with my deception. But I ... I do not know these peoples, and they had fled with Kiayla because of battles on their planet."

Starleira didn't speak, only her cascading tears carried the unspoken words of the fear in losing Kaida again, the fear of losing the Dragon Child and what that would mean. Her heart was breaking.

Rynik understood her tears, her grief, as his heart mirrored his Bonded's. "We will all have to think on this. Kaida must be told. Sooner or later, she must be told. It is my opinion that we can not hold back much longer. Those peoples will return. They already think Kaida is familiar. After some thought, they will come looking for her. She needs to be told so she can be prepared."

The sound of Starleira's sobbing grew quiet. She had been continually rubbing the white crystal orb. She heaved a heavy sigh as her shoulders shuddered in distress.

She looked to her Bonded and then to Zelspar. She took a deep breath and said, "There is something more you should know." Her talon found the hidden spring to the ornate orb and unlatched it. "Let me show you."

"Come over to the table," Starleira said looking at her king and closest friend. "It is time you see what is hidden in the orb." Bending over the table on which she placed a hide of deer, she tipped the orb. The contents spilled onto the soft covering. Heads drew closer to the objects to discern what had been placed within. Queen Mursei delicately used one of her talons to separate the pile.

Zelspar caught something out of the corner of his eye and exclaimed, "This cannot be!"

Rynik tilted his head and saw the same item. "Starleira, what is the meaning of this? Did you add items to the orb?"

"No, I did not. But, there is more." She stirred the contents until it revealed two more items. "Do you see now," she said in a whispers breath.

No words were spoken for several heartbeats. Zelspar's hand flew up to pull across his long face as he stared at the items exposed. Rynik drew his face within inches to the objects, his heavy breath making them shift on their soft cushion. His eyes full of questions looked up to Starleira and then to Zelspar. He took a hard seat on the granite bench.

Finally, Zelspar spoke. "I must talk to the Ancestors. What does this mean? Rynik, you were with the birth mother, this cannot be correct."

"Yes, I was there to help deliver Kaida. I gave the strange orb to Starleira for safe-keeping. She has not altered it, how could she? The talon you see there is gold, as is the snip of scale. We have never known Golden Dragons. There is only one thing that makes sense, it came from her father."

The Queen nodded a soft agreement. Zelspar declared, "By all that is Dragon!"

Both the Queen and King of Mursei replied, "Yes. By all that *is* Dragon!"

Starleira, finally free to speak of the unusual findings picked up the third item to hold in front of them. "I did not know what this was for a long time. I was finally able to get it to shift."

She held a small thin square not much larger than a pebble, made from some sort of flexible metal. "I was curious as to what this piece was and why it was in the orb. I discovered quite by accident when I had to place some snippets from the heritage box into the packet we gave you, Zelspar, so you could make her potion, like you did ours. I placed the metal down next to the items as I was searching through to select bits to put in Kaida's packet. A few on her nail clippings landed on the small square. It unfolds to become almost the size of my hand. There are writings on it that I cannot read but this I am sure of, it holds Kaida's legacy ... from her mother *and* father."

She scooped up pieces of Kaida's nail and gently placed them onto the small square. Without the nail clippings flying off, the metal unfolded beneath itself. As it did, the only sound that could be heard in the still room was the pounding of three hearts. After it reached its full size, Starleira lightly tipped the clippings to the deer hide and cradled the metal in her hands. There, in shimmering symbols were what they recognized but could not read. The metal was separated into two sides, each side showed a list of symbols that grew from the top to the bottom. They each had something similar in their descending order but not made in the same way. This looks to be Kaida's ancestral line. In symbols showing all her Ancestors."

The quiet in the room was deafening. Slowly, Starleira took the pieces and placed them back into the orb. The metal retracted into its more portable size where she picked it up and slid it back into its home. She closed the orb and looked at her companions. After a moment she softly uttered, "Perhaps this explains why she is so adept at Dragon Magic."

Her companions remained silent, at a loss for words and in the deepest of thoughts.

Zelspar paced. He stopped and looked at the orb and paced again. Each time he opened his mouth to talk, it snapped shut quickly. When he could stand it no more he muttered, "This is unheard of. What this ... this orb suggests cannot be, we have no records of something like this taking place, ever!"

Starleira could see the wise White Dragon trying desperately to make sense of what was inside the orb. She approached him slowly and said, "You are correct. *We* have no record of this but as we all are aware of now, her mother and father are from another place. Their ways and records are not ours. We only know of our Hails, of these peoples on Urthe."

"By all that is Dragon, you would think the Great Ancestor would know! I must seek council."

Rynik touched Zelspar's shoulder. "My friend, we do always seek help from our Ancestors but think on this, they are *our* Ancestors. Perhaps they do not know...."

Zelspar, in his frustration, slung his staff down and proceeded to stomp in a back and forth motion, causing his bushy brows to catch the breeze he was making. Then, he abruptly stopped. "The Historian! He should know. He is the keeper of all Histories."

"Of course," Rynik answered. "He would indeed have knowledge of ... these distant peoples and the unknown Dragons. We should find the Historian."

Quickly, Starleira responded. "Not now. You have only just returned. There is no urgent need for answers. What has it changed? She is still the Legend foretold. She is still our little Dragon, only now the bonds are truly closer, can't you see that? Our knowledge only helps us understand how very unique she is and why she *is* the Legend. What better person to bridge the gap between peoples and Dragons but the one who carries the bloodlines of both?"

"Yes, yes ... I suppose you are correct," Zelspar answered as he slowly sat down. "We will have time enough in the future to learn more."

"Agreed," said Rynik.

But there could be no denying, as Starleira looked at her companions, their minds seemed to have drifted a million miles away.

Chapter 31

Perthorn said, "You *saw* the spell and converted it into action. Well done." Perthorn tapped a bony finger against his head. "It's all in there. All the spells, the magic, the murmurings ... but *knowing* is not the same as doing. It will take much practice for the Magic to become second nature and *that* my boy, is what will make you a Master Magician in due course. Levitate again and this time follow through with your ascent and descent. See it, then do it."

Kiel risked a quick sigh before making another attempt. His eyes focused on the wall behind Perthorn and he lifted from the ground. A slow but steady ascent before he descended, lightly touching the cave's rocky floor. He knew he was flawless, he felt it deep within, the feeling of *flow,* where body and mind were one. A smile creased his youthful face.

Perthorn's eyes flashed Kiel a pleased look. Compliments didn't fall from the Master Magician's mouth often, but a particular look was hard to disguise. It was enough for Kiel, that look was as good as a pat on the back. Kiel's smile deepened.

"Now Kiel, do it again and this time I want you to conjure a fireball in your hands as you levitate."

"What? Are you serious?"

Perthorn was idly braiding his mustache under his chin. "I would not have said it if I was not serious. Do you know how to conjure a fireball?"

"Of course I do," he replied with a snort.

"I don't have to ask if you know how to levitate, as you've just shown me. To be even a good Magician, you must be able to do multiple spells at the same time. We started your training by learning individual spells. You have practiced each until they are written," he tapped on Kiel's head and heart, "there and there."

"I know, but...."

Perthorn stared deeply into Kiel's eyes and placed his hands firmly onto Kiel's arms. "If you think I work you harder than any others I have trained, you are correct. I won't apologize for it or lessen the intensity of your training. *You* are *my* chosen apprentice. The apprentice to the Master Magician of the Vale of Valdross. That in itself is enough ... but," he said with a glint in his eyes.

"But?" Kiel asked.

"But, your future holds much more than that."

"What do you mean? That I someday will be a Master Magician?" Kiel's face illuminated with the thought.

"My dear boy, that is a given. I would not have made you my apprentice if that had not been what I wished to occur. No Kiel," Perthorn said as he wore a faraway look in his eyes which seemed to swirl with mist as he spoke, "your future will cast my works into the shadows. That is why I work you so hard, why you must be better than any other Magician ever known."

Chill bumps rose up across Kiel's arms and crawled up his neck, making his hairs stand at attention. Even the rhythm of his heart skipped beats. He did not know what to say and when he tried, his mouth grew dry and his tongue clung to the roof of his mouth.

"What ... what future," he stuttered in question.

"The Book of Days has only shown me glimpses, but this Time was foreseen. It was determined that we would leave our Inner Urthe and return to up above with the Uplanders ... and the Dragons. This is the Time for great

Changes. We were chosen to be here, to be part of it all. Whatever that leads to, I cannot say with certainty but this I do know: the Book has written that from you, the greatest Magic shall come. From you, from your bloodline, the greatest Magician shall be borne. It is my responsibility to train you, to prepare you and I will not shirk from that task."

Kiel's jaw lost its hinge pin and flopped open.

Perthorn rubbed a weary brow. *Thunder and Lightning, I've said too much! How will I ever get him to train now with such a burden to carry?*

As Perthorn's mind flowed to different streams of thought, he felt Kiel start to rise and he removed his hands from the apprentice's arms. Kiel rose and as he did so, his right hand conjured a green fireball and in his left hand, a yellow fireball. He continued to rise and then, in a calibrated pace, touch ground again, clapping his hands to a thunderous *pop!* as the fireballs were extinguished.

A steely resolve danced across his eyes as he looked to his Master. Both wore the traces of a smile that took hold and spread.

The Master Magician studied the apprentice with a new appreciation. He said, "Again."

Before Kiel could do as asked, their attentions were diverted to outside where they heard the sound of the ground shake. Eyes widened. A shadow fell across their entrance.

"G'morning Perthorn and Kiel. I thought we might share some time together, exchanging Magic spells and learning," Zelspar said as the two gathered their hearts from their throats.

"Zelspar, friend! Good to see you, come in, come in," Perthorn said only slightly stumbling over his tongue.

"Better yet, I'm inviting you to our practice session. I'm on my way to get Zlemtec and Kaida and I thought this would be a good time for us to all come together."

"Ahhh, yes. I think your idea is a splendid one. We would be delighted to join you, won't we Kiel?"

"Yes, what an opportunity to learn the Dragons ways of Magic. I'll just grab a few things and we'll meet you ... where?"

A toothy grin met Kiel, "We'll come back here shortly. Then, I'll take you to our training rooms."

Perthorn and Kiel exchanged looks as Zelspar walked away, a tinge of a chuckle working its way up from his belly.

By the time Zelspar made his way to the dwelling of his new friends, Molakei and Flower Bird, their morning fire was drifting out in the gentle breeze. He heard the sing-song laughter of Kaida as she explained the nuances of Dragon language to them. He paused, breathing in the moment, hearing their little Dragon happy once again. He couldn't stop the onslaught of thoughts and worries regarding Kaida's future. *The picture of the new peoples they met one their way home, the ones who looked like Kaida, the ones who searched for her mother. I'm afraid, Ancestors. I don't want us to lose Kaida again*, he thought. He stepped away from the side of the mountain and stood in front of the cave's entrance.

"Zelspar!" Kaida called out full of joy. "What brings you out this beautiful morning?"

He was flooded in joy. Kaida had that effect on those around her, as if she carried the spark of the sun in her soul, resplendent in her love of life. "G'morning all. I have come in search of my students with whom have been away from their lessons too long."

A quiet echoed through the cave, until Molakei broke through it with a hearty laugh.

"Another thing that we peoples share in common with Dragons. Ongoing training!"

"I stopped by to alert Perthorn and Kiel, they will be joining us for today's Magic lessons, would you and Flower Bird like to join us?" He was looking at Molakei awaiting an answer.

"Zelspar, my friend, we thank you for the invitation but unfortunately we had already made plans on visiting King Togar and his Solteriem folk. We know so little of those who live in the world under us, we wanted to become better acquainted and share stories."

"A grand plan, my friend. Learning has many paths and sharing stories is a key to understanding and forming deeper bonds. Please take them my well wishes," Zelspar stated. "Zlemtec, Kaida, are you ready?"

"Yes," Kaida glanced at Zlemtec, "aren't we?"

A soft sigh escaped his lips, followed by a thin trail of smoke wafting up front his snout. "Yes, I guess so. I wanted to stretch my wings some, but it can wait."

"Indeed it can Zlemtec, as we have guests joining us for our training session today. Why don't you and Kaida fly on up to our training rooms, I'll go pick up our guests. I'm sure they are ready by now."

"Come on, Zlemtec! Let's fly!" The excitement shining on Kaida's face brought Zlemtec up and out of the cave where he leaned down to allow Kaida to climb upon his scaled back. She leaned forward, her arms on his neck and roared, "We fly!"

Left behind, Molakei and Flower Bird looked on. Molakei leaned closer to Zelspar and quietly spoke, his words filled with wonder, "I never tire of watching them fly. It is always the same as it was the first time I watched them fly, there is a peace, such a wholeness and unbridled joy unlike any other time I have spent with them."

Zelspar looked on and nodded. *How could any Dragons or peoples think of this as wrong? You only have to watch them to know, at least for the two of them, they move as One,* he thought. Zelspar said his goodbye and launched away to meet Perthorn and Kiel.

"If it's all the same to you, Zelspar, we'll walk to your training rooms," Perthorn said as his eyes displayed a nervous twitch.

The apprentice combed his fingers through his hair. He had a smirk on his lips that he tried to hide from the Master Magician. He thought, *Imagine, the mighty Master Magician afraid of Dragon flight. I think it's fantastic moving above the ground, feeling the power of the Dragon beneath me carrying me along. I could get used to this, with a willing Dragon to be my friend like Kaida has....*

Zelspar chuckled and pat Perthorn's shoulder. "I'm afraid that wouldn't work as our training rooms are high up the mountain. You're not afraid are you, after all the distance we have traveled?"

A coughing fit came from Perthorn. "Afraid? Thunder and Lightning, a Master Magician is not afraid of many things and ... and, I'll have you know I was only thinking of not being a burden on your back."

Zelspar's eyes danced and glimmered brightly. "Not to worry, the two of you cause me no strain. Climb up and let's join Kaida and Zlemtec."

Kiel clamored up a little awkwardly and leaned over to give Perthorn a grip on his arm. The great Magician from the Vale of Valdross wriggled his long mustache, took Kiel's arm and launched himself up onto the back of the white Dragon, muttering something incoherently.

Leaning over, Kiel told Zelspar they were ready at which the old and Wise Dragon took a few enormous gaits and powered off to the sky. The wind whipped through Kiel's hair making his lips spread into a flashing smile. Behind him, Perthorn hung onto Kiel's sides, his Magician's hat crumpled between his grip on Kiel.

Sometimes, the old Dragon got a hair up his snout and this was one of those times. He dipped low to the ground skimming the surface before shooting straight up into the sky causing Perthorn to give Kiel a death-grip as he looked wildly at the disappearing ground beneath him, certain he would fall to his death. His apprentice on the other hand was in sheer ecstasy, grinning and hollering the higher Zelspar flew.

A mighty roar boomed through the air as Zelspar circled the caves below and turned and headed to the training rooms. A broad yellow-toothed grin split his powerful jaws open and he showered the sky with a burst of lightning flame. He glided down to the platform outside the cave and caught hold. Turning his head up to his riders, he said plainly, "Here we are, just a short easy ride." He heard Perthorn grumbling and that caused his belly to jiggle with repressed laughter. *It is a good day to be a Dragon,* he thought with a gleam in his eyes.

The training room was well lit from the wide entrance and the translucent crystal-covered openings high above the chambers. Zlemtec and Kaida went to meet the others at the front of the cave.

Zlemtec looked at Perthorn and asked, "Are you feeling alright? You look a bit pale."

"I'm fine," he gruffed, snapping his hat to shake out the deeply embedded wrinkles caused by the death clutch during his Dragon ride. "I'm simply not accustomed to shooting straight up into the air waiting to get pitched to the ground and having all of my bones shattered!"

Four others in the room did their best not to burst out laughing, with Kaida clutching her sides hard to keep the laughter from traveling up and out into the open. She turned to the wise Old Dragon and said, "Zelspar, you didn't?"

Kiel spewed out, "He did and it was great, my heart was hammering so hard I thought it would fly right out of my mouth." Kaida started to chuckle but caught sight of Perthorn's stern look and stifled it.

With a cough of smoke Zelspar looked around and said, "Welcome to our training room.

Today we will do a bit of Dragon Magic. Zlemtec, why don't you start."

"What do you want me to do?"

"Go invisible."

"Aww, that's easy," he said as he thought of the Invisibility Magic and vanished from sight.

However, the effect was dazzling to watch for the Magician and his apprentice. Kiel gasped as Perthorn rubbed his eyes in disbelief.

Kaida gave a resounding 'hmpff' before she added, "That's not fair, only Dragons can do that."

"Is that so?" Zelspar said raising an eyebrow. "You try it now, Kaida."

"But I can't, you know that," she pouted.

"Have you tried?" asked Zelspar, knowing the answer.

"No, I haven't but I know I cannot do Dragon Magic."

"And you know this, how?" Zelspar scrunched up his chin and peered into her eyes.

"I don't even know how to begin!"

"Ahhh, yes. Well, of course the way you begin is at the beginning. Quite so, am I right?"

"I ... I guess so but I don't even know what that means."

"It's this simple. Remember when you wanted fish and had been playing in the pond inside the cave? All the fish had swam to the bottom. You had no fishing gear but you still wanted fish."

"I remember that day, Zelspar." Zlemtec became animated in the re-telling of the tale. "She got a little sore at me for saying she disturbed our meal and said she would get them anyway. Then, before I could blink, fish were hitting me all over!"

Kaida giggled. "Well, it served you right for making fun of me."

"This is the lesson, Kaida. Just as you urgently wanted to get fish at that moment, without having to go find your gear, you thought about it and called it to be. Isn't that right?" Zelspar studied her face and saw her eyes register the connection.

"I never thought of it in those terms. I just called the fish out of the water."

"That is true. You wanted something bad enough, you hardly thought of an adverse outcome. Your mind and body worked in unison to give you the desired outcome. You could say your 'Will' and 'Belief' were the magic ingredients which conspired together to achieve your goal." Zelspar leaned against his staff watching Kaida intensely. "Kaida, you have Magic within you, more than you are currently aware. To discover a Magic, you must first endeavor to try, otherwise your Magic lies dormant and may even fizzle away without use."

He thought again and approached from a different angle. "There are many pathways through the mind. Find one that meets your need or desire. For instance, if you were in danger from, let's say, the Jodrug Hail," Zelspar paused as he saw her eyes grow wide in alarm, "now, what you *need* to do is vanish quickly, so they won't spot you. What do you do?"

She closed her eyes tightly and clenched her fists so hard, her whole body was caught in a grip of fear. Nothing. She opened her eyes and looked down at her body and said, "It didn't work!"

The White Dragon softly smiled. "What did you think while you were tightened into a stone?"

"I was scared they would find me and kept saying in my mind, 'Don't let them find me. Please, don't let them find me.'" Her voice was trembling with the remembrance of past experiences.

"I see. But what you did was not concentrate on 'being' invisible. Instead you allowed the fear to take hold. Now wishing for something, either for good or for self-preservation is a Magic but it is weak and fights against itself because in your heart, your 'belief' combined with fear and when you combine a positive such as belief with a negative like fear, they combat each other until the weak Magic is snuffed out before it can take hold."

A groan rumbled out of Kaida. Her shoulders slumped in her perceived defeat.

"Don't groan, little Dragon," Zelspar said gently raising her chin so she would meet his eyes. "This was a splendid lesson. It taught you something that will not work when fear sets in. You needed to see it for yourself in order to learn what does work. Now, try it this way. You see the Jodrugs approaching, you do not want to be seen. Tell your mind what you want."

Kaida nodded and thought, *They can't see me, I'm invisible. I have disappeared. I'm safe.* Her lips moved her silent chant as all watched. The spell was broken when Zlemtec leapt into the air saying, "She did it, she did it!"

Her eyes sprung open and she gasped. "I did? Did I really disappear?" Her look of surprise was mimicked by the guests.

Zelspar gave her a hug and said, "You did, our little Dragon, you did indeed. It will only need more practice to perfect it as your hands and feet were still partially visible but ... that was a first rate attempt. Now, you *know* it is possible. You won't be second-guessing yourself. You have strengthened your 'will' and 'belief'. And that, my little Dragon is the basis of all Magic. Upon their strength, you perfect your Magic."

Kaida feeling delighted, spun circles with her hands up in the air, spinning, spinning and shooting smiles like shooting stars across the room.

Zelspar watched her as his heart swelled. *She will have all the Magic she will need,* he thought, *no matter what she must face in the future. I will make certain of that.*

Perthorn inched forward until he was beside Zelspar. He questioned, "How was she able to do such Magic? In my great Book Of Days, it tells of no spell to induce invisibility!"

A smile creased Zelspar's leathered face. "Ahh, it is Dragon Magic."

"But, she is no Dragon. Sure, I understand she is named 'little Dragon' and has been raised primarily under the Dragons' care but that does not make her a Dragon, nor her abilities." Perthorn wore a confused and flabbergasted expression and proceeded to pluck off his tall hat and turn it around and around by its edges.

"Shhh!" Commanded Zelspar. "Your words can only make Kaida upset."

"Pardon me, I meant no disrespect. It is only I do not understand."

"It is well, my friend. She is preoccupied with Zlemtec, for now," he stated, as his bushy brow raised in warning. "Kaida is the things you mentioned but much more. It is hard for any of us to determine all of her talents and abilities because there has never been one such as herself. She is the Legend, the Dragon Child. And as such, it is my role, my distinguished responsibility to discover the Magic within her and train her in the usage of it. Today we have only scratched the surface. I believe she will need to know what resides within her for her to safely accomplish what she was born to do. To become the very bridge of understanding between the Dragons and peoples."

"Yes, yes ... I do see your point. I have a habit of seeing her simply as a strong young woman, not yet Kiel's years but I am quite truly amazed at such a spell. I listened well to your guidance as you brought her to the understanding of the basis of her Magic. I must say, I had not thought of it in that manner. I have to wonder if practicing our spells of Magic would become enhanced through that form of visualization?" Perthorn's forehead furrowed in contemplation.

"Having not had a Magician as a student, I cannot in all certainty, say." Zelspar said and continued, "It is true, that my students first learn by reading the spells, and memorizing until it is embedded into them as much as their name. Then, there is the repetitive training of using spells in order to master them. Most, of which, I am of a mind to believe is similar to the ways you use. However, for Dragons, we have...." his eyes searched the cave's ceiling for the words. "We have a short-cut, an added bonus for learning Magic."

"You see," Zelspar continued, his eyes growing distant in thought, "we have our Ancestors always close and as such, we are given deep memories which are embedded into our very soul. With Dragons, our lifespan is thousands of years long, making our memories a vast resource to tap. Most of the training I do with Dragons is in the opening up of pathway to Remembering."

"I do say, that is an added bonus for you," Perthorn said, jutting out his chin, "but it makes me wonder if that isn't something we might experience. Now, not all Magicians can claim an unbroken line of Magician ancestry ... but there are some," he concluded with a wink.

A smile crept across the wise Old Dragon's face. "I take it that you may have such a line?"

Smirking, with a flash in his eyes, he answered. "Indeed, I do. That is another thorn in Flegmorr's side. His lineage is an unbroken line of Magicians, all from the Vale of Valdross. And I, am an outsider, having not been born and raised within their confines also have the same distinguished unbroken line of Magicians."

"Ahh, I see where that might cause a rift. Where were you raised, if not with the other Magicians?"

Perthorn shuffled a bit and slipped his hat back on. "Oh, I traveled a bit, here and there as is my custom." He gave Zelspar a wink and a nod, "Some say I was born of stardust and crashed through the Urthe ... funny thought, isn't it?"

Surprised by the answer, Zelspar's mouth opened but no words fell out.

"Kiel, time to work," the Master Magician called out on his way back towards his apprentice.

Chapter 32

In the meantime, unknown to the Uplanders, traversing through the collapsed cave Molakei once called home, fingers pulled at the tumbled rocks and sent them clattering down below. The Urthe's shifting and quakes had created a broken stairway, of sorts, in which the vile Magician worked his way through. Pockets of light could be seen sifting through far above, his destiny at hand.

Fingers calloused and torn to the point of bleeding, only made him more calculating in his endeavor. Rock by rock, he made a clearing to inch his way upward. His ever present Flaptail whispered vile murmurings in his ear, goading him on. Misery loves company and so the two unlikely companions trudged on, pushing and crawling through obstacles that would have turned any sane person around ... but then, these two could not be considered in such company.

Only one thing was in Flegmorr's mind. He would *own* the Book of Days. No one and nothing would stop him! He turned to the side and expelled a black wad from his mouth and snarled. "I'll chase you from the depths of Fire to the vault of Heaven, you will find no escape. You thought going up top would save you," he glared through the darkness, "there is no place safe from me."

His Flaptail teetered on his shoulder, as crazed as his master, whispering in words and obnoxious clicking sounds, "The Book, we gets the Book...."

A pile of rocks tore free and light broke through, momentarily blinding the climber and companion. Flegmorr's hand reached a level surface. He pushed rocks aside and opened up a hole. The last streams of daylight were hitting the side of the mountain. The corners of his mouth turned up and he held his position. Night would come soon. He would wait, a little longer. He preferred the drapery of the darkness to make his move, and then, the hunt would begin.

A slight chill poured down and swirled against the opening in the mountainside. Night had fallen and its noises carried with the wind. Flegmorr's hand moved across the rocky expanse, moving an army of black ants the size of his thumb. For night-time creatures it was the time to hunt and Flegmorr was no different.

He slithered through the hole he had opened through the rocks, secured hand holds as he shimmied down the rocky surface, his unseen feet searching for ground. A sudden shifting of rocks catapulted across his shoulder. His face planted into the uneven surface, dodging a direct hit. The Flaptail was knocked free, his penetrating screech rising up into the night.

A few more cautious moves brought the crazed Magician to the ground with a grumble of words spewed from his lips. Glik heard his companion and once again claimed his shoulder, his tail running down Flegmorr's back, vibrating its rattles.

Flegmorr mused, *Which direction?* He leaned one way while Glik leaned the opposite.

"We head this way," he decided as he picked his way close to the mountain to not be seen by man or beast. They traveled in a southwestern direction, looking for shelter, food and the Magician that stole his title and place at the Vale of Valdross. A sneer crawled across his lips as vile as his thoughts, but in the darkness, both remained hidden from sight.

They stumbled across the broken backs of the giants that were once stately trees. Their mangled limbs created a low covering in which Flegmorr used for his shelter. He squirmed his legs deep within the tangle of branches and limbs until he found the center of the slain sentinels and had enough room to sit upright.

A flash of light issued from his bloodied fingertip as he took in his surroundings. With a snap of his fingers a pillow plopped to the ground. He reclined and stared out of the opening until his weary eyes fluttered shut. Glik hopped up onto the bent branches above him and latched on with claws as his tail wound around it, securing his perch for sleep. The sounds of the predators and prey in distant screams worked as a lullaby and brought them into a heavy sleep.

It wasn't long before more rocks pelted around the ground where Flegmorr had recently forged his way through the mountain. Brilliant blue eyes cut through the darkness as muzzles lifted into the air, inhaling the vile scent they followed. They silently turned and crept towards the downed trees, the place they once called home.

The scent was strong in the air. They crept in calculated steps, as to not disturb the branches of the fallen and peered through the pockets of debris. Their necks craned backwards but held their tongues. Pacing to and fro, saliva dripped from their fangs.

Sigrunn knocked her head against Tyrianua to get his attention and softly padded away, glancing over her shoulder to make sure he followed.

When they were a good distance away, she stopped. Tyrianua sat, his lips still in a snarl.

"We could just as easy dispatch of those two."

Sigrunn shook her head. "No, it is not our battle."

A low growl slid up Tyrianua's throat. He did not like having a threat come up from the Inner World, there were threats enough to deal with without having to stalk these two intruders. "What good are we if we do not protect and guide the Future?"

She stood and stared at the fallen trees. "We do protect and guide, but you aren't seeing the picture in its whole. A new light has entered this realm and where there is light...."

He glowered, "there is darkness. Yes, I'm highly aware of the Balance. Where one abides, the other abides there also. But there *was* Magic here before the Master Magician came."

"Yes, but not from Inner Urthe. Perthorn's balance followed. It is the same as all things, it is as old as the beginning and it cannot be hastily disrupted. Especially now."

Tyrianua turned to search her eyes. "What is it that you are not saying?"

She continued to stare off into the downed trees. "I know from where Perthorn comes. I also know this Future was written. It is how it must go. From this moment forward, paving stones are being laid. Each action is tantamount to the Future. It is not ours to ensnare. A great coming of Magic has already been written. Perthorn himself saw the new writing in his Book of Days and that is the reason he came. That is his destiny and that of his apprentice, Kiel. Do you not see? Even the rocks hear the murmur of the new spark traveling to its destination."

Tyrianua paced, his hackles prickled.

Her eyes misted over. "A great Magic is being woven, even now with the initial spark. There will be great loss to obtain the great gift. In thousands of years, the peoples will look back, trying to spot the beginning and we are privileged to be here as it grows and matures with its pains of labor. So my friend, our ultimate task is in protecting Kaida. Only if those two paths cross, are we permitted to interfere."

He ceased pacing, rumbling a low and deep growl. "He will *not* bring harm to Kaida or I will dispatch him until not a shred is left."

Sigrunn studied her companion. "It is agreed, under those terms only. Now, let us go find Kaida. I wish to be there when she wakes."

Tyrianua's tail found joy again and waved through the night air. Their muzzles sniffed at the wind and followed the scent to Kaida. It was time to become her wolves again.

Chapter 33

The first light of the day streamed in broken fragments across the cave's entrance. The wolves trotted towards a sleeping Kaida, stirring on her sleeping mat of leather-laced furs.

Tyrianua lifted a paw and pressed it against her arm only to be met with a hand to brush it away. He pushed against her arm again, this time adding a low yelp. Blue eyes peeled open to find two wolves gazing upon her.

"You are back," Kaida said as she thrust herself into a wakeful state. "I was afraid you had lost your way and became lost in the Inner world." She sat up and leaned forward, grabbing both wolves around their necks, hugging them close to her, planting her face deep within their fur.

Tyrianua, pulled back enough to give her an open-jawed smile and said, "We came back through what used to be Molakei's home."

"How? We fell down through Urthe in it?"

"Yes. It was a hard route but then ... we had unrequested help." He looked at Sigrunn.

"Kaida," Sigrunn said, joining the conversation, "we trailed behind Flegmorr." Kaida's hand flew up to her opened mouth, covering her immediate gasp.

"You needn't worry," Sigrunn continued, "You will be safe, but we should warn Perthorn and Kiel. I will tell you this, Flegmorr is more determined than ever to steal the Book of Days and seeks revenge against Perthorn." She shook at her beautiful white coat of fur and continued, "Flegmorr and his Flaptail carry a

Dark Magic which is like a poison that flows unencumbered through his streams of life. His powers are great. We must discuss this with Perthorn as soon as possible. Will you come with us?"

"Of course, I will. Let me awaken the others so they will also know what you've told me and be warned."

Kaida, along with Zlemtec, Molakei and Flower Bird assembled in front of the fire pit. Tyrianua shifted and padded off to the entry. "Wait. I see Zelspar approaching."

Zelspar smiled, seeing the wolves had returned, knowing they had and continue to protect their Dragon Child. He poked his head through the entry saying, "G'morning all. Have you room for one more by your fires?"

With a shot of urgency, Kaida bolted towards the white Dragon, leading him in. He saw the wrinkled brow on her face and wondered what brought her a burden of stress. He spoke. "Has something occurred that I should be made aware of?"

The two wolves and Kaida all began speaking causing a cacophony of sounds ricocheting from ceiling to walls. Zelspar rustled his wings to stop the chaotic assault.

"Quiet. Please, just one speaking at a time!"

"We must see Perthorn," Tyrianua spoke. "We followed Flegmorr here."

"He is here, where? I'll roast him like a wild boar." Zelspar glared at the news and then back at Tyrianua. "Well?"

Tyrianua paused, "Zelspar, first we take the news to Perthorn. Who comes with us?"

The cave filled with the booming sounds of 'I do, I will and we will.' They all followed Tyrianua out into the sun-drenched ground. Zelspar made quick his way to Perthorn's abode to announce he has visitors.

Perthorn, with his long hair still wild from sleep, knitted his brows close together, surprised to see so many outside. "What has happened?" His head finally darting around the room in alarm, only to find Kiel was there, just rising from his bed.

"It is Flegmorr, isn't it?" He was a quick study of the 'tells:' the special looks and language the body gives off before words flow. Only one thing would bring an alarm to his abode from so many. It could only mean Flegmorr.

The white wolf agreed. "It is so, Perthorn. We trailed him and his Flaptail here. They hid in the broken trees that once towered above Molakei's dwelling. They made it here at nightfall."

"Of course he would come in the night! He is the most horrid of men. Envy and revenge has turned his inner streams a black a putrid coagulation - an abomination, he is," Perthorn spat out as if the very name soured the taste on his tongue.

"I have already told the others to point me the way, I shall char his hide!" Zelspar puffed up his chest, to make ready.

"It will not bring you the results you desire." Sigrunn held a penetrating look with Zelspar before turning to look at all those gathered in close. "When you, Perthorn, came up to the outer world, you set into motion the Laws of Balance, where an opposing force was activated. That initial *Balance* is what must be played out, to morph into that which will remain. This is one of the reasons why outside aid or interference will not impact the outcome. The battle of Balance is between Perthorn and Flegmorr. What we *can* do, is use all of our means to protect ourselves from him and to fortify ourselves against him and his Dark Magic."

Smoke puffed from Zelspar's snout as he fought to keep control of his anger. "I find it hard to grasp that a massive assault being driven by all Dragons against just one Flegmorr, would not have the desired outcome of blowing his carcass to smithereens!"

Tyrianua, having listened to both sides, added in his thoughts. "It is quite hard to fathom, I agree with you, Zelspar. You have had thousands of years strengthening all of your powers to reach the heights you currently enjoy. I understand. So understand us when we tell you these things. We are Timeless. We have been in all places, in all times, when a new pathway is forged. We are not the Change but we come to *guide* such change. We have seen all the attempts to alter the Change that you could possibly imagine. You cannot battle against the Laws of Balance as an outside force. Only those who initiated the Change are effective on the outcome."

Perthorn had remained silent during the discussion, allowing his mind to calculate the possibilities. He was honored by his new friends who had shown their willingness to fight for him, even to fight his own battle. Such friendships are rare and he was humbled to the point of silence, but now it was his turn to speak.

"Friends, all. I am honored beyond words at your willingness to risk all that you are in fighting this battle, but as Sigrunn and Tyrianua explained, it is my battle to fight. I am ready, just show me the way. I have seen the hope of our future in our Book of Days. If I and my apprentice, Kiel are to see this glorious Future, I must secure it by battling Flegmorr. I am ready."

A hush blanketed those assembled together. It was if a dark cloud had already drifted over them and clutched at their very souls.

Once again, Sigrunn spoke. "I mean no disrespect to you Master Magician, but you are not ready. You would battle against a darkly prepared foe. You must elevate your Magic. You need to learn more spells and conjuring to have an equal opportunity. This will take time. For now, join forces with the Dragons. Create a Protection barrier to shield Dark Magic from entering your area. That will be work enough. What Tyrianua and I will be able to do is offer you time. We can create a false way, a ruse, to guide Flegmorr and Glik away from the area. We will be able to monitor them and keep them at bay. We will leave markers along a new path for them to blindly follow. This will grant you time to fully prepare."

Perthorn's shoulders slumped. He had always held himself to the most rigorous of trainings in all aspects of Magic. *How could I not be ready?* he thought. Running his hand down the great length of mustache, he wondered what he had done by coming out of the Inner World, bringing with him his nemesis. *What if Flegmorr hurts one of my friends? What if I can't stop him?* His mind continued to run circles against the unknown.

Kaida broke the silence. "Zelspar! Our stones of Protection you cleansed!" Kaida dangled her necklace out to glimmer in the sunlight. "I know this works for me. Remember Perthorn, when we first met and you tried to hit me with Magic and it was deflected? It's my necklace."

A long yellow talon delicately moved Kaida's stone and memories flooded back at the cause of the event and the capture of the greatest Deceiver of all time, Dargenoin. He was the reason for the stone Dragon Tears in the first place and the reason for the Cleansing Ceremony. "Kaida, you are correct," Zelspar answered, "we all have our Protection, we must get one for Perthorn and Kiel, so I will give them one from my own collection. Perhaps it infused part of my very Magic into the stones. For now, I will weave a Protection barrier around our area."

Zelspar moved out past the line of caves, his lips moving in low guttural sounds, his wings spread wide as his arms lifted and moved across the area. He turned and thrust his arms out towards the mountain where all the Hails had made their lairs. Electricity danced from his talons causing a sudden ripple of blue light as he secured the protective shield all around them.

"It is time to make the others aware of Flegmorr. All should know and all should be protected. These are unusual times and as such, our training will increase to add to our skills. I'll speak to the Queen and King of Mursei. Kaida and Zlemtec, tell King Togar that I will need him and the Solteriem folk to join us for all sessions, starting now!"

The Master Magician cleared his throat. "If it isn't prohibited, Kiel and myself would like to come with you. If there are any questions, I feel our presence would be helpful in answering those queries." His chin rested against his chest as he kicked the dirt around his feet. "It is because of me that wretch has invaded your homes."

"I believe having you and Kiel coming with me is a sound idea but know this, Perthorn, you are not the cause of this problem. If anything, by you coming with us to our Upper World of Urthe, you have given us advanced warning and time to prepare. I will give you all the knowledge and training I have and," his old eyes gleamed, "considering I'm a old Dragon and the Elder of the Qyrdrom Hail," his chest thrust out in pride, "that is a considerable amount!"

Feeling less of a problem, Perthorn nodded and held onto the words of friendship. "Let's inform the others." Zelspar leaned down to accept Perthorn and Kiel onto his back and made ready for flight.

Glancing back at the others he repeated, "All of you make ready to join us in the training rooms. We are about to stir up some serious Magic!" He took a few heavy strides, his strong wings stirring the fine layer of dust, he swooped into the air.

Tyrianua turned to those left standing and said, "Sigrunn and I will travel to find Flegmorr and leave a path for him and his companion to follow. We will stay close to them, watching, learning of any plots they form against Perthorn or for the matter, any of you. Do not worry for us, he can not bring us harm."

Kaida in a flurry of arms and legs, ran to the wolves and dropped to her knees in front of them. Arms laced around their necks, she rubbed her face in between them. "I know and believe all you have said," she whispered choked with emotion, "but you will forever be my wolf pups, my dearest friends that came to me when I felt so alone. Please take great care. You carry with you part of my soul."

Sigrunn panted and showed Kaida a toothy smile, "Remember, part of us is always with you." Sigrunn managed a wink, "we both added parts of ourselves at your Cleansing Ceremony, remember?" A lick to Kaida's face and the wolves got up to go. Sigrunn craned her neck, her fur quickly bristled. Her mind filled with images as her eyes flickered. She thought, *'The Time is at hand.'*

Still privy to the wolves internal conversations, Kaida asked, "What time? What do you mean?"

Turning towards Kaida, Sigrunn stared deep into her eyes and communicated, *'Your Time. Where you go, we can not follow. Learn all you are able from Zelspar and tap into your hidden knowledge. You* are *the Legend. Never forget or doubt it. Every moment of Life has been in preparing you for this Time.'*

A shadow fell over Kaida's eyes. The rivers within her churned and crashed against their walls causing her heart to race and thud wildly against her bones. Her mind careened from thought to thought. *I've only returned home but a brief time ago, do I have to leave my family? And Zlemtec. I don't want to be away from him again, he ... he ...* her mind fought for the right words.

Sigrunn's reassurances spoke to Kaida's mind. *'Speak first to the Queen of Mursei. She has your answers. Ask Zelspar about his Visions. Even know, a beacon has been re-activated. The time grows short. Learn quickly. And Zlemtec? He will be with you, never fear. The strength of two shall be the strength of One. Everything has prepared you for this Time, this journey, but you must know who you are and never falter from that belief, no matter what battles come your way. You are the Legend, the Legend of the Dragon Child.'* She looked lovingly into Kaida's eyes then trotted away with Tyrianua, to lead away the immediate threat.

With a deep breath, Kaida rose, squared her shoulders and ground her teeth together,

"We've work to do! We need to get King Togar and his Faery folk and start some serious training."

There was something about the set of her jaw, the rise from the ground that stirred the hearts of those around her as if someone new had formed from the ground she had been kneeling upon. A new fire blazed around them and that fire was Kaida.

Chapter 34

"But Zelspar, I hardly think so much alarm should be given over only one man," his friend and the Queen of Mursei, Starleira replied.

"I had felt the same as you, Starleira, but the wolves were very convincing." Zelspar shot a sideways glance towards the King of Mursei, who had held his thoughts tightly throughout the discussion. "What are your thoughts, Rynik?"

"What you brought up in regards to the Laws of Balance rings true. We must remember, we also sought Urthe out as a land to bring our ways and our hope of a peaceful existence. We blamed ourselves for not blocking the portals from the ones we wanted to leave behind, the ones that hungered for domination and war. If we consider the Laws of Balance, then we must also realize and accept, we caused our enemies to come here by our decision to inhabit Urthe." Rynik paced in a tight circle, continuing his thoughts.

"It was for us to rectify the dilemma. We initiated the change. In our own beliefs, there is always an opposing force. Where there is one, there is the other. One force becomes the primary force and the other, secondary; for that is the nature of all things."

"I do agree, my Bonded," Starleira answered. "The part I am in disagreement with is what possible threat would one person bring against our legions of Dragons? The mere thought of this, I find outlandish."

"Perhaps so," Zelspar said, "but, as Sigrunn reminded me, we do not have the ability to nullify the threat because we can not affect the outcome. We are not the opposing force. What we can do, is strengthen our abilities to hold that force away. Since the threat comes from a Magician, I believe by intensive training, we can add protection to the peoples and Dragons, alike. Even though Flegmorr is trained in a Dark Magic, he does not possess Dragon Magic. When the battle comes, and it will ... we must be prepared. Perthorn is our friend," Zelspar's eyes locked onto Perthorn's, "he is my friend and I will stand by him, come what may."

Starleira considered her friend for a moment. He has always been the noblest of all Dragons and fiercely independent of thought. For him to make such a stand, she pondered, there must be more to this Perthorn and Flegmorr scenario. *What is it that Zelspar knows and has not shared? There is some ember buried deep within his belly he has not brought to the surface. I do trust his judgment, I always have, but I just can't see the situation as dire as he seems to think.*

"If that is your wish, then yes, do more trainings. I am sure our new friends will benefit greatly from your teachings," Starleira said, offering up a smile of consent.

"I appreciate your support, Queen and King of Mursei. It troubles me that I have brought problems to your doorstep, so to speak." Perthorn shifted on his feet, uncomfortably. "I promise you this, I will do everything within my power to eliminate his threat."

"We will start at once. I have sent Kaida and Zlemtec to bring our other guests to the training rooms where each daybreak we will be meeting and perfecting our skills." Zelspar nodded his goodbyes and turned to leave with Perthorn and Kiel close behind.

Reaching the training rooms, Zelspar nodded to his guests and made his way to Zlemtec.

"Where is Kaida?" he asked, exhibiting a tinge of irritation. "We need to get started right away, she knows this."

"She said she would join us as soon as possible … something about what Sigrunn told her, she had to get answers from the Queen."

Zelspar's eyes flashed. *Not now,* he thought. *She needs more training! If Sigrunn told Kaida about her birth mother, what will she do? By all that is Dragon, I should be there to hear what is going on but now I have guests, depending on my teachings.* His brows pinched together with his inner turmoil.

"Very well," Zelspar's gruffly answered. "We will begin. Today, I would like to start by Perthorn showing us his abilities. In this manner, I will learn what I can offer to add to his line of defense. Please start, my friend"

Chapter 35

Kaida stopped at the entrance to the Queen and King's lair.

The Queen of Mursei looked up to see Kaida hesitating at the entryway. "Come in, Kaida! I had expected you to be with Zelspar this morning, continuing your lessons in Dragon Magic."

Kaida stood fixed to her spot. Part of her wanted to run to her Queen mother but the other part knew she was here to find out the answers Sigrunn had told her to find. She knew the answers would change everything, that somehow, she herself, would change. She took a step forward and shivers traveled the length of her spine, making the hairs on her neck prickle. This one step felt as if she traveled millions of miles to get here. She let out a rush of pent up breath.

"Sigrunn said I should come. It is time I know the secrets you hold about me." Kaida's stare was unwavering.

The Queen's palm flew to her chest, startled.

"I must know. Sigrunn and Tyrianua told me that my Time was at hand, that something has started and I must be prepared. I need to know what you know."

The King joined his Bonded and held her hand, gazing at her reassuringly. A small tear slowly traveled the length of her face, no words found her tongue, only a slow nod of her head answered Kaida.

"What is it that you know Sipta Queen? What worries you to tell me?" Kaida persisted.

"Oh, Kaida. You have been ours since the day you were borne. You took my heart and soul the moment you clasped your fingers around mine. Yes, I knew you were borne as the Legend foretold but more, you ... you became my daughter." A rush of emotions tore at the Queen's heart as Rynik reassuringly patted her hand.

"Starleira, it is time to show Kaida her heritage box." Rynik saw the flicker of pain in his Bonded's eyes before she turned to retrieve the box from its protected niche. When she returned, she had something tightly clasped within her hands. It was, to her, that she held her whole world in her hands, but she also held Kaida's. She slowly opened her hands like a blossom unfurling, and exposed the gleaming orb within.

"I've seen these," Kaida gasped. "The strange peoples we met on our way home were wearing orbs just like this one. Remember, Sipta King?" It only took her a second to recognize the look on his face and then it hit her like a gale force wind and she stumbled backwards a step. "You mean ... this means, they are my peoples?" Eyes wide and jaw hanging open, Kaida stared at the object, piecing together the mystery. "They had called me by the name of Kiayla. I just thought they mistook me for another."

Rynik spoke. "They did, our little Dragon. They mistook you to be your mother." He paused as Kaida began to process the news. "Those new peoples had traveled here through their gateway, looking for your mother. I recognized their orbs to be exactly like the one your mother had, the one I gave to the Queen after your birth mother died giving birth to you. You heard the story they told, how they had to escape with the princess due to an upheaval in their kingdom."

Kaida's knees buckled and she suddenly dropped onto the carved granite bench. "That means my mother was the princess they were trying to find. Why didn't you tell them? Or me? I could have ended their search, their ... hope...." Her words died out as her knowledge began unraveling the ramifications of this new information.

"We had no idea, in the beginning, who your peoples were. You were like no others we had ever seen. I only realized when we came across them, that they are your peoples but you have to understand, I couldn't say anything at that moment. We, we hadn't prepared you. Hearing that they had to escape with the princess, well, I was afraid for you, worried at what kind of turmoil this kingdom was going through ... and more than that, I was afraid they would insist on taking you away." The King's head fell to his chest.. A mightier blow could not have hit him as hard as this did.

The vision doubled before Kaida's eyes. The knowledge bit into her with savage fangs. She longed to block it away, to return to yesterday when she was the odd hatchling, the girl who was safe and at home with her family, the Dragons who raised her. She blinked away the tears, blinked away her childhood and clasped her knees firmly. She leveled her eyes to meet the Queen and King's.

"Sigrunn said I must prepare. My Time is at hand and she said a beacon had been re-activated. Since this is what brought the peoples ... my peoples here in the first place, that can only mean they will return to find ... they will find me. In time. I will spend what time I have left in learning and developing all that Zelspar can give. Then, Zlemtec and I will leave to do what I was borne to do."

The Queen and King exchanged looks of despair. Gulping back a sob, the Queen said, "I knew the day would come, eventually, when you would meet your destiny. I always thought there would be more time. If I could take this burden...." The Queen could not speak any further, as she fought back her grief; a battle she could not win.

Kaida slowly rose and stoically walked to the entryway, then turned. "I could not have asked for better parents than the both of you. Do not be sad, I now understand the nature of things. We are all borne for a purpose. I am fortunate that I now know what mine entails and I can plan and prepare for it, or at least be as prepared as time allows." She summoned a small smile and began a new journey as she crossed over the threshold from the past to present.

A cyclone of thoughts whirled in Kaida's mind. *Who are these peoples that looked like me? Where did they come from? I only know they used a portal, or what they called 'a gateway' to get here. I'm ... I'm borne of a peoples and who is my father, is he alive?*

All the questions tortured her soul, needing to find the answers and yet: *I have my family, my place and it is here with all those I love,* she thought. Kaida shook her head as if she could clear her mind of the bombardment of unanswered questions.

Making her way to the training rooms, without a second thought she uttered, 'lift' and her feet left the ground. She descended onto the ledge outside the cave and entered to see her friends in feverish training, sharing knowledge of their Magic skills. Zelspar saw her, all at once aware of a change in her. He puffed out a mouthful of smoke, steeling himself for the questions to come and made his way to her.

"We could not wait, there is much to learn in a short amount of time. Are you ready?" he asked.

"First, Zelspar, I want to know what you can tell me of my peoples and any Visions you had about me; Sigrunn said to ask you. I must prepare for what comes, for what awaits me ... for my future."

"Kaida, I know you have questions but time is limited. We must use time wisely. You need more training and I must discover what lies hidden within you, to bring it out and help you hone your skills," Zelspar stated firmly but with affection.

"You are right. Time is fleeting but that is why I need my answers now. I may not have the benefit of extensive training but I will have the benefit of your knowledge if you will share it with me now."

He could not deny this warrior her needs. Her blue eyes were locked onto his and unflinching. In a wingspan of time Zelspar took quick inventory of the young woman in front of him. Her feet were planted firmly to the ground, shoulder width apart, her stance as rigid as a true arrow. Her hatchling days had sloughed away leaving the form of the warrior in front of him. An involuntary groan burned in his throat and he knew she must do what she had been borne to do.

"You are the Legend, our Kaida and your hatchling days are over. I will give you all I know and all I have seen."

Zlemtec gazed over to find Kaida speaking to Zelspar and started to approach. His legs stopped abruptly as he noticed the exchange taking place. He did not know his heart could both leap and mourn at the same time. A fierceness now met his eyes as he took in Kaida's being, having replaced the soul warming sunlight she normally beamed. He knew in his heart, grave challenges must surely be a breath away. He returned to the group, trying to concentrate but his sideways glances compromised his attempt.

"Let me start by saying this, I have spoken to Molakei and Flower Bird and they shared with me a dream you had which filled you with night terrors. They were concerned there were Dragons that wanted to harm you, for that was what you dreamed. I went to the Ancestors, to ask them to help me understand your dream. They gave me a Vision and this is what I saw."

Zelspar's eyes clouded as he drifted through the Vision. "I saw a different world, full of Golden Dragons, their scales glinting as a multitude of suns. A world of peace and happiness unlike my original home on Verlaunde or even here, on Urthe. Then, turbulence came, shaking up their world from outside forces. Strife set in between two neighboring worlds, once welcoming but now a great divide worked between the two. I saw the blonde-haired peoples fighting against one another on their planet and Dragons fighting Dragons on the other planet. It did not take long before each world blamed the other for the sudden chaos each found in their lives."

"The world you saw, that is where my peoples live?"

"Yes, Kaida. That is the reason the peoples fled your home world and took your mother, to safeguard her against the rebellion. Your birth mother and her guardians at first escaped to the world of Golden Dragons, for they had been friends and they had formed life-long friendships there. They had found safety in the storms of chaos for many months until...."

"Until what, Zelspar? What happened?" Kaida leaned in, absorbing every detail.

"Kaida, the two worlds had once been very accepting of each other but the division in small factions had started taking root. The peoples and Dragons alike began to fear that each were losing their uniqueness, were becoming too 'blended' and were afraid of losing what each felt were their true heritages."

"I don't understand, why?" she asked.

"Why?" replied Zelspar, shaking his head. "That is a question for Time itself. The short answer is fear. The fear of not being what they once were, the fear of the unknown, the fear of change itself. There are no good answers for this type of battle. It springs up from a rotten well, a well that seeks to wash over each one, bathing them in limiting hearts and minds, promoting a dominating attitude: one of superiority over another."

"I understand this is hard to grasp, because Kaida, you were raised here but even you saw when you lived with Molakei, the Urthe peoples despised Dragons. They formed their opinions on how other Dragons had treated them. It caused them to hate all Dragons, because of their fear. It is the same on these two worlds. Fear had burrowed deep into them, growing and growing until something snapped.

Kaida's eyes never ventured away from Zelspar's face. She absorbed every minute detail; each, a thorn piercing her skin, a burden which had been foretold for her to carry. "What caused the snap?"

An old hand slid over scales, and traveled slowly down to his muzzle. "You must understand Kaida, not all are able to accept change. I will now tell you the answers to your night terror." The White Dragon took a deep breath and exhaled slowly.

"Your birth mother and father had known each other for many years. When the uprising came to your mother's world, her guardians took her to the world of the Golden Dragons to seek asylum. They had many long-standing friendships there. It was going well for many months, but then the search for your mother brought trouble to the Dragons' world.

A lone puff of smoke rose from Zelspar's throat as he choked out his Vision. "Your birth mother and father were in love. They never hid their love for one another and were often seen flying across the sky. They became Bonded to each other but in a way unknown before. Their very Rivers of Life merged. They became more together than they were as individuals. They were still two, but One."

A flicker crossed Kaida's eyes, a recognition validated. She blinked her eyes rapidly to return to what Zelspar was saying.

"It wasn't long before changes happened. Your birth mother showed signs of ... of carrying a child. The uprising from her world had come to the Dragons' world, complete with accusations of them kidnapping Princess Kiayla. Of course, this was not true, but the seeds of turmoil had been planted. A group of Dragons made their way to the caves where your father's family had taken in your mother and guardians. They saw your mother in her advanced stages of pregnancy and became even more enraged. They wanted her gone!"

"They chased her from the enormous arched structures in which they made their lairs and pursued her relentlessly across the jagged terrain beyond dwelling spaces. Your father chased after them, and his family joined in. They fought against their past friends to defend your mother. A Golden Dragon, full of rage swooped down and was ready to char her in his flames. Another Dragon cut him off so she could escape. The fire-breath killed the Dragon. It is thought to have been your father."

Kaida's soul quaked and her lips trembled. She tightly squeezed her eyes shut and forced the pools of water to cascade down her bronzed face.

Soft-voiced, Zelspar continued. "The horde of Dragons suddenly halted in their pursuit. Never before had a Dragon killed a Dragon. Not on their World. Killing was reserved only in finding food. Roars of agony ripped wide rifts into the air. While the Dragons gathered around the charred remains of the slain one, your mother had found a portal and disappeared. Her guardians escaped also, but did not find the same portal. Life had been irrevocably altered not only by the killing of one Dragon by another, but in the Bonding of a Dragon to a peoples ... and now that woman was with child. This was too many hard changes that none could or would accept."

It tore at Zelspar's soul to watch Kaida hear his words. The little Dragon that knew nothing of hate, who loved all, unreservedly. She had slumped against her staff, the weight of hearing her beginning, threatened to knock her over.

White-knuckled, she pulled herself upright against her staff. Her arms swiped across her face, wiping away the tears. Reddened eyes met Zelspar's, her face now drained of color. She croaked out, "Train me hard." Then, through a clenched jaw, added, "I've a battle ahead."

Nodding slowly, Zelspar turned and they made their way to the training grounds.

Chapter 36

Flegmorr moved a gnarled hand through the air exposing a near invisible twinkle of magic along the path ahead. A curl of his lips shaped a smirk. "They passed this way. For a so-called 'Master Magician', he should have banished his trail of Magic. An error of a novice!"

The Flaptail squirmed across his back, his nose flaring but the scent of the Magician's matted hair abolished all other scents. Clicks chimed close to Flegmorr's hat, an affirmation to his Master followed by the droning sound of "yessss ... find himz."

"A simple task, Glik. The thought of revenge emblazons my soul and he cannot escape what Magic I wield. His weak conjuring will be no match for the true Magic I possess. His time is over."

"Hiszzz friendszz...."

"They had better stay away or I will finish them off, as well!"

"Dragonszz?"

"So? Nothing but large bags of flimsy flames. I can out do them with fire. I have the Flames of Nether, filled with the writhings of confined souls. There is no match to my Magic as they will soon see." Strengthened by his own thoughts of revenge and superior ability, he marched on, following the trail of Magic.

Sigrunn and Tyrianua climbed over tumbled boulders, leaving a trail which lingered in the air, miles ahead of Flegmorr.

"That way," suggested Tyrianua, "through the caves. They wind through the mountain and should open out the other side. We'll gather dried wood from the Pyce tree and set a fire pit inside. The smoke from it will deepen the deception and show that Perthorn had rested inside."

A nod from Sigrunn and they trotted towards the entrance, collecting the broken branches along the way.

The heat of the day bore down on the travelers as they climbed the tumble of rocks the quakes had thrown down the mountain. Flegmorr paused to remove his hat, swiping a dirty arm across his brow, soaking the edge of the wide sleeved robe he wore. He gazed upward, finding the trail as it disappeared into a cave.

A bruised and battered hand raised and pointed. "Up there. The trails leads into a cave. Either they are in the place in which they will die or we will rest inside and follow their trail after the sun moves lower in the sky." At that moment, Flegmorr wished for the latter as the arduous journey over the rock slides had taken its toll.

A scurrying beetle, splendid in its red markings, darted under a rock. Flegmorr quickly tossed the rock aside, snatched up the wriggling bug and popped it into his mouth, savoring the crunch of its shell as the twitching legs succumbed to the pounding of teeth. Extracting a leg caught between his teeth, Flegmorr cast it aside and made his way to the cave.

Charred remains of a fire permeated the air inside. It took Flegmorr no more than ten strides to locate the fire pit. He snickered, "They were here," he said pointing down the remains in the fire pit. Shaking his head he scoffed, "Foolish oafs!"

With a shake of his dusty, sweat marked hat, Flegmorr sat down, inspecting the fire pit. "The stones are still warm. They will be close enough to find. A brief rest and we will have them." In the subdued light of the cave, a gleam of anticipation glowed in his eyes.

Glik flapped up to the ceiling and clung to the rocks overhead, his long tail gently rattling until he found slumber. With the smoke still wafting through the cave, both travelers breathed in its fumes, causing a heavy sleep to entrap them.

A distant howl rung into the air. Tyrianua turned towards Sigrunn, "Overconfidence in the self will always turn the tides."

Sigrunn replied, "Yes, but in our favor." Both wolves trotted down the back side of the mountain, streaming behind them the trail of Magic to follow their ruse. Their yips faded as the distance from the cave network grew, leaving behind them the Magician and his foul friend, snared in the clutches of a sleep that would keep them immobile for several days.

Miles away, two howls entwined, as the wolves picked a treacherous path to leave for their followers.

Chapter 37

Fireballs of green and red exploded on the far wall of the training rooms.

"Impressive, besides the fire, does your Magic in the fireballs do anything other than to burst into flames?" Zelspar curiously asked.

"Thunder and Lightning," Perthorn retorted, "I would think that would be plenty of damage," His eyes narrowed and jaws clenched, as he glared at Zelspar.

"Perthorn, my friend, I mean no disrespect. I'm only trying to gauge what other elements you and all of us should add to our arsenal of Magic. Remember, there are no egos at stake between friends, and we are all friends. What is at stake, however is a lunatic aimed to spread his type of Magic, to let it seed and fester in our world and we will do all within our combined powers to stop him."

"Yes, yes. I see your point. Flegmorr is getting under my skin. I had looked at him as merely a delusional nuisance before but now ... after all the talk the wolves brought us, well, I must confess he has wormed his way into me. That alone frustrates the day's light right out of me."

"Understood, Perthorn, but now back to what I asked, if you would."

"Well, no. Our spells of Fire are just that. We create the fireballs to throw at a enemy in times of great danger. The green ones work devastatingly well at close range where the red ones travel a great distance."

"Do you have Lightning Magic?" Zelspar asked.

"Yes, we do but not as potent as what I've seen you do."

"Then, we will all work with Dragon Magic, agreed?"

Heads nodded and most of the guests were chattering excitedly. Kaida had not joined in and Zlemtec frowned. He moved next to her and tilted his head close, saying "You'll never have that worry, I will help you with any Dragon Magic." His eyes flashed their blends of blues, purples and whites and gave her his most splendid of smiles. There was a long pause before Kaida even seemed to notice he had joined her.

"Oh, I'm sorry Zlemtec, I was lost in my thoughts."

"What is bothering you? I could tell something seemed ... different when I saw you talking to Zelspar earlier."

Kaida batted away a stray tear that had formed and sighed.

"I've learned about my peoples and my heritage. Zlemtec? Is it wrong of me to wish I never knew? To wish I could go back to just the Kaida raised with Dragons?"

His hand reached over and moved her hair from covering her eyes. His voice urged on with tenderness, "You'll always be that Kaida. You can tell me anything, I'm not going anywhere."

A frail smile finally broke the tightness of her concentration. "But you will, be going that is."

Blinking quickly, trying to assess her comment, he could only stare and wait.

"Zlemtec, do you remember those strange people we talked to on our way home?"

"Of course," he answered, "I was worried when I saw they had surrounded you. But why worry about them now? We all saw them leave."

"I found out," she paused. The words were hard for her to say but she finished by adding, "they are my peoples."

Zlemtec's chest expanded, "Look Kaida, those peoples may be as you say, they could be the peoples of your parents, but we are your family!"

"Thank you Zlemtec. That is what is making it so hard. Everyone here is my family. I don't want to feel torn but I do."

"Just because you know your peoples now is no reason to feel torn. You are ours. We are yours. That won't change."

"It's not as simple as that. There is more to tell and then you will understand why it is I seem different. It is because I am."

"Kaida, Zlemtec. Enough talk, we are here to learn. Join us and work with the Dragon Magic. Lightning Fire! Let's go," Zelspar said, an edge grating in his words.

After hours of tedious training, all present were able to cast a Lightning Magic. Flimsy at first but after much repetition, it was admirable what had been achieved. True, none could manage the Lightning Magic as well as Zelspar, but he had his Ancestors to thank as well as thousands of years of practice.

Zelspar leaned against his staff and a small smile creased his face. *They have learned well. It is difficult to teach Dragon Magic but I am well pleased. Even Molakei and Flower Bird were able to work the Magic. I must thank the Ancestors for helping them,* he thought. His eyes wandered up to the ceiling where a thinning of fog had dispersed and smiled as he thought, *Yes, I felt your presence and my thanks to you.*

"That's enough for today. We've all worked hard. Rest up and we will start again at first light. Let's make ready to leave."

The group relaxed and grabbed up their things to take the trip down to ground level. Between Zelspar and Zlemtec, all were delivered safely to the ground. As each group made their way home, Zelspar headed one way and Zlemtec and Kaida, another.

When Zlemtec and Kaida found shade against a tree, Zlemtec asked Kaida to finish her story, which she did, mostly.

"You mean your mother was a princess? No wonder they were trying to find her. That doesn't mean they will try to take you does it? They had better not or...." Kaida had to interrupt him.

"It does mean they will come looking for me but not for those reasons only. You see, I thought the Legend I was borne for was set here on Urthe, but it isn't, well not completely. There is a great upheaval on my planet and...." She looked deeply and searched Zlemtec's eyes as she told him, "and in the world of the Golden Dragons. Where my father was from."

Zlemtec caught his breath and a smile cracked his face wide open. "Kaida, that's great! No, I'm sorry, it's terrible that everyone is fighting but you know of your family and your father was a Dragon! That explains a lot, don't you think? Why Dragon Magic comes easily to you, why you have always been like the rest of us, why we feel ... um, I mean why it's natural for us to fly as One and everything. By all that is Dragon," Zlemtec started laughing, "Yes, by all that *is* Dragon!" He rolled onto his side, laughing harder at his last comment.

Kaida grinned and tears flowed at the same time. *He doesn't think I'm odd at all for having a mother as one of the peoples and a father that was a Dragon. He's happy!* She dropped down against him and hugged his neck tightly.

"I was so worried you would think I was strange. The peoples, my peoples, and the Golden Dragons ... well not all of them but the majority are not happy my mother and father were Bonded. This is part of the reason the worlds are fighting both against each other and also between themselves."

"So...." Zlemtec had stopped laughing and caught on to the implications.

"So, that means, I must go there to work on helping them reach an understanding, to help end this battle while it is still new, before it can become ingrained into their beliefs. I know this is what I must do."

"What *we* must do, because I won't let you go without me. Never again. Where you go, I go, understood?" His eyes danced with their flashing colors as his hand smoothed Kaida's hair.

Her smile was enough to set the sun in shame. "Yes, that's exactly what I mean, this is what *we* must do." She thought for a moment. The smile faded away as the seriousness of what loomed in the future crossed her thoughts.

"This is why we must train so hard. There is no way of knowing what we will be up against, or even if ... or even if we will survive. But, if I can only get them to listen, to know me, to hear how I was raised and all the good things I have been shown, then they might change. I might be as the Legend foretold, I could be the bridge to understanding and acceptance."

"You will be, Kaida. Maybe we can bring Queen and King Mursei, Zelspar and...."

"No, Zlemtec. Sigrunn made it clear. This is my battle. You are the only one that goes with me. It will be up to us to get them to listen, to understand."

"We will be enough." Zlemtec's chest puffed out.

"Zlemtec?"

"Hmm?"

"Let's fly!"

Kaida could think of no better way to celebrate the elation her heart felt with Zlemtec's acceptance or to shake off the thoughts of their upcoming battle. For this moment, she simply wanted the joy that overtook her when she flew as One with Zlemtec, to feel the lift of his Wings beneath her and how the air moved through her hair, the soaring of her heart. Flying did all this for her, and flying with Zlemtec? It had no known words, only feelings.

Chapter 38

Upon leaving the training rooms, Zelspar immediately left to talk to Starleira and Rynik and caught them as they were leaving their lair.

"Zelspar, good to see you," Queen of Mursei said seeing her old friend.

"Could I have a moment of your time, I need to air my thoughts."

"Certainly Zelspar," the King answered, "We were going to check in with you on how the training has been going with our guests."

"All that in good time. First, I must clear my head. I need to speak of Kaida."

Starleira stifled a sniff as her eyes watered knowing where the subject would lead. "Yes, come join us in the lair, you have our undivided attention." They turned and all three found comfortable spots for the conversation.

"Kaida came to me and wanted to know more about her birth parents and asked of my Visions in regards to her. She was steadfast and would not be put off. I told her all I had seen in the Vision, how her father, a Golden Dragon had been Bonded to her mother and the trouble that forced her mother to find a portal to escape."

"Was it..." Starleira began with voice choked in emotion, "terribly difficult for her, hearing what you told her? We too, talked with her before she came to you. I cannot express how much inner turmoil it has caused us, Zelspar."

"No need to try to explain, my friend. I find myself reeling with the same turmoil of which you speak. I find myself in a quandary." Zelspar was wearing a rut in the floor of the lair, preferring to pace rather than to sit. "Just as Sigrunn had let me know Perthorn's battle is his alone against Flegmorr, she informed Kaida the same holds true for her." He stomped his staff against the ground, obliterating an invisible foe. "How can we let her go to these peoples, to the world of her father, a Golden Dragon? What we know is a battle has begun because of Kaida's mother and father and she is to go there ... without us? How can we allow it?"

A new river of tears washed down Starleira's face, and she did nothing to stop them from their path. "It is almost more than I can bear, I feel my heart will wither away. Zelspar, she has only just returned to us a short time ago. I'm afraid, the prophecy didn't say...."

"Yes, I know. It never said the outcome and what would happen to the Dragon Child. I've been thinking in that regard, I wondered if Pravietis, the Future Walker, could give us an answer?"

Both Starleira and Rynik chimed in, "Yes!"

Zelspar shifted from side to side, an unease set into his old bones. "He does see into the Future, whatever it shows."

Starleira reached out and grabbed Zelspar's arm and abruptly stopped his pacing. "No, don't ask. I ... it's just that, I don't want to hear what troubles await. I don't think I could stop her from going or stop myself from following."

"Quite so, quite so. I don't like this one bit. I have never been so frustrated in all my life, and that's been a good long time." Zelspar roared his agony against the wall of the cave and they all grew quiet.

After a long pause Rynik ventured, "Do you believe her peoples are on the way here?"

"I do not know, Rynik. Kaida mentioned a beacon had been set in motion. I'm certain it must mean the beacon her peoples followed here long ago."

"The orb! Kaida's heritage box. It must send a signal when it is opened." Starleira said as her hand slammed over her mouth. Her words fell softly as she remembered. "It shimmers when opened...."

"Hmm." Zelspar said, his thoughts running circles in his mind. "It won't be long, then. She is training well but there is still so much to show her, to find out what Magic lies dormant inside. By all that is Dragon, it could take years to discover all she has and needs to develop. Time we don't, rather time she does not have."

Rynik mustered up all the courage he could find. "We are speaking about her as a mere hatchling child. She is more than that. She is more than our little Dragon for she is the Dragon Child. We had no idea that the prophecy would mean an actual child borne of a Dragon and a peoples, only the way she would be found. We had never known of such a birthing and I do believe she is the only one or we would have heard of such news. She is much more than any of us have given her credit for being. And because she is who she was borne to be, we must trust in her. We must support her and not try to stop what she must do."

The room grew quiet of words but not of groans and tears for what none of them had the power to change. Three Dragons huddled together, leaning against each other for support. All had come to recognize they must now learn how to let go, to allow the prophecy to be fulfilled. None of them found any comfort in the recognition.

Chapter 39

The flight through wisps of clouds and shimmering sunlight rejuvenated Kaida. Her golden tresses streamed in ribbons behind her, resembling a banner of fabled kingdoms on distant worlds; and a kingdom it was for her, the kingdom of Dragon flight. The gentle rocking of wing beats calmed her soul and became a rhythm that merged with her own heartbeats.

Zlemtec carried her past the mountains of home, out west and over the vastness of blue waters teeming with life. His wings dipped down as they spotted an enormous Sea Dragon, its humps breaching the white caps in a undulating line that more than tripled Zlemtec's length. The Sea Dragon with his sleek scales of greens and blues spotted them, roared and his powerful body shot up from the water, greeting the sky Dragon. Zlemtec answered the greeting with a resounding roar, dipped and circled the Dragon, allowing Kaida to see his majestic form up close.

They chased the sunset, two flying as One, until they turned to set their heading towards land and home. Kaida hooked her feet under Zlemtec's scales and rose to a full standing position. Her arms extended from her sides and head thrown back, a primal roar pierced the air. Her spirit was free! The whole of her being celebrated, having at last, come together completely. She had found the missing piece. She was Dragon-borne and reveled in it. She was the blending of two different lifeforms where neither became diminished, both entwined to become greater than the one.

In overwhelming gratefulness, her head swayed from side to side as more roars tore from her throat. Zlemtec's roars sung with hers. The two were One, fires burning in their eyes, bathing in the reds and purples of the fading sunset.

Landing, Kaida slid down and breathed in the air, holding the feeling long, before making any movement that would break her remembrance of flight, of this moment and of self-discovery. Zlemtec intrinsically knew to pause in the moment. Both held tight to the memory before they made their way home in the splendor of silence.

Molakei looked up as they entered the cave. He was awestruck by what he saw, not just the glimmer surrounding their bodies but something that defied description. The closest explanation would be they held a 'warrior' look, the look of assured confidence in themselves and the battles they would fight. A mixed medicine of faith and trust, radiated from them.

"Welcome." Molakei said.

"Molakei, Flower Bird, we've been flying," Kaida announced in her lilting voice.

"I would have known without your telling, Kaida. Happiness glows from your skin!"

Molakei chuckled.

Kaida turned to Zlemtec, "I'm hungry, are you?"

"Starved!" he replied.

"It happens that Flower Bird has prepared many fried fish and berry cakes. Eat your fill," Molakei swept his hand over the assortment of food as the two began helping themselves.

The Elder warrior looked on, pleased to see them filled with a renewed happiness. Ever since the wolves had talked with them, the mood had grown tense. Now, it seemed like joy had returned to their cave and made a home by their fires. His heart was well pleased.

The evening passed with stories, laughter and friendships shared by the fire's side. Their spirits were fed and nourished by the bonds. One by one, they made their way to their sleeping mats. Zlemtec curled next to Kaida, his wing, a gentle covering and his arm, the pillow for her head. Sleep found her quickly as her breaths deepened to the sound of Molakei's chanting to the glowing embers in their fire pit.

The chants lifted up with the wisps of smoke carrying his thankfulness to his Ancestors. His song was long this night for his gratitude overflowed. His deep resonating sounds softly subsided as he finished and stared into the flickering embers. As the embers faded, he made his way to his mat. It had been a good day.

The stars still sparkled in their indigo blanket when Kaida stirred in her sleep. Images ricocheted through her mind. Tall, arched buildings with pillars for entryways, shimmered with gold coverings over their domes. Golden Dragons flew the skies, their wingspan as enormous as were their size. Large spikes rose from their backs and tails, like swords gleaming their deadly potential. Suddenly a horde of Dragons descended towards a great arched building, fire crackled the dome. Dragons poured out and peoples fled.

A moan crawled out of Kaida's throat. The images came faster and faster and more violent. Kaida shot up from her sleep screaming, awakening those around her. She could not still her heart from the heavy hammering against her bones. Molakei called to her but she answered, 'night terrors, they've gone' and she lay back down nestling closer to Zlemtec. The soothing sound of his heartbeat washed over her, allowing her eyelids to flutter to a close against the remnants of the night. Zlemtec kept one eye open until her breathing mixed with deep sleep, then closed his eye and gently pulled Kaida closer to him. Day's light and training would come soon.

The night broke with long pale yellow streams of light moving against the interior of the cave. Kaida rustled from her sleep, stretched and sat up. The aroma of woodsmoke and sweetbread wafted through the cave, waking up Kaida's appetite.

"Flower Bird, that smells so good. What are you cooking?"

"Good morn, Kaida. I call them corn cakes. I make them differently, depending on the season and what I have left in the storage baskets and pots. Today I mixed in acorn, walnut and the black berries. It will give us energy for the training today."

"Do you need help?" Kaida asked, eyeing the stack of cakes already cooling on a flat basket.

A soft smile greeted Kaida. "Yes. Bring me the golden liquid we have from the beehives. It too, will bring strength because it came from the fierce small warriors. Its sweetness even tames the corn."

The whole cavity of Kaida's mouth filled with water, anticipating their deliciousness. Her stomach growled in longing. She brought the thick golden-amber liquid and squatted next to Flower Bird.

"Take this cake and add the liquid over the top. Tell me if the ingredients merged their spirits in a nice combination." Flower Bird's eyes sparkled. She knew her cakes would delight the mouth much more than the smells delighted the nose.

At first bite, Kaida's eyes grew as large as her stomach's gratitude. "Oh, this is so good, Flower Bird. The spirits blended well and the thick bees liquid makes it melt in my mouth. Your hands make Magic in the food you make. I am grateful."

"You make my heart sing. I am pleased it brings you delight as well as nourishment. I learned this combination in a time when great sadness made its home in our cave. Days would pass with no smile breaking the sadness in my father's face. I made these cakes with walnuts and the blue berries. I added the golden juice on top and set it by the fire's side before my father awoke. I watched as he came to the fire and looked at the cakes. Soon, he took a bite. It was the first smile I was given since my mother had left to join the Ancestors. Yes, I think Magic lives in the small cakes."

Molakei and Zlemtec woke and joined the two at the fire's side. "Daughter, you have made the sweetcakes this morn. It is good. It not only brings strength to us but the taste makes this old warrior want to sing." Flower Bird bowed her head but her spirit soared.

Zlemtec's talon pierced a cake and plopped the tiny morsel in his mouth. "Delicious! It awoke all my hunger. I will return after I've had my fill of the greens nearby. Save me a few of those cakes to make my fire sweeter," he chuckled as he left the cave.

After he fed, he was making his way back when he saw Zelspar.

"Good morn, Zelspar!" Zlemtec shouted a greeting as they glided to a stop close by.

"A good morn to you, Zlemtec. Has everyone awakened?"

"Yes, all are up and eating the first meal of the day. I was about to go back, will you be coming with me?"

Zelspar exhaled, long and slow. "Yes, I want to speak with all."

"Is it about our training today," asked Zlemtec.

"We will discuss that after I have a chance to speak to all together, then we can decide."

"Come then, we will all be interested in hearing what is on your mind."

Zelspar was lost in his thoughts on the way to the cave. He reflected about his previous visit with Starleira, Rynik and Galdean. It had been a long evening for all, each torn by thoughts of the future for Kaida. He was called upon by Rynik before first light had stirred. The night terrors visited each of the four of them, in varying themes and torments. He had been called to decipher their meanings, and the collective night visions all pointed to Kaida. He must now go to her to discern if she had also experienced the night terrors and what the visions could mean.

Entering the cave, Kaida ran to Zelspar and attempted to physically drag him to the fire pit. "Zelspar, Flower Bird made these wonderful cakes! Come, share the fire and food with us, we are getting ready for the training session today. These cakes will give us extra strength and energy."

Her twinkling blue eyes flashed so brilliantly, Zelspar only wanted to see her this way and not to bring her sadness or worry. He felt his belly fires churn and worked up a smile, even though it was short lived.

Molakei noted the stiffness of the old Dragon and how his face seemed more drained than he had seen before. He greeted Zelspar by saying, "Welcome friend. What is on your heart to say?"

Kaida gave a quick look towards Molakei and back at Zelspar. She stopped dragging her Teacher and friend and gazed up into his eyes. "What has happened?"

"Kaida, all ... I did not wish to bring worry to your home and you are correct Molakei, I do have much on my heart this new morn. I thought it is better to lay out the thoughts in the open and see what is discovered. I will ask now if any had night terrors last evening?"

The room was so quiet you could hear the wood popping in the fire pit.

"I did." Kaida replied, her eyes locked into the small dancing flames of the fire.

"I did too," replied Zlemtec to Kaida's surprise.

A trail of smoke drifted out of Zelspar's snout. *It is as I thought. These are not random night terrors, not for them to touch so many.* "I would like us all to explore these night terrors. I believe they are more than terrors. I think we were given Visions."

Kaida merely nodded as she took in a deep breath.

They gathered by the fire's side and each recounted what they remembered of the Visions. Zelspar shared the Visions he was told about and his. They all shared the same basics with slight variances, typical of each one's own experiences and interpretations. When all had been shared, the room again grew quiet. There was nothing left to interpret as the combined Visions painted a clear picture.

Kaida stood. She was latching her long yellow hair back into a leather holder and tied it tightly behind her head. The flames of the fire intensified the chiseled jawline; the strength of her character shone all around. "What next? I must leave, right?"

Zelspar's hands reached out and held Kaida by the shoulders. "That is for you only to decide."

"How do I know the right answer? I think if I stayed, I might train harder and longer. But if I stay, trouble will come here," she said with a sigh which escaped her grasp.

Zelspar continued to hold her shoulders and his look bore deep into her eyes. "Be the Dragon you were borne of and raised to be. Think the way we do. Begin as all Dragons must."

He spoke with softened words, like wisps of smoke that filled the head. "You must find your answers by returning to the beginning. Let them layer and blend and bleed together. Your answers should not be jagged stones, they would never fit into a smooth wall. Our Visions are the jagged stones; your journey, the wall. Your answers should flow like the sunset, where the light is scattered and the pieces are caught up in the clouds. Notice how the colors of the sunset are not distinct and separate? It is a smooth blending of one color to the next."

A yellowed talon lifted her chin. "The answer is you must return to the beginning, like the sun's morning rise. By the sunset, the sky's palette will smoothly blend the scattered pieces together."

Without knowing, Molakei had softly began singing the warrior's chant. They had all felt it in their beings, the time Kaida had been borne for had come.

"I will gather my things." Kaida moved to her bed of furs.

"Not so sudden, our little Dragon. We must have a Dragon's send off if you chose to go."

Zelspar had been surprised at her immediate thought of leaving.

"Zelspar, and family, it is hard enough to leave, not knowing ... I think it would be harder for me to spend the day in celebration with the Hails and the peoples, it would work a thorn under my skin and give me second thoughts. Zlemtec and I will fly to the portal we saw the peoples take to return to their world, to my birth mother's world. We will leave before the sun is straight overhead."

"The Queen would torch my hide if you left so abruptly. You prepare here and we will meet you back here before the sun is high in the sky." He gave her a small squeeze on her shoulder, "Understand?"

She leaned into his wide arms and hugged him ferociously. With only the slightest hint of a quiver in her voice, she said, "Understood."

Flower Bird hustled around, gathering food and extra clothing for Kaida: the sister not borne of her blood. Molakei rose and went through his packs looking for something honorable to give to the one who brought happiness back to his home, the warrior who would not walk away from a battle. He lifted out his warrior's knife and turned it over slowly, feeling the weight of the blade, the fit of the antelope handle, smoothed by time and use. It had saved him from the huge woolly beast when he was sent out to find meat. It never failed him in battle. He nodded and placed the knife back into its leather pouch which would be tied around the warrior's waist, the warrior who will fulfill the Legend.

Rolling up her sleeping mat and furs, Kaida tied them with leather bindings which she could fasten to Zlemtec during travels. She put other pieces of her life in bags and small containers as she allowed her eyes to swipe a look around the home she must leave. A well of emotions bubbled to the surface causing silent tears to surge over her lower eyelids. Such an involuntary action irritated her. *I won't do this, I AM the Legend and Legends don't cry,* she thought. *Oh, but how my heart aches. It's as if a part of me is being torn from my chest, still beating. To leave everyone and everything I have loved,* she paused in thought looking at Zlemtec preparing for their leaving, *well, not everyone, thank the stars of luck, I'll journey with Zlemtec.*

Preparations had wound down, with all of Kaida's belongings placed by the cave's entrance. Warm yellow fingers reached into the far depths of the cave: the sun announcing the time of her departure grew close.

Molakei approached Kaida, feeling twice his age, he leaned heavily against his staff. His eyes slowly took in each speck of her, memorizing her in this moment. "I have brought you a gift," he said, eyes dampened with the full weight of his heart. He slowly reached around her waist and tied the leather sash around her tunic.

Kaida looked down, and slid the knife from its holder. Her jaw hung open. "Molakei, this is your warrior knife...."

"Yes, the last daughter of my hearth. It has honored me all my life, may it honor you now. My own father made this knife, it is tempered with the spirits of warriors and of my Ancestors. It will give you great strength in battle."

"This is too great a gift, I cannot take it and leave you without it. It is a part of you, and what if you will need it?"

"Precious Kaida, you must take it for the very reason it *is* a part of me. You will carry me in Dragonflight, through portals to other worlds and ... into battle if necessary, where *this warrior* will once again rise with honor to fight with you. You have brought me many blessings and smiles that reawakened my spirit. You also have given to me the friendships of the many Dragons. They will be my knife now. There is no greater protection I would ever need."

Kaida, overcome with his words, sheathed the knife. "It brings me great honor and strength, Elder warrior. I will take you with me." She leaned in to embrace her protector of the peoples, her Teacher of the tongue and ways of the peoples of Urthe. "You hold a piece of my heart, for you took me in when the others feared and shunned me. You made a place at your hearth for this girl of the Dragons. I will bring you honor, in my ways. My greatest hope is to return, to share the fire's side with you and Flower Bird, after...." Her words stopped short. All present knew the difficulties ahead, and let the words stall.

Flower Bird slipped a pouch over Kaida's head where it came to rest on her side. "You are a sister to me, and I am honored you came into our life. Father is correct, you have brightened our days. It has been as if Magic moved across our fires and spirits, because before you came, our world filled with the darkness of grief. We could not find the path of Light, but you showed us the way. Since you brought us Light again, within your pouch, under the sweetcakes, is a small bag of crystals. They came from the inner cave of our Ancestral home, the one with the Rivers of Life flowing through it. The crystals will bring you peace in times of trouble and clear your head when too many thoughts try to overpower you."

Kaida said, "I do not have all the words to share with you what my heart knows. You will always be my sister and the source of Magic you carry. Everything you create is filled with the Magic of your spirit. I'm highly honored with your gifts. May your crystals from your Ancestral home guide me through my journey and home again."

Zlemtec's voice cut through, "Kaida, come outside with me. Molakei and Flower Bird, join us.

Waiting for them outside, were three Dragons of Blue and Gold and one old White Dragon. Clustered around them were Perthorn and Kiel, King Togar and a flurry of the fluttering Faeries, known as the Solteriem folk.

Kaida's hand flew to her heart, the sight of her family, caused her heart to skip its beat. She went towards them and became circled between them. Each adding a special gift of remembrances to her. Her tears became a rushing river of the love she felt. She swiped away at the tears, but they kept running their course.

The King of Mursei called Zlemtec to join them. "Zlemtec and Kaida, we pass along your Heritage boxes of the Mursei. In it is the legacy of all we are plus the pieces collected since your hatchling days. Take these with you so you'll always have us by your side. You will carry with you pieces of Verlaunde, where we came from and Urthe, our new home. May it bring you comfort in the days ahead and guide you safely back to us."

The Queen of Mursei stepped forward, her hand shaking as she uncovered the white orb of Kaida's birth mother. "My little Dragon, you have another Heritage box to carry with you. It was the one your mother wore when she ... when she came to us. It holds pieces from both your mother and father's heritage plus pieces of your hatchling days. This one, you should wear as your mother did. It will show you are her daughter when you reach the place of her birth." After the Queen placed it over Kaida's head, she pulled her close, trying to engulf her scent, to embed her into the Ancestral memory, to hold forever Kaida in the Mursei Hail of Dragons.

Everyone collected the bags and parcels to strap onto Zlemtec and made them ready for their journey. Kaida's heart near bursting, she climbed up on Zlemtec's back, his scales brought comfort to her heart. "Family, all. I will...."

Zelspar's thunderous voice burst through. "Save your words for your return, Kaida. You won't be leaving us yet." His old eyes sparkled as he spoke, "We are all escorting you to the portal. A Dragon does not go into battle without the support of their Hails."

Tears pooled around her eyes. She had not thought of them flying with her to the portal.

She watched silently as those around her joined the Dragons for the long trip to the portal. Her mind exploded with thoughts. *Why is it only now I realize so deeply all that I have when I'm about to leave them behind? How can my heart be so full and yet feel all the loss not yet here? I don't know why I have to experience abandonment over and over or why has the fates constantly have chosen to tear me from my family. To be borne as 'the Legend' has been cruel, I would not wish this path on anyone.*

Five Dragons, four peoples, the Faery King and his Solteriem folk plus one Dragon Child, took to the air, gently leaving the ground to fall away under them. Mighty Dragon bellows sliced their way forward being answered in kind with the mixed shouts of their riders.

For this flight, Zlemtec took point, the dazzling blues and golds of his scales flashed in the sunlight. Kaida once again, found her rhythm and wholeness of breath. She rose on Zlemtec's back, toes locked firmly beneath his scales. With her staff in one arm, she thrust it at the sun overhead and ripped the sky open with her own Dragon roar.

A ripple tore lose overhead and a force of wind whipped up behind them. Kaida's staff sparked like it held the heart of lightning. With one smooth move, Kaida slid down onto Zlemtec's back, tucked her staff under her arm and leaned forward.

Her roar was met with the roars of the Dragons following alongside. Sounds of crushing rocks rose up as the ground moved; the great rifts in them being pulled closed with a thunderous rumble. A bright finger of sunlight stretched out to illuminate the golden haired warrior and point her towards her destiny.

A surge of energy rolled across her arms, leaving her hair standing on end as it traveled up her arm and to the nape of her neck. It was raw power, and it was Time. The Legend Child had arrived for her point in History, her preordained Fate, and she was unshakeable.

Chapter 40

For the Dragons and the peoples traveling this journey, it was bittersweet. To witness Kaida's transformation into the full embodiment of the Legend left them in awe. They rode towards Destiny, and to a pivotal point in the History of peoples and Dragons. However historic this flight would become in their future, one thought remained: Kaida and Zlemtec were going to a place they could not follow, a place where the Future would be shaped by what the prophecy foretold.

Mountains and valleys became rushing landscapes in their passing. Zelspar silently implored, *Great Ancestor of all Dragons, this warrior, this girl you see flying as One, she is the One foretold in the prophecy; guard her well! We have been her guardians, her protectors on Urthe, I ask for your protection of her and Zlemtec once they leave our fold.* Hesitating a wingbeat, he added, *My years are stacked high, behind me. I have no fear of Death. My fear is this could be the last time I see them and it torments my soul. I ask of you this selfish desire: that I, that we all, live to see the day of their return.*

Heavy mist gathered from all directions and formed a looming vision in the distance. The Great Ancestor appeared from the swirl of mist, his head the size of mountains. Thunder rolled in an otherwise cloudless sky. The Great Ancestor's body continued to form, drawing up from the Urthe the vapors hidden in its depths, unexplored. Colossal wings spread out as the rest of his form took shape. The vision turned, exposing a tail that whipped across the sky, streaming a path towards the portal.

Explosive roars filled the air as all Dragons and riders followed the apparition. Zlemtec swung his head over his shoulder expecting to see Kaida's ever present smile but was met with eyes of blue lightning, and a jaw clenched with determination. She glanced down to meet his gaze, leaned in against his neck, driving him on.

As the sunlight retreated behind them, the landscape grew familiar to all but the Queen.

Destiny lie ahead and they all felt its grip.

The scattering of trees opened to reveal the one towering tree above all others, the tree that holds the portal the yellow-haired people used to return to their home. Zlemtec honed in on the sight, his break-neck speed blurring Kaida's vision. Closing in, he circled the tree once and then landed with all others close behind.

Sliding down Zlemtec's side, Kaida's dismounted and waited for the others to do the same. As they did, she found herself not only surrounded by her friends and family but engulfed with a fervor of love. She embraced them one by one, voicing not the thoughts in her heart but let her embrace speak her volumes of words.

Dragon tears pelted the ground. It was left to the noble Zelspar to give the parting words.

"Our little Dragon. Your presence in our lives has marked us all. Not a day we have shared could have been filled with more pride. No matter how far your journey or what you find there, we are your family and we will always be your home. As I told you before, to find the answers, the solution, you must start at the beginning again, as all Dragons do, to seek their inherent knowledge."

As all eyes watched as he continued, "This is then, by definition, your beginning. We will celebrate it as your re-birth, a journey of discovery and a metamorphosis of Change, for you were borne of the very seeds of Change. When our words have all ended, stay your footsteps, allow us to give you and Zlemtec our tribute, the circling of Dragons overhead, honoring our warriors."

Fighting the overwhelming avalanche of emotions, both Kaida and Zlemtec nodded briefly. The Queen of Mursei fidgeted with Kaida's necklace, ensuring it was placed in full visibility. Each of the peoples made a slow pass and embrace of the two warriors, then each of the Dragons had their turn.

Zelspar added, "Both of you use your Invisibility Magic before you go through the portal, you will not know if it will deliver you in the very midst of danger. By opening your Heritage orb, you can alert your birth mother's guardians to your presence, but if you find yourself in danger, search for the way to the Golden Dragons. You are Dragon-borne and they will sense it. Seek out family, for they will shelter you even if danger follows you to their lair. Rely on your Dragon Magic. Trust your instinct." His eyes bore holes through Kaida's with his fierce scrutiny. "You have been given all that you need to assure your victory. Know that. You *must* own it!"

His eyes softened their blaze, as did his voice. "You will write into History a glorious Future, the chance for peace between all. This is not an ending, but a beginning. Now, Kaida, Zlemtec, we will honor you with a warriors' salute."

The peoples once again climbed onto the Dragons' backs, looking at the two standing by the towering tree.

First, the King of Mursei lifted to the air, followed by the Queen, Galdean and finally, the Elder of the Qyrdrom Hail, Zelspar. They made one slow circle above Kaida and Zlemtec, then circled higher. Each Dragon thundered their strident roars. They circled slowly a total of five circles, and watched from above as Kaida and Zlemtec used their Magic and then, disappeared into the tree's portal. The sky became ignited by Dragon-fire as their roaring traveled up from the lowest pit of their bellies, the place reserved for the deepest attack of loss.

The Queen broke rank and dove for the tree, all other Dragons chasing her. She landed with a resounding thud, steps away from the portal. The King quickly darted in front of her path with Galdean and Zelspar behind her.

"Move!" she commanded to her Bonded. "Move or I will go through you."

Grief had covered her in its suffocating hold, and her eyes glazed over in its grasp.

"Starleira!" Her name boomed from in front and behind. The three Dragons surrounded her, wings outspread: a fortress she could not break.

A weak and trembling voice croaked out, "Please ... oh please let me go...."

Tears fell from all, fighting the urge. "No. We cannot let you. For if you went, we all would follow and it cannot be."

Unknown to Kaida or Zlemtec, wailings of grief assaulted the outside of the gateway they had taken. They could not hear, for they were already separated by Worlds.

Chapter 41

Kaida and Zlemtec cautiously stepped out of the portal and into a new world. Senses heightened and eyes wide, their legs could not move. Spread out before them was a foreign world with large flat islands jutting up from the enormous gorges below. Water cascaded down the rims of several plateaus, creating unfathomable waterfalls, jolting the ears with booming rumbles.

All the landforms were connected by shimmering arched bridges of a pale blue polished stone. Kaida looked behind her at the portal and noticed it was similar to the one they had taken from Urthe, being a towering tree with gnarled bark and huge sweeping branches. The landscape seemed to favor these giants. They grew in clusters across all the plateaus within their sight.

Besides the rosy tone of the sky, their interest was captured by the spires rising up out the landscape, conical in shape, and filled with openings emitting a diffused golden light.

Kaida whispered, "Let's explore where we are before leaving this area. We need to form landmarks so we won't lose our portal to home."

"If we flew, wouldn't we have a better grasp of where we are?"

"I like your idea Zlemtec, but still, I would feel safer by keeping to the ground to explore this area first, and we may not have much time."

"That is fine with me but climb up, we'll cover the ground faster with you on my back."

Climbing up, Kaida adjusted her staff and weapons, to be ready. They moved with hesitant steps towards the cluster of trees ahead of them, which could help hide them if there Invisibility Magic faltered.

At the edge of the tree line, they peered inside. Water bubbled up out of the ground, creating small pools of water. Edging the waterline was a thick carpet of a sponge-like mat of a fuchsia moss which sprouted flowers of drooping green petals: their perfume reminiscent of slightly spicy bee nectar.

Zlemtec leaned closer to the water. Within it crawled rock-like creatures with a cluster of vibrant blue legs surrounding their rounded shapes. Kaida took a sip from her water bag, not wanting to risk harm from the water or the creatures in it.

Easing their way forward, their sounds cushioned by the moss underneath, they saw another spire through the trees. And peoples: the yellow-haired peoples much like the ones she spoke with on Urthe.

A low rumble rose to Zlemtec's throat. They kept still and observed them. A group of men lifted rocks and pulled out long squirming creatures that were a deeper color than the moss they stood upon. Slipping them into large tightly woven baskets, they secured the lids, smiling at one another. They were still too far away to pick up their talk but Kaida saw one man lick his lips. *Food,* she thought.

Zlemtec started easing backwards.

"What are you doing?" Kaida bent over and whispered close to his head.

"Getting some wing room. We have seen what lies in this direction. The only way forward is to come close to the peoples, we don't need that right now. I say we turn back, take flight and get a perspective from up above, plus, if we are attacked, we can move far easier in the air."

"All right, but help memorize this place from above before we venture out too far."

"Of course, Dragons have a highly developed skill of cataloging our surroundings to the tiniest of details but it is much easier from above."

He was right, she thought, as they left the ground below them, the picture of the world was so much better to see. The plateau they soared above held various spires, all generally the same size. She counted six spires in all. On the far side, past the spires, the land smoothed and people were collecting items from the growing plants. One large section had low-growing vining plants with large spiked leaves. Out of the spikes, fist-sized plum protuberances were being snapped off and cast into their bags.

After circling this landmass, Zlemtec soared higher. He pointed down to draw Kaida's attention to the details. From the ground the plateaus seemed random and disjointed but from the air it was easy to see the chunks of land were not only joined by the arched bridges, but they formed a spiral with the center being the largest landmass with an enormous spire of gleaming stone. Around this triangular shaped building, were broad fields being grazed by woolly beasts with three horns extruding from their chins. They scooped up the plants, tossed them up and caught them in an opening at the top of their heads. Kaida shuddered and wondered what kind of animal it was.

Tall thick walls surrounded the fields on all sides, making an enclosure around the building. Atop the walls: a narrow walkway that led to towers set into each corner. A shiver shot up her spine, *This must be my mother's birth home.* Zlemtec responded to the sudden change he felt from Kaida and rose higher, sweeping a slow wide circle over it.

Unexpected movement came from the towers as loud sirens pierced the air. Fearing they had been spotted, Zlemtec darted away. He dove down towards the gorge as he arched his head upward to see if danger followed. The noise of the rushing of wings alerted all his senses and his body reacted, swiftly turning and climbing the air. Hundreds of Golden Dragons streamed from the fifth plateau in the spiral and headed towards the center, towards Kaida's home.

"Find the Dragons portal while they are still coming out!" Kaida dug her knees into Zlemtec's scales and held on. He dipped off to the right and flew behind the ground where the Golden Dragons emerged, watching them trail out of an arched portal towards the edge of a cliff. Zlemtec landed nearby and watched from the trees until the Dragons stopped coming out.

"Take the portal while there is time! We need to find my father's family. We may be able to find out what is going on without ending up in the middle of this battle. There is no time to go to my mother's people now, we would not be heard. Be ready, Zlemtec, we may be flying into our worst night terrors but we must try."

Chapter 42

Outside the portal, four Urthe Dragons stood in vigil, denying both sleep and flight. Their energies had been consumed after Kaida and Zlemtec left. Grief had closed them in a steel trap, immobilizing them.

The Queen had been in a madness of panic, watching them disappear. Having failed her attempt to follow them, she had refused to leave the portal tree. Her bellows of grief shook the ground and sent nearby avians into flight.

She paced savagely. Torn between the knowledge of a warrior, the prophecy of the Dragon Child and the gut wrenching despair of a mother who could not protect her children; her torment raged through mind and soul. Thoughts bombarded her without ceasing. *What are they walking into? Will Kaida's family accept her? How will they treat Zlemtec?* On and on, the questions assaulted her mind. When her Bonded tried to coax her away, she refused.

"I cannot leave. What if they are met with immediate battle? They may return to us. I want to wait here, to be here if I'm needed...."

"I understand your heart and your words, my Bonded," began the King, "all of us do."

The Queen lifted her eyes to meet his, then for the first time, she turned her head to watch the peoples trying to console one another. She had forgotten what a large impact Kaida made in all of their lives, not just her own. She walked towards the peoples and extended her wings, enfolding them; grief shared would not diminish it, but there were more shoulders to carry its weight.

After sharing each other's grief, the decision was made to delay their return home, so as dusk turned to a blanket of stars strung overhead, they kept vigil. Each, in the way familiar to them, sent thoughts of a successful journey to Kaida and Zlemtec, searching the stars, wondering which one they traveled.

The first hints of day's light crested towards the east, and still no return of Kaida and Zlemtec. All who had gathered around the portal began to move about and stretch, an effort to shake the numbness that had crept over them during the night's passing.

Rynik spoke with his Bonded and she gave a slow nod of agreement. He then turned and spoke to the rest. "We have stood our watch over our warriors. We can do no more by waiting here so we will make ready to fly home. If you have hunger, eat. We will leave soon."

The peoples began putting their packs, bags and parcels onto the Dragons; it seemed none were interested in food this new day. Before the light covering of dew had left the grasses, they were loaded, mounted and ready for flight. Zelspar, with his riders of Perthorn and Kiel, took point with Galdean, King and Queen of the Mursei, close behind.

It was a silent and solemn flight with the sunlight chasing their tails. The landscape began to change under their wings as the miles passed under them. Hills gave way to outcroppings of mountains. Seeing the familiar mountain landmarks, their journey was almost complete. Weary and drained, they flew on knowing home was within reach.

A crackling noise cut through the air, moments after a bolt of Lightning had hit its mark. Zelspar went into a tumbling roll, his riders held on with death-grips. In the sudden confusion, the Dragons behind were dazed and then spotted Zelspar whirling fast towards the ground. They dove, wings tight against their bodies and passed Zelspar by. They then surrounded him, reaching out to grab onto him, to break his fall. His right wing had taken the hit.

The Queen, the only Dragon free of riders, flew under him. Her body bounced as Zelspar tried to make contact mid air. Galdean was able to grab hold of his left arm and stopped his spinning. He made another attempt and collided onto Starleira's back, the impact jolting her. She gritted her teeth and groaned under the weight. She braced for impact and hit the ground with a hard thud.

Zelspar slid off her side and laid, belly down. His face was swathed in beads of sweat. He was mumbling a spell and a broken shield of protection began to form. Perthorn jumped off and immediately swirled his hands above them, adding another layer of protection.

Kiel slid down and asked still in a daze, "Was that Flegmorr?"

Perthorn, in his fury, could not answer. His face had turned a blistering scarlet, inflamed by the attack. The attack that hit his friend.

Zelspar continued his low tones, calling forth the remnants of his exhausted energy to add a spell block over them and then with a shudder, closed his eyes.

Starleira didn't know she had more room for grief but it rolled over her in an avalanche. Her sobs came in mighty roars even the highest heavens could hear as her tears rained down across Zelspar's head. A worse blow could not have been hurled against them. Still quaking from their grief of Kaida and Zlemtec's departure, their energies drained, they had flown without the Invisibility Magic and directly over a trap.

They had come to rest miles from the attack. The King of Mursei, Galdean, and Perthorn scanned their area, looking for the foulest creature ever created and they were looking for revenge.

Off in the distance, the form of Flegmorr emerged from a cave, with a smirk of satisfaction smeared his face. Glik landed on his shoulder, clicking rapidly. Flegmorr's smile broadened. "Yes, my friend, it has been worth the journey, to see Perthorn fall from the sky. My Magic may even have hit that meddlesome Dragon, too. A better outcome than imagined. What?" His laughter rose up from his poisoned well, "Of course I'm sure. Didn't you see them fall from the sky? They were higher than these mountains. Nothing could withstand that impact." His spirit soared as he leaned back and laughed again, his dark laughter catching the wind.

The Dragons assembled around their friend, the old White Dragon. Memories flooded their minds of all he had done for them.

Galdean spoke, "If it wasn't for him, I would not be with you all today. He brought my Spirit back to me. Oh I know, it was all in a plan designed by the Great Deceiver, Dargenoin, but it was Zelspar who brought me from the land of the Ancestors and it was he who found the Magic that removed the poison Dargenoin created to kill us all. It would be my greatest honor to go find this Flegmorr and annihilate him from the face of Urthe!"

"Not without me, you won't," growled the King, "the lowest slime from the great waters is far better than the walking slime known as Flegmorr, for him to have attacked the greatest White Dragon ... the only Dragon capable of capturing Dargenoin and removing his destructive forces against us, all I can say is he does not know the wrath he has unleashed." Smoke freely spewed from his snout as he began pacing to and fro. "I say we go now!"

Sudden movement came from behind them and all turned, prepared for a fight. Tyrianua was the first to cross through their protective bubble, followed by Sigrunn.

"We saw the Lightning flash from behind us but we were too late," commiserated Tyrianua. "Flegmorr had been following the ruse for several days and had entered a mountain of tunnels we had marked. We were just leaving through the other side when he evoked his Dark Magic. We came as soon as we could."

Sigrunn looked at Perthorn, then down at the ground where Zelspar lay motionless. "Ah, Flegmorr missed his mark."

227

Stares of disbelief met her response, Starleira's eyes bloodshot from tears, abruptly shot up as she sprang from the ground and went toe to toe with Sigrunn, "Is that all you have to say? You both had kept us from incinerating that useless bag of bones, now look what he has done! We have strived at all times to not bring harm to any of the peoples, but he *will* answer for this attack!" Starleira's muzzle dropped close enough for Sigrunn to smell the sulfur rising from it in large plumes of smoke.

Before the heated exchange could continue, thunderous booms broke through the sky causing a great wind to swirl, tearing up the ground in front of them. The Great Ancestor of all Dragons began to take shape, his face composed of dirt and swirling debris. Behind the Great One, more forms of the Ancestors formed. The cacophony of sound drove Dragons and peoples alike, to their knees. Their roars were deafening: the sound of Universes colliding.

The unison of voices tore out from the swirling visions of the Ancestors. "We demand retribution! The Undefeatable deserves justice, he has not yet accomplished what his future holds."

A great pause happened in places where neither peoples nor the common Dragons roamed. The Weavers of the Strings held their hands immobile, waiting. The Historian, Wyrtregon, stared down at the great Book of History, opened to Zelspar's entries, his massive leathered palm covering his face. In the great waters of Urthe, Pravietis, the Future Walker, erupted from the waters, causing great waves to set into motion ripples that would punish the Urthe, and he continued to crash in anger against the waters. Zelspar had been a friend to all, a White Light to every soul and they all mourned his unwarranted attack.

The Great Ancestor of all Dragons spoke, "Cease talking. Zelspar yet lives, breath is still within him. His Time has not yet arrived. My plans for him are great, the greatest of all Dragons that have ever flown the skies or turned in the waters. He is the greatest Healer on Urthe yet in *his* time of need, who answers?" The sky-renting voice declared, *"I do!* Stand away from Zelspar, all, lest you be consumed in my touch."

Peoples and Dragons scurried off in all directions, leaving Zelspar exposed. The swirling form of the Great Ancestor moved across the air and hovered above Zelspar, whose shallow breathing could not even move the sand beneath his snout.

Thunder boomed and Lightning flashed within the swirling form. "Zelspar, your weakened spirit called and *I* have come. I have come to answer the injustice worked against you, I will bring Healing to you. Your path is incomplete. It is the hardest path of all but it is the path of greatest reward. Never will a Dragon arise that will meet your spirit, for it is the most noble of Dragons of the past or future, a spirit that has been granted to always live on. Dragons all pass away, spirits return to the Ancestors, but for you, Zelspar ... your spirit will always continue until the very End of Days. You will inhabit many lives and impact the world in ways currently unknown to you. Your path has been forged and *will not be altered!*"

A great finger of Lightning reached out from the swirling mass and struck Zelspar on his right wingtip. A blue Fire traveled its length and moved across to his shoulders and then wrapped around his body. The ground hissed underneath him and smoke burnt the nostrils of even the furthest Dragon.

He stirred. Slowly, his shoulders rose as he hoisted himself up onto his shaking arms until he could sit upright. His head shook, trying to clear itself. A hoarse whisper crawled out of his throat, "By ... all ... that ... is...." and then stopped, seeing the sky was filled with his Ancestors and the Great Ancestor of all Dragons. He gawked speechless at such an astonishing gathering. "Great One...." Zelspar croaked out as the swirling mass of the Great One retreated.

In that moment, the sun glowed brighter and if you were very still, you could feel the Urthe catch its breath, it was as if the Balance had returned to its designed calculation and all within its confines, rejoiced.

"Zelspar," the Great One of all Dragons whispered, causing a tingle to crawl across skin and scales alike, and an invisible smile permeated the air. "Your health and strength has been restored, for it was unjustly taken." Zelspar's eyes narrowed with the memory and smoke emitted from his snout. "I caution you against retribution at this time." His swirl extended, drawing all eyes and ears to his voice. "Seek instead the strength of Mind and Magic. This battle against the one carrying Dark Magic has not arrived. All must prepare for that day, for not one alone can withstand his Magic."

Having returned to all the fullness that was Zelspar, he spat out, "Not one perhaps, but we are not one. We are many and can bring many more. He meant to kill Perthorn and I will not allow...."

A roar resembling a good natured laughter rippled the air. "There stands the Zelspar the worlds have known." After a softened pause, the Great One continued, "No, Zelspar. It is *I* who won't allow. It is *I* who holds *your* future and it will be *I* who will *allow* your retribution when the Time comes. *Any* who attempts to change my directive will die in the attempt." His voice had steadily increased its volume until the last words had boomed and echoed into the ears and hearts of all before him. "Return home and do as I have spoken. The dark Magician is blinded from seeking you further. He believes he accomplished his goal and his mind carries only the thought of being the victor."

A mumble escaped Perthorn's lips, "But the Book?"

Thunder crashed against his ears. "Your Book of Days is in your keeping, it is ... forgotten to the dark Magician, closed from his thoughts. You are being given time to prepare. Be wise, as you have glimpsed a Future which holds on but by the thinnest of threads, a Future only written because you have helped the Dragons. For that, your Destinies are entwined."

Then, the winds died down, the dirt fell once more to the ground and the Ancestors vanished leaving in their stead, a drumming silence full of the thud of heartbeats.

Chapter 43

With stealth and quick reflexes, Zlemtec and Kaida entered the portal they had watched the Golden Dragons exit.

As they left the portal, they found a new world, a world of the Golden Dragons, Kaida's father's homeland. The sky washed everything around them in crisp tones of apple-green yet the trees glistened in hues of iridescent pale blues and silver. Every sight proved to be more breathtaking than the last. Large lakes rippled their lavender colors to gently break against shores of golden sand.

Kaida murmured, "What a fascinating world."

"Let's fly above to take a better look." Zlemtec responded.

Taking to the air, Zlemtec fixed the location of the portal to his mind. They looked down upon this foreign land, noting the enormous swaths of forests and the landscape full of a bounty of broad leafed plants, lavender lakes and colonies of cities with their golden domed buildings supported by massive gleaming pillars. Mountains cut through the skyline, thousands of feet high. Large gold rocks littered the ground, the same color as the Dragons flying overhead with their wingspan dwarfing any other known Dragon Hails.

"How are we going to find my father's family? We know some of the Dragons have rebelled against him, because he became Bonded to my birth mother. We can't just show ourselves and ask. I don't even know his name." Kaida's voice carried her doubts, tension making her stiff in flight.

"We'll find them. You are not given a quest without the means to go about it. We will watch them and learn more of this world, soon enough the answers you need will present themselves."

Zlemtec felt Kaida ease more in flight, knowing his words brought her the reassurance she needed for the moment.

"Fly to the mountains, let's hunt for a place where we can overlook the buildings below. We might even find a cave where we can rest," she suggested.

Upon closer approach, they noticed a sheen from the mountain as huge slabs of white crystal ran in towering bands with solid rivers of gold branching through the white. Most of the mountain surface was jagged with crystal spurs but there were dark voids scattered across its expanse indicating at the least, shallow caves.

Zlemtec found one where a upward jutting slab partially obscured the hole and a small platform in which to land. He guided them down and landed smoothly, all senses on high alert. They crept in. Kaida felt bumps rise from her skin as a chill crawled up her spine. They were not alone. Grating noises scratched at her ears in a punishing assault. Zlemtec pushed Kaida back as he bellowed Fire out before them, igniting the chamber in blue firelight.

Gasping, Kaida pointed to the creatures on the ground. The beetle like creatures turned to look at the intruders. They were covered in an armored gold and white swirled shell, with mandibles protruding by their mouths. They had been chewing through the rocks in the mountain, creating large dugouts all around them. Their grinding halted. They turned to seek out the intruders, their mandibles making clacking sounds on their approach. Kaida fired off an arrow which shattered on impact, still the beetles marched forward. Zlemtec gushed out a thick blue flame which was met with a shrill screeching noise that pierced their eardrums.

"It worked! They've stopped," Zlemtec said, thankfully. Smoldering beetles that were knee-high to Kaida, had stopped in their tracks. Zlemtec approached, sniffed, then ate one. "Not very flavorful, but crunchy."

"How do you know they are edible?" Shocked, Kaida asked.

"There isn't much that upsets a Dragon's belly. Besides, we are in the land of Golden Dragons, I imagine just about everything we come across will be edible. You did happen to see how large they are, didn't you?" he chuckled.

"Crack open one for me, I'll try it."

Zlemtec picked up one and using both hands, snapped it back shattering its shell into pieces. Kaida reached inside and tore loose a chuck of meat.

Her mouth chewed on the new food, chomping down and pushing it around. "All I taste is smoke and grit." She wiped her lips on the neck of her tunic.

"Well, they are rock eaters, what did you expect?"

Kaida grinned as she looked around in their watchtower. "I expect," she laughed, "is now we have a great place to watch the city below! It will be nice not to keep up with the Invisibility Magic. I never know when it wears off in time to cast the spell again."

"So true," Zlemtec agreed as he scraped a stuck chunk of ground beetle and gravel from one of his back teeth with his talon.

"Hey look, this powder by the wall … it looks like the same stuff we use on Urthe to melt into the liquid to pour into molds," Kaida said with excitement.

"It does, Kaida. Well usually have to pulverize rock to bits and fire them until we can extract enough to use and here it's all over the ground in piles. Those rock beetles did all the crushing for us. I'm surprised the Golden Dragons haven't found this, every Dragon loves this shimmering metal."

"I'm sure they have plenty, just look at the tops of their buildings! They are all covered in the same shiny gold color."

"Then I bet this world is thick with it! That takes a lot of pulverized rock to get that amount." Zlemtec said, gazing out over the city below them. The sky had shifted to gold with a burnish of orange spreading over the city.

"Oh, look at the sky!" Kaida pointed out from the cave, it must mean their sun goes to rest."

"The Dragons are returning, you must be right," he said as he watched the enormous Dragons fill the air and seek their hidden lairs.

"To think...."

Zlemtec turned to Kaida and asked, "To think what?"

"To think some of those Golden Dragons are ... could be ... my family." Her eyes filled with the twinkling of excitement.

Zlemtec looked at her in a new light. Sure, he new her birth parents weren't the Mursei, but he always considered Kaida a Mursei. His heart felt a sudden pang. It was his first moment to wonder, *What if she wants to stay here, with these Dragons? What if she finds them more to her liking?* A groan worked itself out.

"What's wrong, Zlemtec?"

"It's nothing, really. Just thinking."

"About?" Kaida probed deeper.

"I was wondering, what if you didn't want to return home, to Urthe, I mean. You might like your family's world better and...."

"Oh Zlemtec, I couldn't stay and leave you, no matter if I were to grow to love this world or even my mother's world. You are the family I know and love...." Kaida shocked herself as well as Zlemtec by her tumbling of words. "You know, I love all my family on Urthe, even Molakei and Flower Bird...."

Zlemtec's face softened from the shock of Kaida's confession and his eyes danced their flashing colors. *She said it, she actually said she loved me!* They both turned and watched the first sunset on this new world. The sky turned from burnished orange to copper and then a deep magenta filled with brilliant diamonds. He would always remember *this* sunset. They stood looking out into the night, tied together with an invisible ribbon that wrapped around them and through them. A new Bond had formed.

"I think we should investigate. Most are already inside their lairs, at least that is what I think those huge domed buildings are. If we use our Magic of Invisibility, we could get close to each building to hear what their discussions are. It might even lead us to where my father's family is located," Kaida said.

"Good idea but I want to remind you, we are in dangerous territory. I know we are here to fulfill the prophecy but ... if we are in danger, Kaida, realize I will fight with everything I have to protect you, protect us. We won't have the time to ask questions. They might even be part of your family."

Dropping her head, Kaida nodded. "I'm prepared to do the same. My first goal is the same as before: to bring about an understanding between the peoples and Dragons. With that challenge, I understand the danger we will be brushing against but I am hopeful we won't be stepping into a full blown war."

"Then, I say we go take a look. Let's make sure our Invisibility Magic is strong before you climb up, Kaida. Complete your spell."

Kaida wove the spell. Zlemtec checked her from front to back and head to toe.

"Excellent! Now, look me over."

Kaida looked from one side to the other and said, "I would not have known you stood here, if I were a stranger. I'm glad that we can still see each other, though. I would hate to drop the spell if we got separated, so you could find me." She dug her feet along his scales and positioned herself for flight. "Ready when you are."

They soared out into the magenta evening sky, first circling the city from high above, looking for any lingering clusters of Dragons. Having found it safe to land, they chose to land in an area that offered enough space to escape if they were discovered. They were a short walk away from one of the domed buildings. As they approached they could see it was lit up to the point, even the dome glowed warmly in the night sky.

Kaida raised her hand to pause movement. She slunk around a pillar and approached the entry, waving Zlemtec forward, they peered inside. A fire pit stood in the center, its embers still flickering, but what was most unusual were the torches held by blackened metal prongs along the walls in front of the chambers. The torches were long silver branches that were not in flames but a pale blue light that burned from within. Not finding any gathering of Dragons, they selected another building.

As they crept up from the side, they heard voices. They halted in their steps. Scanning all around, not seeing any Dragons, they used great caution not to kick up loose stones.

The voices became louder the closer they got to the entryway. They became an invisible backdrop to the front wall. Kaida's eyes bulged as she looked in. There were three Golden Dragons clustered inside, huge beasts whose heads were adorned in a full crown of elongated spikes, growing shorter as they ran down to near their eyes, where they took the shape of twisted horns. Kaida's eyes followed the horns to the side of the neck where the spikes held together a webbing of scales, which fanned out to where the shoulder blades began. Even the underbelly was ridged with armored scales. The pointed spikes carried down the back to the tail where they stopped, giving way to a long thick smooth tail. At the very tip of the tail it split into five pointed barbs, a whip that could easily deprive an enemy of its flesh.

A vibration surged through her staff which was held tight in her hand. She whipped her head to look at it making sure it did not cast a glow through her Invisibility Magic. It did not. The Dragon rumbles became words. Zlemtec and Kaida leaned in closer.

"Yes, I saw them take the gateway to Paradys! They are intent on bringing us all into battle. They should be punished for what they are doing," spoke the one on the far side of the fire pit.

"And you think the Paradysians shouldn't be punished? They came here, to our World of Amas, and killed one of our own, said the second Golden Dragon.

The third Dragon bellowed so loud it rang outside like a deep clanging bell. "You know that isn't true, Drengor! We killed our own! Do you hear me? A Zentoor Dragon killed its own!"

"He was driven to do it by chasing down that ... that Paradysian woman, the one who brought the troubles to us," retorted Drengor.

"Kiayla had been a friend to the Zentoor Dragons always." Krelen's eyes glared at the second Dragon.

Kaida clutched her staff with such force it restricted blood flow to her fingers. *They knew my birth mother,* her mind echoed. Zlemtec placed his palm against Kaida's shoulder, partially in support but ready to clamp down in the case she decided to stomp into trouble.

"A friend?" Drengor spat the words, looking fiercely at Krelen, "A friend does not bring us to the brink of war because she fled her own planet to hide amongst us, Krelen. A friend would not throw a whole family and now our whole planet into chaos by coming here."

Krelen replied, "Drengor, you know as well as all of us do, she came to warn us ... she came for Braaf. They were inseparable, they were...."

"Do not say it, Krelen," said Drengor, "How could a Paradysian and a Zentoor Dragon become Bonded? It is an abomination to say so. We are two completely different lifeforms, don't you get it? If that were to happen, it would mean the end of Dragons!"

Kaida pressed hard against Zlemtec, fighting back both tears and a growing rage.

Krelen did not back down. He addressed the second Dragon, Drengor. "Yes, I completely 'get it' but I fail to see how you can make such an assumption. You must know what happens when you make assumptions? You prove yourself an ass!"

Muwert, the first Dragon, exploded into a fit of flames, the room shook with his bellow. Krelen snorted plumes of smoke, his laughter snaking up from the pit of his belly, soon the others joined in.

Krelen gave a sharp-toothed grin. "Sorry Drengor, but you were getting so one-sided and irritable, I had to poke your scales. Even you, my magnanimous friend would have to see such thoughts are foolish. The end of the Zentoors? Impossible. We are the largest Dragons of all known worlds, we have the capabilities other Dragon Hails could only dream of. We live on a world full of riches for trade, and through our wisdom, have turned those golden shelled Jerbits into an asset by harnessing their appetite for rock-crunching into a production line for our trade. It is only one Zentoor and one of the Paradysians who chose each other, not whole planets."

Drengor stewed over his friends words. His broad shoulders slumped as he looked into the fire's embers. "Even you, on an occasion, have golden words," he admitted with a half smile, "but what I said is what all the other Zentoor Dragons are saying."

"All?" Krelen repeated, his large brow bone hoisted in question.

"Sometimes, Krelen, I could twist that muzzle of yours completely off of your face."

"I see we have the same thoughts," bellowed Krelen, slapping a knee. He shifted his thoughts and asked, "Do you know if any told Trezlor about the ones who went to Paradys?

Both Drengor and Muwert shrugged their shoulders.

"We should go talk to her, as Braaf's mother, she should be made aware. If they start trouble while on Paradys, it could very easily come to rest at her entryway." Sadness flashed across Krelen's face, then he continued. "Last time, there had been no warning. Because of that, she lost her loved one and barely evaded death herself."

Nods of agreement circled the fire pit. The Dragons rose and headed towards where Kaida and Zlemtec were standing.

As quickly and quiet as possible, Zlemtec and Kaida scurried to the back side of the building, barely escaping being plowed over and being discovered by the Golden Dragons bumping into things they could not see. They watched as the night sky glimmered against the golden wings, and followed behind them.

The Golden Dragons, the Zentoor Hail as Kaida had learned, lead them to the place of her father's family. By the Dragons discussions, it was the home of Trezlor, which meant Kaida's birth grandmother was inside. Kaida felt her stomach churn with nervousness and buzz as if she had swallowed a bee hive of the tiny warriors, fighting to get out.

Krelen stood before the entrance and called for Trezlor to awaken. Drengor and Muwert cautiously stepped backwards leaving Krelen at full exposure.

From the inner chambers, Dragons entered the central room, roaring in great displeasure. Sweat beaded up on Krelen's brow.

The matriarch, Trezlor, thundered. "Krelen, the Fool! That is the name I give you for risking waking me!" Her glare burned holes through his eyes, her fury, however just, crippled Krelen's speech and his ability to retreat.

"You risk losing a wing by disturbing me, so speak of what flew you here to suffer that consequence," she thundered.

Behind Trezlor stood four more Dragons, broken sleep burnished their golden faces, muzzles snarled and teeth bared.

"Trezlor," Krelen forced his words out of the steel trap which locked against his throat. "I apologize profusely for this disturbance but...."

"Fool. Spit it out, my patience left with my sleep."

Trezlor may be old but she was one of the most fierce Zentoors Krelen had ever known. He blurted out, "The rumors are some of our more troubled Zentoors have left to retaliate against the Paradysians. They have not yet returned."

An ear-splitting roar came from behind Trezlor. "No! Who does this attack? We have assured the Paradysians, we would only return there for the Trade Cycles. They will cause us great danger."

Trezlor roared out, "Tell me, who?"

Krelen's jaw came unhinged, his words spun in a dry mouth. "It ... I ... we don't know. Only know, were told, many left through the gateway...."

"Shizitsus Comi!" Bellowed Trezlor, causing a shudder to ripple throughout the Dragons. It was an oath of the greatest assault. It meant, *Burn the Dragons.*

Trezlor turned to the still shocked Dragon who now stood next to her. "Braaf, this will bring a battle to our doorway again. Be prepared!"

Kaida gasped. *My father! My father lives,* her mind exploded. Before Zlemtec could shake away the sudden shock of knowledge, Kaida bolted into the chamber, dropping her Magic of Invisibility at the entrance. Zlemtec stumbled quickly behind her, shedding his Magic as well, prepared to shed even his life.

The sudden commotion caused a great shift in the room. Heads spun as all Zentoor Dragons stared at the intruders. Kaida watched their lungs expanding, filling with great gulps of air to fan the flames that were on their way.

"Father!" Kaida yelled and took one step forward, staff trembling in her hand.

Sputtering and coughing echoed loudly, radiating outwards in the chamber.

"What ... what did you say?" Braaf coughed out as all those around him could do nothing but stare.

"You...." Kaida started and trembled until the words dried up.

Zlemtec met Braaf's eyes and said, "This is the daughter of Kiayla who came to our world, Urthe. During the great quaking, she found our cave, our homes, the dwellings of the Mursei Hail. Look at her! Can you deny her resemblance to her mother or the Paradysians? She wears the orb of her mother." Zlemtec did not know what Ancestor had torn the words from his mouth, but he was grateful.

Trezlor's tongue stumbled, "How ... how can this be?" Her eyes scrutinized every detail of Kaida, eyes widening as she did so.

"Kiayla ... did she come?" Braaf asked, hardly above a whisper.

Tears streamed down Kaida's face as she shook her head from side to side. Her words choked out, "I never knew my mother. She died as I was borne. She ... she left me this," she said as she lifted the orb for all to see.

Trezlor sucked air as Braaf roared out his grief. Suddenly, as if the dust fell from his eyes Braaf reacted. "Daughter? I have a daughter? Dragon-borne of Kiayla, my Bonded...." He wept so hard he shook.

Kaida was fused to the stony floor, not knowing what to do next. Zlemtec nudged her forward. A second nudge got her feet to work again. She stood in front of Braaf and slowly reached out to touched his arm.

Zlemtec was on high alert and moved behind her, his gut rumbling the vast fire pit, made ready to flame.

A golden talon reached out and slowly traveled down Kaida's arm. Braaf raised his head and looked into the blue rivers of Kaida's eyes, the same eyes of her mother.

A circle had begun to close in, locking Kaida and Zlemtec in the midst. Zlemtec extended his wings of Blue and Gold, a Mursei banner of protection. The Zentoor Dragons gave space.

Kaida spoke, heaving her pent up emotions into the air. "Greetings, my family of Amas."

The center room erupted in roars of joy overtaking Zlemtec and Kaida both. The circle tightened as they sought to touch, smell and hear this newest member of their family. A gurgle of laughter, like the tinkling of crystal bells flowed from Kaida's lips.

Zlemtec's eyes of purple, blue and white filled to the brim with tears for his Kaida. His chin quivered just before the dam broke and his tears flowed freely.

After the first moments of her family's acceptance, Kaida pushed back a step. She said, "Please meet Zlemtec. He is from the Mursei Hail. We were raised together as hatchlings and ... and we are...." her eyes searched her father's, "we are the same as you and my mother were." Zlemtec placed his arm on Kaida's shoulder, making the connection, feeling the surge of electrical currents binding them together.

The Zentoors now scrutinized the smaller Dragon, eyes narrowing, sizing him up.

Zlemtec thrust out his chest as he boldly said, "Tell me mighty Golden Dragons of the Zentoor Hail, have you heard of a legend?" He met each eye picking away at his bones, "Have you heard of the Legend of the Dragon Child?"

A chaos of words exploded around him, mixed with gasps, questions and garbled thoughts. He continued, "Not only is Kaida your family member but she *is* the foretold Legend. We are here because of it. I too, have been marked by the Legend. It was deemed I would be with her through this journey. We fly as One."

Braaf's eyes shot wide open. He ventured, "The Legend? All Dragons know of the Legend. My daughter ... Dragon-borne." His thoughts suddenly shifted. "When you fly ... you mean you carry a rider?" His eyes narrowed to watch the response.

Zlemtec immediately answered, "No. I mean we fly as One." His eyes never left Braaf's, making sure he got the full intent. "We become more together than separate."

There were more definitions but Zlemtec knew he hit at the heart of it all by the flicker in Braaf's eyes. There would be no further questioning whether Zlemtec from the Mursei Hail would be enough for the Dragon-borne Kaida. The assessments had been given, marked and catalogued in the eyes of all the Zentoor Dragons present.

Braaf extended an arm and clasped Zlemtec's forearm. "Zlemtec of the Mursei, you are welcome here." Zlemtec grabbed onto Braaf's other arm in a steely grasp, forging a unbroken line of continuity.

Unlike a circle that goes on and on, repeating itself, the square line of continuity is forged of unbroken lines which will not break, but open to receive others in. The bond had been established.

Zlemtec beamed, "Thank you for your welcome and acceptance." His heart hammered wildly in his chest.

Kaida placed her arm on Zlemtec's and watched the square open, as her father now placed his arm on hers, forming the circle which grew as each Golden Dragon repeated the gesture forming a circle that goes on and on, repeating itself, marking its symbol in the room to be inscribed in the sky above. All such

243

symbols are recorded and remembered, by whom, only the Future could answer. For the now, all present were marked by the circle which begun within the square lines of continuity.

Chapter 44

The Ancestors had left, and it was time for Zelspar to again lead through his knowledge and wisdom of the ways of the Ancestors, even though it ruled against what boiled in his own cauldron. He turned back to look at those behind him, clustered tight like a nest of Dragon eggs, eyes still wide from the encounter of the Ancestors. They were all staring at him, waiting.

"We all heard the Great One. There is little left to contemplate, we must follow the directive to fully prepare while we have the gift of Time. While I acknowledge Flegmorr's attack hit me instead of his preferred target, it was a coward's fight. That alone is enough for me, for the all of us, to want to seek him out to destroy." He deeply sighed and shook his head. "It is time to return home. Sigrunn, Tyrianua, will you come with us?"

Sigrunn answered, "We will join you soon. First, we will backtrack Flegmorr to assure he has continued his search for Inner Urthe. If he can find no secondary entrance, we will create one."

Zelspar's brow knitted together like a pile of yellowed grasses cleaving to each other. "You can do that?"

"It would not be hard, the Urthe has already received a harsh shaking and the many mountains have shifted their insides. We only need to focus on the Shift. We will find where the Inner energies escape and mingle with the Outer. Once we are sure Flegmorr enters his own realm, we will seal the opening and return to you."

Dragons, the peoples and the Solteriem folk made haste to return home, leaving behind their portal watch for Kaida and Zlemtec and their path to avenge the attack waged against Zelspar. Dragon memories are long and will not slip away as a loosed scale, but are recorded in a ebb and flow of their internal rivers.

An inner drive pushed them forward, roars of thunder cracking the air as they flew. Each of those returning home joined the warrior cries, all heartbeats drumming to the same cause. A battle brewed. They had been warned it would be a grueling battle with much at stake. As all Dragons do, they returned home to the beginning, the place where the questions unravel and the answers are extracted, forged and tempered as new weapons against their adversary. Their flight home did not go unnoticed. Many watched and waited.

The Weavers of the Strings once again wove, their nimble fingers twining the strands of each Tapestry, eyes blind but senses keen, they dared not snag a strand.

One such Weaver had been moved to the front line during the long pause of caught breaths. His vastly extended Tapestry now lie folded neatly in an ornate basket of finely woven gold, his fingers trembled to keep taut the strand. Beads of perspiration escaped down his neck. The strand had come close to breaking from an outside force, a darkness so deep, even the blind could see. His assistants worked feverishly unwinding the threads upon the many spools that supplied the Weaver. The gurgling of the fountains did little to calm the Weaver, nor the perfumes of the always blooming flowers swaying on the hills.

Hidden deeply within a winding cavern, Wyrtregon's hand slipped down one of his three heads, red eyes fixed to the opened page of the book. The print so fine and the language ancient, it would take eons to decipher all the knowledge held between his hands. His six red eyes rested upon the secreted doorway to his chamber. Rising, he sent his writing bench crashing to the floor, his massive body moving to the doorway. One hand found the obscured stone, he pressed into it his palm and opened the way through the winding cavern. Unusual circumstances called for unusual actions. He would return to the place of his memory.

Flashing colors of all the minerals of stardust and Urthe, glinted off of the back of Pravietis, the mighty Sea Dragon, as he swirled in the great waters. His crashing against the waves had subsided but he was still tense with the swirling of recent events. It had even muddied the waters of his sight. As the Future Walker, this wrought great turmoil which he could not ease.

Broken images swept past him in the ripples of the water. His sight took him to distant shores where castles rose and fell, their banners changed with the rulers of those kingdoms. Triple Crowns and a Golden Dragon waved on flags and banners on the new castle, where the power of great Magic pooled. He gripped the Vision with all of his mind, following the thread backwards to find its beginning but at each attempt, the Vision dispersed into vapor, cascading down all around him. He searched for the meaning of the Future so distant, his Vision could not hold. The fires in his belly churned into multiple Dragons, clamoring to be loosed. His head sunk to water level as smoke wafted from his snout. He felt trapped in a Volcano vent, ripe to explode. He must find the way back to the beginning.

Chapter 45

T he sound of thundering wings broke the circle. Trezlor and her first-hatched son, Braaf, stood in front of Kaida and Zlemtec, sheltering them from view.

A Golden Dragon rushed through the entrance with several Dragons left standing outside the entrance. "Trezlor, Counselor to the Zentoor Dragons, a wave of our Dragons came through the portal pursued by the Paradysian King and his army! Tell us now and we will dispense of them all on our own soil!"

Trezlor's eyes burned holes through the Golden Dragon. "We will not. Our Dragons have broken the bond of no interplanetary travel except on Trade Cycles. Our own Dragons brought the Paradysians to our doorstep and if they shed blood on Paradys, their blood is forfeit by their own doings!"

Unable to swallow his anger, Braaf's ear-splitting roar shook even the pillars to their domain. He stepped forward one step as the other Dragon receded to the entrance with his friends behind him.

"You heard Trezlor! If a single Dragon has caused harm against the Paradysians, that Dragon or Dragons will be judged by *their* laws, we will not oppose."

Swiftly, heads wrenched to the skies. "Our Dragons come!"

Braaf stepped out and looked as a cluster of nine Zentoor Dragons began their descent. His head whirled back to his mother. Kaida and Zlemtec had been partially exposed. "Family! Take to your chambers, I'll address these renegades." The fear in his eyes registered in Trezlor's, *he wants his daughter and companion hidden.* His brothers and sister shifted to obscure Kaida and Zlemtec, then hustled them into Braaf's chamber but Trezlor, the grand dame, refused to leave the center room.

Once ushered into Braaf's chamber, Kaida became incensed. Blue lightning flashed in her eyes as her uncles and aunt tried to bar her from leaving. "Let us go, we will help my Father!"

"Quiet, daughter of Braaf, we are trying to save your thin hide. If they see you...." Her aunt dropped her eyes to match her voice.

The breath caught tight in Kaida's throat. *They think I'm ... what? An embarrassment, an abomination? My own family thinks this way?* "You wish to hide my existence? Am I such an embarrassment to the Golden Dragons that I should be hidden into the back chambers when my Father, *your* brother, could be in danger and highly outnumbered?" Kaida spat out her words as if fire from a Dragon's belly as her eyes smoldered. "Zlemtec! Invisibility now!"

At her words, both she and Zlemtec used their Magic of Invisibility to the shocked gasps of her family. They moved about frantically searching, but could not see nor find Kaida or Zlemtec. As soon as the passageway opened in front of them, they darted out, leaving her aunt and uncles behind.

Zlemtec grabbed Kaida's arm and whispered, "Kaida, they were only trying to protect you. I would have done the same." Kaida softened her posture and squeezed Zlemtec's arm. He continued saying, "Now, climb up if you want to stand a chance of seeing what is going on." A soft chuckle came out as he said, "Your Father is huge!"

An elbow to Zlemtec's side did little but push a scale but he could tell Kaida's fire was safely contained. They needed to use their wits to ensure the best possible result. Kaida climbed up and took her place upon Zlemtec's back, at once, finding her peace and energy with the connection made against the softened leather beneath her. A small smile creased her face as the thoughts danced in her mind, *I'll never be able to explain to others how or what this is with Zlemtec and myself. The connection, the fusing of two into One. The sheer beauty and peace of it.* She softly exhaled and fixed her sights outside the home of her family.

Trezlor now stood next to her son, the other Dragons had moved out to the common ground, awaiting the landing of those flying overhead.

Zlemtec moved towards the edge of the building where they could get a better view. Kaida tensed on her seat as the enormous Dragons stirred up rocks and dirt with their wings as they landed.

Their leader, a massive Golden Dragon with torn neck flares, approached. "Braaf! The trouble all started with you. With you and that Paradysian girl! We were at peace before you decided to go against tradition, against the normal...."

"Hold your vile tongue, Akkren. Your words are as untrue as your nature. What did you do on Paradys? Did you harm a person?" Braaf said, gulping down his own contempt in order to see what chaos had been wrought against the Paradysians.

"I can see that is your primary concern, not in the asking of our welfare. Why even bother to come to the Counselor's domain?" His liquid amber eyes glowed in anger.

The great dame, the Counselor herself, stepped forward. "Why indeed, Akkren?" She hissed with seething rage. "You have broken the agreement we had with the Paradysians, you have led a rebellion against them, against co-existing with other lifeforms. You want Separatism!"

"And why shouldn't I, why shouldn't *we*?" he spat his words, glaring. "They are no match to us, we can rule over them!"

A hush penetrated the group. Finally, Akkren's true nature was shown, even to his own followers who mainly followed to enjoy the thrill of breaking the rules.

During the dispute, no one had noticed what was occurring behind them. The King of Paradys, King Ynir, led a mass of over one hundred soldiers seated upon great woolly beasts. As they came closer, the noise of the mammoth hooves hitting the ground caused the Dragons to turn.

The one beast which could bring fear to the Zentoor Dragons was the Triglors. A ripple effect moved through the Dragons. Not only were the beast menacing but they held a Magic that could render its opponent to stone.

King Ynir advanced, his unplaited white hair fell loose around his silver and blue cloak which clasped in front with a detailed brooch of their star cluster, the Seven Sisters. His eyes, an icy blue sought out the Counselor.

"Trezlor, step forward. You must answer to the invasion of your Dragons against our agreement. Not only have they tormented our people but they have ruined many of our harvesting grounds and now my people want retribution. Our peace between planets has been a precarious hold in recent years, and now this?"

She boldly stepped forward and lightly tipped her head to King Ynir. "I have just recently learned of the broken agreement. I was speaking to one of the offenders when you arrived."

"I have carried all the weight of my people, who even before this, wished to break off relations with the Zentoor Dragons. As you know, their fear has been in, well, diluting our heritage...."

Akkren sprung forward, causing several Triglors to snort and paw defensively at the rocky ground. "Dilute! If it wasn't for your own daughter parading around with one of our own, their would be no 'diluting'!"

"How *dare* you!" King Ynir screamed through clenched teeth. "Kiayla has always been a friend to the Zentoor Dragons, even when the rebellions began."

"If you have an argument, Akkren, you face ME with it," roared Braaf. "You will not speak that way about Kiayla. I will rip your face from your bones!"

Zlemtec had maneuvered around the Zentoor Dragons to watch the exchange and to see Kaida's grandfather. Kaida's head turned from side to side, her jaws tense hearing the exchanges between the two groups. Zlemtec had only a wingbeat of warning before he felt Kaida rise and stand on his back, throwing down her shield of Invisibility. He too, discarded his.

"Stop! Stop this fighting against one another!" Kaida glared through river-blue eyes, face streaked with tears from the implied insults. Shocked faces all turned to look at the speaker.

Dragons, beasts and Paradysians all moved and talked at once.

"Kaida, no!" shouted Braaf, alarmed.

"Who is this person and foreign Dragon?" demanded Akkren.

Trezlor moved towards Kaida, "You were to remain hidden, child."

"I am not a child and I will not be hidden! I am not an embarrassment...."

"No, Kaida, I did not mean that, child. Only we wanted to protect you," Trezlor's voice cracked with emotion.

Kaida looked at her grandmother Trezlor, to her father, Braaf, and finally at her mother's father, King Ynir. She thrust her chin forward and reached for the white orb which dangled beneath her tunic. She placed it on top of her clothing for the light to shine against it.

"I am Kaida, the daughter of Kiayla, the granddaughter of King Ynir. I am also the daughter of Braaf, a Zentoor Dragon and granddaughter to Trezlor, the Counselor of Amas." Kaida looked upon every eye, with defiance.

King Ynir spoke. "Kaida? What are these things you claim?"

In an instant, Kaida slid from the protection of Zlemtec's union and strode directly in front of the King still mounted on his woolly beast. The Triglor sensed an attack and his flared nostrils blew the Stone Magic onto Kaida.

Without a thought, Kaida raised her hand, deflecting the magic backwards and the King's mount became rigid, then turned to stone.

A clamor of commotion stirred all those watching. "I have heard enough of your words against one another," spat the riled Princess of Paradys, the granddaughter of King Ynir and granddaughter of the Counselor of Amas. "When and where your dispute originated is not of my concern. Only the 'why' concerns me. I have come to you for more reasons than to find my birth families. Yes, it *is* true. I am Dragon-borne."

The ruckus grew to a fevered pitch. "Quiet!" demanded the Dragon-borne, her staff held high, lightning flashing through the stones. "You will listen. I have been judged by both sides and I will have my say, which is long overdue."

King Ynir was captivated by the staff, his memory flashed to a conversation with the guardians of his daughter. *The one who looked like Kiayla, rolled back her head and the sky thundered. From out of the sky a staff was thrust into her hands. She held a staff that rippled with lightning which enabled us all to understand, Paradysians and Dragons alike, she said she was not Kiayla but there is something so familiar about her....* He returned his attention to the fine details of her face, the color of her hair, the stubbornness of her soul. *She must....*

Kaida sounded her staff against the ground. "You will know me and my heritage and why I am here. You will grant me all my words, then, and only then, you will make your own decisions. But know this, all of you. This quarrel ends here. If you decide to wage battle, you will battle against *me!* I am more than prepared, you can not fathom the Magic I hold."

Zlemtec, standing by her side, let a low rumble out, giving his wings a stretch, he dazzled a smile to his Kaida. He was willing in this moment to fight them all. The energy flying off of her made his snout flare with excitement. He could feel it with every pulse of his coursing rivers within his scaled body. It was not simply the energy radiating from Kaida, it was the now, the moment, the

History in the making. He felt his energies stretch out and spiral with hers. They would make their stand.

"I have only just learned of you, my family from distant planets. My parents, the ones who raised me as their own, Queen and King of the Mursei Hail of Dragons, gave me the information after our meeting with who I now know as my birth mother's guardians. They had traveled to my planet, Urthe, following a faint beacon from my Heritage orb." Kaida lifted the white translucent orb and lightly sprung the lid, watching King Ynir's eyes widen.

"This orb was worn by my birth mother. Our Urthe went through a great shaking and a 'peoples', as we call them on Urthe, stumbled out from her cave and sought refuge. She found a place where the mountains did not shake and crawled inside. It was the grand caves of the Mursei Dragons. She was heavy with child and very weak. A large group of the Mursei flew out of the caves on their way to battle their enemies. It was then, Rynik, the soon to be King of Mursei found her. She was giving birth...." Kaida fought back the quivering of her voice, but could not wrestle back the escaped tear traveling down her cheek.

"She ... she could not finish, she did not survive. She passed on to her Ancestors as she gave birth to me, her hand clutching the orb I wear. Rynik had to complete the birth as I had not fully come into the light. Here, I show you this!" she pulled the tunic down to expose the scars on her left shoulder, the mark of the Dragon.

Faces filled with awe as Kaida told her story. Some eyes filled with compassion while others held shock.

"Now, perhaps you will understand the rest. I, myself, had to return to my beginning to fully understand. You have heard of 'The Legend.' I speak of the Legend of the Dragon Child. The one who was foretold to become the bridge of understanding and peace between the Dragons and 'peoples.' She would carry the mark of the Dragon. She would be found by the 'peoples' by her fifth year, alone in the forest, with no parents to be found."

Loud whispers filled the air and every eye was cemented on Kaida.

"I *am* the Legend. I will fulfill my Destiny. I have learned much in a short time of *who* I am and the deeper understanding of *why* I am. It is not only because I carry the mark of the Dragon, as I had thought, nor that I fulfilled the prophecy by being found by the 'peoples' in the manner foretold. It is because of you. It is because my birth mother, a Paradysian fell in love with a Zentoor, a Golden Dragon, and they became Bonded. They shared a rare and unique relationship, one of symbiosis. A relationship where the two become One," Kaida said as she turned and smiled at Zlemtec, "the same relationship I have with Zlemtec."

"The Legend exists not only because I carry the mark, it exists because I am Dragon-borne. How could I come to you proclaiming to be the Legend without carrying a piece of each of you in my being? The fear of each other started here. It tore my mother from her Bonded, it forced her into a new world, alone and carrying me inside her. Without your knowing, you, the Paradysians and the Zentoors, created the Legend. You created me."

Tears flowed from the eyes of the Golden Dragons and the yellow-haired people of Paradys. Heaving shoulders leaning against each other, tracing their fears and cruelties back to their points of origination. Back to the instance when the Future could have been rewritten, to where there would have been no need of the Dragon Child, back to where the stories would have been erased.

Kaida and Zlemtec stood center, as a great enveloping closed in. At last, Dragons and yellow-haired people embraced in love, in mind and in soul. They embraced their own.

Kaida reveled in the embrace of her family, the thoughts of nonacceptance sliding away like used up storm clouds, bringing to light the depths of her soul. She slowly untangled herself from the arms and wings of them and stepped back.

"Family and new friends, by your loving gestures to me and Zlemtec, is it true you are willing to embrace one another again, to build upon your old values?"

King Ynir was the first to respond. "Daughter of my daughter, nothing would bring me greater happiness than to follow the old path, therein lies great Wisdom."

Trezlor, who's smile radiated like her golden scales, added, "Agreed. We have been friends for many long years. I was a friend to your father, his father and the father before him. I will hold a meeting this very day of all our Zentoor Dragons and make it clear...." she said as she cast a scrutinizing look towards Akkren, "if our policies are not adhered to, those Dragons will be shunned and sent away from our world."

Akkren felt his golden scales grow hot and turn to the color of burnished bronze. "I know I have no right to ask, but I ask for forgiveness for my ... behavior. I allowed a hatred to grow instead of seeking reasoning. My friends and I would return to Paradys to make amends by clearing the damage we caused to your growing fields and sharing a month's horde of our gold to your treasury. Perhaps that might allow you to buy new plants to fill your fields again."

The Counselor was pleased by the earnestness of his heart. She cast her eyes towards the King, hoping he felt it also.

"Yes, Akkren, you will be allowed to bring your friends and help restore what was destroyed. I must forgive you, for I, myself, fell into the same mire you wrestled through."

Kaida climbed up onto Zlemtec and relished the moment. "We will return to you again to see what progress you have made."

"What?" The question came from different locations surrounding her.

"I had wished to bring you back to our home, Kaida." King Ynir blurted out.

"We have only just met, daughter of mine," replied her Dragon father. "I want to share our home with you, to hear all about you." His eyes leaked his hopes and dreams down his cheeks.

Kaida was feeling the same pangs as her family and told them, "Give me some time. I left my home and Urthe family at a critical time. There is a new threat coming against a respected peoples of our community, and if he is not stopped, would inflict radical changes in our lives. When the conflict is dealt with, we will return to share stories by the fire's side."

Her words were met with sniffles, nods and understanding. She waved and turned to Zlemtec and said, "Home!"

The flash of Blue and Gold glinted in the sun as the two who were One, became airborne, following the path to the portal that led to home. One step into the portal and a few wing beats of time, then they stepped out of the portal to familiar territory.

"We did it, Zlemtec! We did what was given to us to do and now we are home!"

"Not quite there, but closer than we were. Rest or fly?"

"If you are rested, I am ready to fly."

He chuckled, "How did I know that would be your answer?"

"Because you know me so well," Kaida said as her hand brushed the side of his muzzle.

The fine light hairs on Kaida's arms bristled. She twisted around looking for the reason of the alarm she felt stab at her spine. Whispering, she said, "Invisibility Magic, now Zlemtec." Unaware of what danger lurked or where, they took to the air, absorbing the colors around them.

After a short flight they were met with a sight that struck fear through them both. Outside a cave stood the Magician known as Flegmorr. His hands swirled overhead and then thrust towards the caves. In a sudden blast, the cave exploded in on itself, dust and rocks flying in the air.

"Hurry Zlemtec, we must tell Perthorn and the others what we saw. It looks as if Flegmorr has grown even more powerful."

Zlemtec fought his roar down and flew silently with the great surge of his wings. "I only hope Zelspar has trained them well, we all need to be prepared for the danger approaching."

"Knowing Zelspar, he has trained them all down to the tiniest detail." Kaida swiveled her head back to look at the receding figure. A shiver traveled her spine. "We need to be quicker. I do not like this. Something ... ominous radiates from that Magician, like a darkness of a gathering storm. And that storm is heading to our home."

Flegmorr's eyes, the color of dark souls scanned the horizon. He reached up and scratched Glik's chin and said, "Soon. The battle will begin!"

Glik clicked his mouth and answered, "Yessss ... soon."

The End

ABOUT THE AUTHOR:

You can find out the latest information regarding the author's future books by following her on Facebook at www.facebook.com/CherylsFantasies

The first in the series is *The Legend of the Dragon Child*.

It is available in both printed book and e-book through Amazon or wherever fine books are sold.

www.amazon.com/dp/B0789RR61F
www.amazon.co.uk/dp/B0789RR61F
www.amazon.ca/dp/B0789RR61F
www.amazon.com.au/dp/B0789RR61F

She had stumbled across his path long ago, in a time when two moons lit the night sky. She had been on one of her excursions, collecting Dragon scales for armor when she saw his eyes. Piercing eyes lurking between the boulders which guarded the mouth of a cave. Their eyes locked. Neither moved.

Ah, but first you should know something about her, of the Legend. You see, she carries a mark across her left shoulder, four deep slashing scars. The mark of the Dragon.

The villagers had found her in the forest, alone and bleeding. She had been curled around a Dragon's scale of Blue and Gold. She was no more than five years of age. No parents were ever found. They took her in, half out of pity, half out of fear. She carried the mark. They had heard the stories. She might be the one they told would be found.

The Legend of the Dragon Child...

Now that the second book has been released, she is currently working on the third book of the series in which myths, magic and her wonderful Dragons entwine. Stay tuned for her announcement of a new children's book to be coming soon.

A Note From The Author:

Thank you for reading my book, *The Legend: Revealed*. I hope you enjoyed it as much as I did in creating it, as well as the first book, *The Legend of the Dragon Child*.

It would mean a great deal to me if you would leave a short review, sharing your thoughts of my book on Amazon. I do personally read all reviews in the effort to deliver the best quality for your reading enjoyment.

I look forward to our continued journey together as I work on Book Three, *Zelspar and The Magicians*, to bring you a wonderful combination of myths, magic and Dragons that I am eager to share with you.

Sincerely,

Cheryl Rush Cowperthwait

Made in the USA
Monee, IL
24 June 2021

72201613R00146